Erebus
Rising

Daniel Mershon

In memory of Micheal Mershon
March 9, 1991 – May 2, 1998

ISBN: 978-0-9860974-0-9

Library of Congress Control Number: 2015901394

CONTENTS

PROLOGUE

September 2065

The sun's rays had just begun peeking over the distant hills creating multiple shades of purple within the clouds. A wooden fence surrounded a beige house with crimson trim. The house's shadow blanketed the backyard. Shrubberies, small trees, and beds of flowers complemented the well-kept lawn. Dewdrops soddened the grass. Small birds chirped and ruffled their feathers, taking breaks to feed on the seeds placed in a small wooden hut. Three crows swooped in. The sparrows flew away and perched on the wooden fence.

The door to the house swung open and a man with light brown skin and straight black hair stepped onto the deck. He wore a plain t-shirt, frayed khaki shorts, and leather sandals. He yawned, stretched his arms, then walked to the side of the house and twisted a nozzle connected to a hose. Water spouted from the nearby sprinkler. The man walked back to the deck and opened a gray plastic tub that rested on the wooden deck. From the tub he took a bag of birdseed, and proceeded towards the bird feeder. He stepped onto the grass. Dewdrops trickled from the grass to his toes. As he reached the gently swinging bird feeder, he lifted the bag above his shoulders to fill the feeder. A sharp, abrupt pain permeated his lower back. His heartbeat hastened. He felt a lightweight on his chest, a hand, though it was not his. His breaths became shallow. He dropped the bag and fell to his knees. The pain intensified with every heartbeat; it was fiercer than any pain he had ever felt. Despite its intensity, his whole body, toes to tongue, froze. His knees buckled and within a few seconds he lay face down on the grass. His eyes grew heavy. It took every ounce of strength to keep them open. From the corner of his eye he spotted two raggedly dressed boys flee and climb over the fence.

~

An hour later, the sun was shining. A young girl, no more than ten, with straight dark hair, stepped onto the porch. She scanned the yard. "Father?" she said, with a hint of concern and surprise. She squinted in his direction. "Father?" she said louder. Her eyes widened. She ran to him and kneeled at his side. "Father!" she shouted, shaking the body. "Wake up! Please!" She kept shaking, but to no avail. His skin was cold and his shirt saturated in blood. She tilted his head to see his face. His eyes were closed. Dark veins stretched across his pale face. His lips were purple. Tears flowed from the girl's eyes. She tightly hugged her father's body and sobbed uncontrollably.

1

Friday, September 30, 2067

Rain spewed from the sky and hammered the pavement. A few minutes prior there was only a light mist. It was abruptly interrupted when the water came pouring in, creating an aquatic clamor across the landscape. According to the weather report, four inches of rain were expected over the next three days. In Cammalot, it always rained in October. Sometimes it was nice at the end of September, but not that year.

A boy scuffed his shoe against the ground. The Cammalot Middle School coat of arms, a decorative silver and blue knight helmet, was painted on the cement walkway, though much of it had faded. Several other boys and girls flew past the boy. Some inadvertently bumped into him. A few bumped him on purpose. Most walked straight into the rain without hesitation. When you live in Cammalot long enough, the rain does not bother you.

"Adam," said a boy from behind. Adam recognized the voice, but instinctually turned to see who called his name. It was Peter, one of his few friends in Cammalot. "What are you doing this weekend?" A slight twang emanated from his voice.

Adam shrugged his shoulders. "Henry and I have been building a robot, so we'll probably be working on it tomorrow, and I think we're going to my grandparents Sunday afternoon."

"How's Henry?" said Peter.

"I guess he's fine... nothing new—he still reads a lot and is learning multivariable calculus."

"What's multivariable calculus?"

"I'm not sure. He's on the computer all the time. If I walk over to see what he is doing, he points at the screen and says 'watch this.' When he showed me yesterday, I saw him click a button that said multivariable calculus. Dad says it's probably college math."

Henry, brother to Adam and two years younger, was a savant. He could easily complete Adam's math homework, as well as his older sister Hannah's math homework. His sharp memory allowed him to quickly read and recite novels, but his social disabilities placed him in special education classes. To an outside observer, he had the mental capacity of a three year old. The special education classes were plagued with kids who lacked the propensity to work and would spit and swear at teachers who tried to make them learn. Many of these students were diagnosed with a behavioral disorder. As long as they practiced barbarism and performed poorly in school, their parents would receive a disability check from the federal government. At least that is what Adam's father claimed. Henry's inability to socialize made him a pariah. On a good day he would be smacked on the back of the head and greeted as "retard." On the more unfavorable days, other kids would "make the retard dance" by throwing small firecrackers at his feet. He was bullied on a regular basis. The elementary school was no place for Henry, so his mother pulled him to be homeschooled. She registered him with an online education program, and spent a small fortune on books (he was a fast reader and he absorbed new information like a sponge). Occasionally, some of the books would be available at the library, but most were textbooks. His mother tried to save money: she would buy used textbooks and outdated editions, and then resell them.

"Sounds boring," said Peter. At that moment, a sleek blue sedan rolled to a stop. A lady with dark hair sat in the driver seat. A couple people in Cammalot had autonomous vehicles—self-driving cars. But for the general population, they were unnecessary and had yet to become affordable. "That's my mom, I need to go." Peter scuttled a few steps, then turned back to Adam and asked, "Do you want a ride?" Adam shook his head, and waved. He would have loved a ride, but his parents taught him not to burden other people. "See you Monday." Peter entered the sedan and the car departed.

Dark gray clouds as far as the eye could see provided no indication that the rain would recede. Adam shrugged his shoulders, pulled up his head, and journeyed towards home. He scurried across the street to the Cammalot Natural History Museum. It was like all the other buildings nearby: the metal roof was rusted from the rain and mildew grew on the walls. He had only visited the museum once, two years ago when he moved to Cammalot. The small, isolated town of Cammalot was supposed to be named after King Arthur's legendary castle, Camelot. Unfortunately, the person who submitted the name did not bother to check the correct spelling, and the people of Cammalot never voted to change it. When Adam heard the story at the museum, he laughed, but after meeting some of the people in Cammalot and spending two years living there, the story became a sad epitome of the town.

Adam continued his trek on the crumbling sidewalk. Small patches of grass and moss decorated the cracks. He walked past the park, where every building and structure was sullied with graffiti. He passed a group of boys with baggy, dirty clothes sitting on their ostensibly undersized bicycles. One of them puffed on a cigarette, while another spat, producing a dark brown slime. Adam overheard them spewing vulgarities and f-words. His mother always said that cursing was evidence of a limited vocabulary, a feeble attempt of a frustrated mind expressing itself. The boys were taller than Adam, and their faces slightly more defined. He thought they might have been in high school.

The rain continued.

He passed one of Cammalot's "gated communities." Inside the gates were weathered singlewide manufactured homes and trailers with vines growing over the wheels. The locals called this place "Little Jamaica" because it housed a large black community. It may have been one of the only "gated communities" where the gate was meant to keep people in. Past Little Jamaica were several houses. Each lawn was littered with toys, but the children were nowhere to be seen.

After a fifteen-minute trek he arrived home, thoroughly soaked. His house was one of the few in Cammalot with a kept lawn and no rusty, broken cars on the premise. When he entered, Henry instantly greeted him. Henry made no sound, hugged Adam, and then ran back to the computer.

His mother cast a smile in his direction. "How was school?"

Adam shrugged his shoulders. "Fine," he said.

"I want to hear all about it."

Adam recapitulated the main events of the day. "Remember the pictures of the dinosaurs I drew a couple nights ago?" His mother nodded. "Yesterday, I went to the library after school and paid to have copies made. Today, I sold most of them before the first bell rang."

He continued describing the day: an hour after class started he was excused to use the restroom. In such a small school one is not afforded the opportunity to choose the most luxurious restroom, and teachers always ask students to use the closest restroom. Adam respected his teacher's request, and used the restroom closest to the classroom, even though it was the most disgusting restroom on campus. The stalls were covered with disdainful writing. Misspelled words, inappropriate doggerel, and improperly drawn Swastikas were etched into the walls. Nobody ever flushed the toilets. Even if they did, bodily excrement usually tainted the seat. If the sinks worked, they only spouted cold water, but most of the time paper towels clogged them. One wall contained a round, dark yellow, brownish stain. According to popular rumor, the stain came from an insolent student who peed all over the wall, but it was more likely from a busted water pipe.

Every time Adam stepped across the dirty bathroom tiles, the coins in his pocket rattled. He chose to use the stall so no one would catch a glimpse of his coins. When he left the stall, a tall and stocky dark-haired boy approached him. Adam purposefully looked away from the boy's eyes, but kept the boy in his peripheral vision. The boy was twice as big as Adam, and staring directly at him. Adam washed his hands and attempted to leave, but the boy blocked the door. Adam's father always said to judge a man by his character, not his appearance, but Adam grew shaky.

"Give me your money kid," demanded the boy.

Adam knew it was wrong to lie, but his immediate reaction was to reply, "I don't have any money."

"Don't lie to me Jesus-freak. I heard your coins rattling."

Jesus freak. A pejorative term used to describe those who still adhere to the archaic teachings of Jesus of Nazareth. A label that shouted provincial, backwards, and superstitious. How did this boy know Adam was Christian? Did he see Adam enter the single church in Cammalot? Adam never told anyone about his religion. If anyone asked him about his faith, he would say, "I don't know what I believe," even though it was a lie. It was easier to lie than deal with open ridicule and confrontation.

"I'm not one of those Jesus-freaks and I don't have any money," Adam said stiffly.

The burly boy stepped closer to Adam. Adam stepped back, and felt his heel press against the wall. His arms and legs trembled. His heart pounded. He knew there was no way he would win a physical fight with this boy. If he were lucky enough to land a first strike he might have a fleeting advantage, but that would quickly disappear. Maybe he could pretend to drop the coins, then, while picking up the coins, uppercut the boy between the legs and run. Perhaps he should just give the boy his coins and accept his losses.

As his thoughts raced, the bathroom door swung open and another student entered. The burly boy stepped back nonchalantly, pretending as if nothing happened. Adam hastily exited the bathroom with his money and dignity, and without any bruises or broken bones.

Mrs. Carter responded, "Oh, I'm sure he wasn't going to take your money," as if Adam hyperbolized the entire story.

Adam rolled his eyes, disappointed at his mother's attempt to marginalize the situation.

"Well, what did you learn today?"

Adam paused for a moment. His eyes drifted upward to the left, as if he were struggling to recall information. "I don't know…"

"What happened in class?"

Adam described silent reading time, which was never silent. Many of the seventh grade boys could not read, not because of any specific learning disabilities, because they lacked the proclivity to concentrate for more than one or two minutes straight. That is the inevitable outcome for children raised by digital "babysitters." The teacher tried multiple strategies such as asking them, "How would you feel if you were trying to concentrate and someone was shouting at you?"

The boys would shrug their shoulders and indifferently claim, "Wouldn't bother me."

She also had a reward and punishment system, but some of the boys competed to see who could get the most punishments. The teacher always had lessons that should have been captivating, but nothing ever worked. The principal never helped either. The teacher, Ms. White, politely asked a student to return to his seat and be quiet. His response was "God, you're such a bitch." He was immediately sent to the principal, but returned to class within five minutes with a candy sucker.

"Wait a minute," interrupted Mrs. Carter. "The boy went to the office and came back with a piece of candy?" Adam nodded. She gently cleared her throat. "Well I'm sure the principal has his reasons." If there was ever an incident, Adam's mother always tried to take the side of the teacher or principal. Some parents were reluctant to believe their kid could do anything wrong. But children are more observant than adults give them credit for. As soon as they realize their parents see them as angels, they start acting like devils. They lie to their parents, knowing their parents will always defend them, and they have no fear of punishment because there are no consequences. Adam's mother realized that the principal was offering some perverse incentives, but did not feel it was her place to criticize him—at least while Adam was present.

Adam continued retelling the events of his day. History was history in name only. Instead of learning about America's strategic victory at the Battle of Midway or how Julius Caesar was betrayed by his most trusted advisor, Brutus, Adam's class made posters. Adam had once asked Hannah if history was better in high school, but he was disappointed to learn that they also spent most of their time making posters. Most of the students loved history, probably because they never had to think.

No subject caused as much agony as math. The math they were learning was all review from last year, at least for Adam. The previous year, in sixth grade, Adam's test scores qualified him for the gifted program. Unfortunately, the program was cut the next year due to lack of funding and lack of interest. His older sister Hannah, fourteen, was smart but pretended not to be. It was the only way not to be ridiculed in an environment where everyone was racing to the bottom and celebrating stupidity. Whenever he thought it was impossible to move at a slower pace, his expectations were exceeded. He never blamed the teacher. She was frustrated and forced to teach to the lowest common denominator. Many of the students were outright antagonistic towards math. They would say things like, "Math sucks," and, "I'll never use this," or, "Do I look like a nerd?"

Maybe these students were not proud of being stupid, but they sure acted like it. Worse, their comments were meant to bring down anyone who had a chance at being successful. They wanted to lower the bar as far as they could, and still try to get under it; the epitome of "race to the bottom." Most of these kids came from generational poverty and never learned how to act properly. Adam wanted to feel sorry for them; they did not get to choose whom they were born to. Many of them were born to drug-addicted parents, some were beaten on a daily basis, and some had it even worse. Naturally, it is difficult to feel sorry for someone who is incessantly nasty towards other people. These kids may have had depressing home lives, but there was no way to justify their behavior.

Not long after lunch, Adam was called into the principal's office. The principal informed Adam that selling things without permission was against school rules. Multiple students had supposedly spent their lunch money on one of Adam's drawings, and then cried when they had no money for lunch. Adam did not believe that story, because most kids at Cammalot qualified for free lunch. When the principal's reprimand required a response, Adam replied with a sullen, "Yes, sir," and feigned apologies. He received no punishment, but was appalled that he was reprimanded because other students made poor choices. After all, there were students at the middle school selling their prescribed medications. And some of Adam's classmates would brag about stealing and smoking their parents weed. "I wish they would get reprimanded by the principal," complained Adam. "Or that when they get in trouble, they would actually face immediate consequences. They only get a slap on the wrist."

"I know," said Mrs. Carter, "but they have it far worse. Their parents never try to make them better people." Adam paused to think about that statement. No one ever tried to make them better. It was the worst punishment they could receive, and it was apportioned over their entire lives.

~

At five thirty, Adam's father returned home from work, wearing a pair of dirty but sturdy coveralls. A faint odor wafted in. Henry ran to the door, hugged his father, made no sound, and then ran back to the computer. Their mother was in the kitchen chopping vegetables for supper. "How was work dear?" Her voice reverberated across the room.

Mr. Carter unlaced his boots, walked into the kitchen, and gave her a kiss. "I'm just glad to be home," he said, his voice heavy with exhaustion.

Thirty minutes later Hannah arrived home. Her blonde hair was tied back in a ponytail. Her cheeks were red, and her forehead lined with beads of sweat. Henry ran to the door, hugged her without making a sound, and then scurried back to the computer. Typically, Hannah was given a ride home from volleyball practice with a friend two to three days a week. The other two or three days, her mother gave her and her friend a ride home.

Supper was served at six thirty. The Carter family gathered around the dinner table. They all bowed their heads, and Mr. Carter spoke: "Bless us Lord and these gifts which we are about to receive from thy bounty, through Christ our Lord. Amen."

The family echoed in unison, "Amen."

A few minutes into the meal, Mrs. Carter asked, "Have you found anyone to fill the job opening yet?"

Mr. Carter finished chewing his food before responding. He wiped his mouth with a napkin, and then said, "No, we've had it posted for three weeks, and only a handful of people have applied."

"That's too bad."

"None of these people want to work. We hired a guy a month ago. Seemed like a decent fellow. But turns out he just wanted to lean against the wall all day. The guy never followed through with assignments, he was late almost every day, and he never got any work done. We had to let him go. The last five people we've hired have been like that, and when we look through the applications, they're the cream of the crop."

"I don't get it," said Mrs. Carter, "I could probably think of a hundred young people in Cammalot who could use a job that pays a decent wage."

"Problem is, most of them can't pass a drug test, so they don't bother applying. Or, like the last five people we've hired, they just don't want to work. It's pathetic, sad really. It's not like these jobs required special skills."

Then Hannah suggested, "Maybe the ones that want to work are smart enough to get out of here." It was no mystery; small towns like Cammalot had been experiencing a "brain-drain" for over fifty years as industrious people moved to the cities to find good jobs.

After supper, Adam and Hannah cleared the table. Henry was still too young to help. He was boy of many talents, but clearing the table was not one of them. The house contained a dishwasher, but their parents insisted that washing the dishes by hand helped build character.

"Hannah, what are the classes like in high school?" asked Adam, as he scrubbed the glassware.

"Ninth grade isn't much different than seventh grade. In history we watch movies and make posters. Everyone hates math, so they automatically hate the math teacher. Our school doesn't even offer calculus. Most of the kids smoke pot and drink. Some of them even do synthetic drugs."

Adam frowned at Hannah's remarks.

"There's also a lot more drama. Today, Ashley beat up Jenine for sleeping with her boyfriend. Ashley was pregnant last year, but had an abortion. Yesterday she was bragging about all the abortions she's had." Hannah's eyes drifted up, as if trying to recall a memory. "Oh, and everyone is obsessed with sports. Even though most of them are failing classes, the school still lets them play." She paused. "Oh, there were also three fights this week. But that's pretty normal, the boys fight over everything."

The thought of high school gave Adam chills. "You remember our old school, right?" said Adam. Hannah nodded.

"Was it any better?" asked Adam.

"Way better. I try to tell mom and dad, but they always disregard it, as if I'm too young to know the difference between a good and bad school. But they have no idea how bad our schools are."

"I wonder how bad the senior high is," remarked Adam.

"More drugs, more drama, more degenerates. It's Cammalot, what do you expect?" Perhaps that was the problem with Cammalot; no one had expectations.

After washing dishes, Adam trod into the living room. His father sat on the recliner, reading a tablet. His mother swept the hardwood floor while the television played the news. "Dad," said Adam. His father looked up. "Will we ever move back to the city?"

Mr. Carter closed the cover of his tablet and set the tablet on the side table. "I wouldn't say never. You never know what might happen. But we don't have any immediate plans to move."

"Oh." Adam looked down.

Mrs. Carter ceased sweeping and looked at him. "Don't you like it here?" she said with a concerned tone. She rested her broom against the wall and stepped towards Adam.

"I don't fit in here. We don't fit in," said Adam. "I just want to live somewhere where people care." Adam slowly shuffled to the couch and sat.

"Look," said Mr. Carter, "I know Cammalot has issues. But the fact is, every place has issues." Mr. Carter stuttered and fumbled his words before gathering his thoughts coherently. "What I'm trying to say is the grass is always greener on the other side." Adam looked down at the floor, and his father continued: "The older you get, the more responsibilities and worries you'll have. You probably don't remember much about living in California because your main focus was fun and play. We lived in a nice suburb of L.A. Sure, people had more money and higher levels of education, but they weren't without issues. People here settle their disputes with physical aggression. In L.A., they use lawyers and try to destroy each other's reputation. It's more 'civilized,'" he mocked with his fingers, "but the idea of bullying and coercing is the same. The L.A. high schools and junior highs still suffer from drug and alcohol issues, they just do a better job hiding it."

"The kids are trained to act more respectful," added Mrs. Carter, "but they're just as entitled. I doubt you remember this, but your old friend Jake—"

"I remember Jake," said Adam.

"Well," continued Mrs. Carter, "Jake intentionally destroyed some of Henry's toys. Your father and I were trying to figure out what happened. He blamed you, and you were in tears, pleading that you didn't do it. When Jake's father arrived, Jake walked over to him and lied right to his face."

"And his father believed every word!" said Mr. Carter in disgust. "That was the last time Jake came over to our house."

"But that's just one person," Adam objected.

"True," replied Mrs. Carter, "but he was from a pretty typical, snobby family. I was surprised how common kids like Jake were."

"Is that why we moved here?" asked Adam. "To get away from the snobby families? I would rather take the snobbery over this."

"Not exactly," said Mr. Carter. "For one, it was too expensive for a meager army paycheck. What's the point of living in a nice area with all the luxuries and amenities if you're barely making it paycheck to paycheck?"

"Plus," said Mrs. Carter, "We felt it was important for you to grow up near family. Seeing your grandparents once or twice per year just wasn't enough." A crash sounded from another room. Everyone turned their attention towards the direction of the sound. "I should go check on Henry." Mrs. Carter set her broom aside and exited.

Adam looked back at his father. "Any other reasons?" he asked, not convinced.

Mr. Carter chuckled. "Call me paranoid, but the thought of being constantly monitored by sonar surveillance drones gives me the shivers. Cammalot is drone free."

Adam arched an eyebrow. "What are sonar surveillance drones?"

Before Mr. Carter could answer, the telephone rang. "I should probably get that. We can continue this conversation later." His father stood and walked towards the phone. Adam shrugged his shoulders and egressed to his room. He tried to let the issues go. Out of sight, out of mind. It was Friday, the gateway to the weekend. He could spend the entire Saturday building kit-robots with Henry. Then, after church on Sunday, they could play in their grandparents' orchard and eat supper. Whatever worries he had could be postponed until Monday.

2

Sunday, October 2, 2067

The gravel crunched as the tires slowly rolled. The car stopped and Hannah, Adam, Henry, and their parents piled out of the old gold colored sedan. Directly in front of the car stood a two story beige house with crimson trim and a brown roof. The front door opened and an elderly couple stepped on to the porch. "Grandma!" shouted Henry, which surprised the family given Henry rarely spoke more than a few words. Hannah yawned and stretched her arms, while Henry and Adam ran to the front door, their muscles unbothered by the thirty minute cramped car ride.

Henry hugged his grandmother, and then ran back to the car. "How are you kids doing?" asked the graying man.

"Good," replied Hannah and Adam in unison. Mr. Carter opened the sedan's trunk and shut the driver door. Mrs. Carter walked to the back of the car and pulled a covered dish from the trunk. Henry stood next to his mother.

"Henry," spoke Adam, "let's get the robot to show Grandpa and Grandma." Henry nodded, and grabbed the remote, while Adam picked up the box containing the assembled plastic robot. The family approached the porch. As they approached, the grandpa produced a hoarse cough.

The grandma smiled. "Come inside," she said, holding the door.

"Thank you," said Hannah. She wiped her feet on the doormat and walked through the front door. Henry followed, but forgot to wipe his feet.

"Oh, right," said Adam. "Thank you!"

The grandma smiled again and took everyone's coats. "Where's your coat Adam?"

He looked at himself, and shrugged. "I guess I forgot it."

"Kids, could you get the rest of the stuff from the car?" spoke Mrs. Carter. They nodded and ran outside.

Mr. Carter looked at the grandfather. "Have you been watching the market lately? The Dow dropped two percent on Friday. It's down nearly ten percent this month."

The grandfather nodded and cleared his throat. "Don't panic and sell," he said. "Can't time the market."

"I know," replied Mr. Carter. "But it's tempting to sell and cut my losses. Things are looking pretty bad with the nationwide layoffs."

"Ignore the headlines and buy on the dips."

"I don't know dad," said Mr. Carter, scratching his head. "This one isn't looking good."

The grandfather calmly replied, "I've been through a lot of upswings and downswings. There's no reason to worry. Just park your money with some good companies, and forget about it for ten years. Wouldn't hurt to get some gold either." He covered his mouth and coughed harshly.

"Can we talk about something other than stocks?" interrupted Mrs. Carter, slightly irritated. Mr. Carter shrugged.

The grandfather looked at Mrs. Carter and asked, "How are the kids doing in school?"

Mrs. Carter paused. Her eyes shifted. "Well," she said, "Hannah has straight A's. Most of the teachers had positive things to say, though a couple said she talks too much."

"She ought to apply for the Locke Grant," suggested the grandfather. "Her grades are good enough."

"Unfortunately, it's not merit-based, it's need-based. We'll make sure she applies," said Mrs. Carter, "but we make too much money on paper. I wouldn't cross my fingers."

"Well, hopefully someone will make good use of it. I keep hearing about kids squandering each and every opportunity. It'd be a shame for such an opportunity to go to waste."

Mrs. Carter nodded in agreement.

The grandfather coughed, and then said, "How's Adam doing in school?"

"Adam has been getting good grades as well, and the teachers always say positive things about him. Though he did get reprimanded this week for selling his drawings."

"Do you think Adam will be able to get into algebra next year?"

"He could easily get into algebra, but the school doesn't offer it. They offered it last year, but that math teacher left. The new guy they hired doesn't have a math endorsement, so he can't teach algebra—or so I've heard. Supposedly they hired him because he has a good track record coaching football and basketball."

"Well that's a shame," said the grandpa. "I wish I could say I'm surprised, but our culture values brawn more than brains. Not that I don't enjoy watching a good ballgame."

The kids returned with items from the car. "Grandma, would you like to see the robot Henry and I made? We've spent hours working on it!"

The grandma's eyes twinkled. "I would love to see it," she replied. The grandma, mother, and children, walked into the kitchen, while the father and grandfather continued talking on the porch.

Adam opened a cardboard box revealing a metal and plastic construction with six legs. The whole device was about as long as a forearm. He placed it on the kitchen table and handed the remote control to Henry. "Watch this," he said. Henry pushed some buttons on the remote and the robot moved its legs, walking across the table. "Now watch what happens when it gets close to the edge." The robot crawled towards the edge of the table. It lifted one of its front legs and started to step off the table, but the leg stopped, and the robot moved a step backwards. "Did you see that?" said Adam. "We made it so the robot can't walk off the table. Its sensors notice if there isn't a solid surface nearby, and its response is to take a step back. Isn't it neat?"

"Very neat," said the grandma. She smiled. "Looks like I have a couple of junior engineers for grandchildren."

"They worked on that thing all summer, and spent the entire day yesterday trying to work out some kinks," said Mrs. Carter.

"Well, I hope they are proud of themselves; it's quite an accomplishment." She bent down and ruffled the boys' hair.

Mrs. Carter smiled. "Why don't you kids go play outside while I help Grandma with supper."

"Okay," said Hannah. Adam and Hannah's departure was interrupted when they noticed Henry fiddling with the robot. "What about Henry?"

"We can watch him. He will probably keep himself busy with the robot."

The grandma interrupted. "Can you pick some apples for me while you're out there?"

"Yes, Grandma," replied Hannah. She grabbed a woven basket from the counter and walked outside with her brother.

After the children left, the grandmother turned towards Mrs. Carter and asked, "Did you hear what happened to the CEO of Goldman Sachs?"

"I heard something about him getting a DUI—nothing more."

"That was just the tip of the iceberg!" spoke the grandmother. "Supposedly, when he was arrested, officers scanned his fingerprints. The fingerprints were automatically entered into a database, and they found a match: his fingerprints were identical to those found at the scene of an unsolved murder."

"You're kidding!"

"Not just any murder—a murder committed over forty years ago," said the grandmother.

"Wow! Well you know what they say, one out of every ten Wall Street employees is a sociopath." The grandma chuckled. "If he is guilty, I hope they put him away for the rest of his life."

"Someone with that much money?" said the grandmother. She scoffed. "I give it a few months before his trial is dismissed."

~

Adam and Hannah stood on the creaking front porch. The wind whistled past Adam's ears. He gazed across the acres of apple trees. Leaves of the apple trees bristled under the wind's touch. The late afternoon temperature was mild, but the autumn breeze caused Adam to shiver on occasion. A t-shirt and denim jeans offered little protection from the elements. The sky was overcast, but the rain was absent. Perhaps because the orchard was thirty minutes west of Cammalot. The clouds to the east were darker. It was raining when they left Cammalot, and would likely be raining when they returned. At least they had a temporary reprieve from the rain.

"Adam, Hannah," spoke a hoarse voice. "I have an important task for you. Think you could handle taking out a few crows and magpies for me? Those blasted birds have been feeding on my apples." The graying man extended his arms towards Adam. In his hands was a .22 Ruger Carbine.

Adam nodded. "Yes sir," he said, as he gripped the rifle.

"You don't need to 'sir' me. 'Grandpa' will do just fine."

"Yes, Grandpa."

"The magazine has seven rounds in it. Come back when you need more. Don't go pointing it towards any cars or the house. And especially don't point it at any people. I'll make sure Henry stays inside with your mother and grandmother. Keep to the north side, mind your bearings, and you should be fine." With the .22 rifle in hand, Adam and Hannah departed into the apple orchards to fend off pests.

"Do you expect them to bring back any birds?" said Mr. Carter.

"No, but it should keep them busy until supper." He coughed.

"And if he does return with a few birds? Will you make him gut, clean, and cook them like you made us do when we were kids?"

"No, I don't think I will," he said hoarsely. He cleared his throat. "When you and your friends killed a few birds out of boredom, that was wasteful. Taking out pests preserves our crops."

"If you say so."

Adam had practiced shooting with his grandpa on many occasions. They would set up targets, sometimes using aluminum cans, other times marking circles on a cardboard box. If the small scope on the rifle was sighted properly, hitting a can from 50 yards was easy—shooting right or left-handed. No other twelve year old in his school could shoot as well. In fact, half of them had never even seen a gun, except for in the movies. Despite Adam's success shooting cans, he had never attempted to shoot a moving target, much less a living one. Killing spiders was one thing, but he wondered if he had the guts to kill a bird.

A peaceful silence filled the air, strewn with the occasional crow caw and gust of wind. Mud slowly crept up Adam's shoes as Hannah and he slowly walked about the orchard.

"Adam," spoke Hannah, breaking the silence. "Have you noticed anything peculiar lately?"

He shrugged his shoulders. "Like what?"

"About grandpa."

"What do you mean?" asked Adam.

"It used to be that we only came out here once a month. Sometimes not even that often. Now we're coming out here every Sunday."

Adam pondered for a moment, then spoke, "Maybe dad isn't as busy with work."

Hannah frowned. "I don't know. The way he talks, he sure sounds busy. He's still working the same hours." Hannah paused. "Have you noticed how frequently Grandpa has been coughing lately?"

Adam's face grew solemn. "You think Grandpa is sick?"

"Wouldn't that make sense?" asked Hannah. "I also noticed that Grandpa has been giving me a lot more advice. He used to ask me more questions, but now he doesn't ask nearly as many; he lectures me more. He says things like 'Watch out for those boys. At that age, they're only interested in one thing.' Or 'When you do find someone, make sure he's a godly man.' Things like that."

"Seems like good advice."

"Of course it is, but that's not the point." Hannah threw her arms into the air and halted. "He's been acting differently, and our parents have been acting differently, too."

Adam paused and looked down. He twisted his shoe in the dirt then looked up again. "Don't you think they would tell us if Grandpa was dying?"

"Did they tell us when Grandma was sick?"

Adam looked up and stared bewilderingly at Hannah. He shrugged his shoulders.

"Maybe you were too young to remember," said Hannah, "but I remember. They didn't tell us until she was in the hospital, a week before she died."

"Have you asked Mom or Dad about it?" said Adam with a concerned, but suggestive tone. He looked directly at Hannah. Maybe it was from the wind, but he noticed her eyes had become teary.

"Every time I ask," she said, as her voice became shaky, "they try to avoid the question."

"Maybe they don't want us to worry about it," said Adam. He immediately realized the irony: by not informing Hannah, the parents created a deep angst within her. A single tear ran down her cheek. She took a deep breath.

"Let's keep looking," she said.

They wandered around the orchard for at least thirty minutes before being presented with a decent shot at a crow. "Look," said Hannah, pointing at the tree.

Adam looked ahead and spotted a small murder of crows. He counted four of them in an apple tree, not twenty yards away. Four or five more crows perched in the tree next to it. One of the crows turned its head toward Adam and cawed. Then the other crows turned their heads towards him and maintained penetrating stares. Did they recognize him as a threat? What would they do if he shot at them? His steps became slow and deliberate.

He paused and tilted his head towards Hannah. "Do you ever wonder why it's called a 'murder' of crows?" said Hannah. "I always thought that term was suggestive. You know? There must be a good reason why a group of crows is called a murder."

The fact that a group of crows is referred to as a "murder" concerned Adam. Adam remembered watching a video in science that illustrated the intelligence of crows. They used sticks to dig insects and grub from trees, and dropped acorns in the path of cars so that the cars would crack the acorns. Crows learned to use traffic light patterns as signals to grab the cracked acorns. They could even recognize individual faces. Even if someone only aggravated a single crow, somehow that crow communicated the information to other local crows. That person who tormented a single crow would find himself being dive-bombed by many different crows.

"You know," said Hannah, "some ancient myths claim that crows are the souls of murdered men." Hannah giggled inside as Adam shivered. "In other cultures they represent omens," she said.

While these thoughts permeated Adam's mind, he and Hannah had slowly approached the crows, and stood ten yards from the tree where they perched. He raised his rifle, and aimed at a crow. A clean shot. His heartbeat increased. His index finger lightly brushed the trigger, but did not pull it. He paused and took a deep breath, then lowered the rifle. The occult and intelligent qualities of the crow made Adam hesitant to shoot one, or even shoot towards one.

Hannah laughed at her brother. "You worry too much," she said. "I'm going to go pick some apples. Have fun hunting." With her empty woven basket, she departed east.

Adam continued meandering for several minutes until he came across a magpie. The bird perched on a branch of an apple tree.

Adam gazed left and right, and thoroughly scouted ahead, making sure that if he overshot, the bullet would be innocuous to the nearby environment. He kneeled in the grass, pressed the rifle butt against his left shoulder. With it's black beak it ruffled its pearl white and obsidian black feathers. Adam centered the scope's crosshair on the magpie's chest. Another clean shot. No obstructions, not even a branch. With light pressure, his finger could pull the trigger and prevent the bird from destroying his grandpa's apples. His mind wandered, reminiscing of the time his older sister nursed an injured magpie back to health, and even taught it repeat phrases—just like a pet parrot. Adam momentarily closed his eyes and squeezed the trigger. A light thunder resounded from the gun barrel. The leaves next to the magpie danced while the magpie flapped its wings, fleeing into the sky. He lowered his rifle, and stared at the branch where the magpie previously perched. He could not help but wonder, *did I subconsciously miss on purpose? Am I a coward? Do I have the guts to kill a pest, or am I simply a bad shot?* He decided it was time to go back to the house. Perhaps supper would be ready soon.

On his way back to the house he noticed Hannah in the distance. She reached for an apple, and then gently placed it in her woven basket. A boy in a crouched position slowly followed Hannah. The boy positioned himself behind a tree, and continued watching Hannah. He looked older than Adam, but from a distance, Adam could not tell for certain. His sister, Hannah, was fourteen. The boy, white in complexion and dark haired, stood slightly taller than Hannah. His somewhat hazy, but boyish features suggested he could be the same age. Hannah reached for an apple from a tree, and the boy remained in a crouched position, but inched towards her. Adam scratched his head, stood still, and observed. He attempted to justify the boy's presence. The nearest house was a half-mile away, and it was Sunday; no apple pickers were on the premise. Adam looked at his rifle. He knew it was never appropriate to use a gun's scope like a pair of binoculars, but he found himself peering through the scope at the boy. The boy wore a white ragged t-shirt and denim jeans. Hannah, like many of her friends, was fit, but Adam had never seen anyone that age as toned and athletic as the boy with the ragged shirt. Something dark was on the boy's right side, attached to his belt. Adam observed as the boy reached for the dark object. As he gripped the object and slowly lifted, a metallic blade slid from the sheath.

The boy fully wielded the knife and slowly resumed his approach toward Hannah. Adam's heart rate increased and his eyes widened. His palms grew clammy as he clutched the rifle. He tried not to be paranoid. He tried to think of a logical explanation for why the knife-wielding boy was following Hannah, but only one explanation crossed his mind. The boy was stalking her. He was a predator, and she was the intended prey.

Adam shouted for Hannah's attention. Hannah and the boy both looked at Adam momentarily then looked at each other. As soon as their eyes connected, the boy sprinted at her. She screamed and dashed in the opposite direction, heading towards the house for safety. Dozens of apples rolled on the dirt as Hannah hastily dropped the basket. The ragged boy ran substantially faster than Hannah. Adam bolted diagonally towards the boy, hoping to intersect his path. Hannah kept peering over her shoulder. Every time she looked back, the boy was closer. The distance between Hannah and the boy narrowed at an alarming rate. She glanced back again, but when she looked forward a low tree branch impacted her face. She fell flat on her back with a hard thud, and then scrambled to stand up. The boy converged on her position, and maintained a close proximity. He looked her up and down.

The house stood less than thirty meters away, but Hannah had no clear escape path. The boy assumed a combat stance while Hannah positioned herself behind a tree. They circled each other for a moment, and then the boy darted towards Hannah. Using one hand to grab the tree for balance, he swung around and kicked Hannah on the backside of her leg. Her knee buckled and she fell in the dirt surrounding the tree. She turned over and deliberately thrust her knee into the boy's crotch. He stepped back and paused for a moment, then spat and stomped towards Hannah. She scrambled away from the boy, but he deftly slid to the right and kicked her in the side. She cringed and gripped her side as tears ran down her face. The boy straddled her and tightly gripped his knife. Hannah spit directly into the boy's eyes. He blinked, wiped his eyes, and hammered Hannah's face with his fist.

Adam realized his inability to converge on the boy. Even if he did reach his sister in time, the boy would easily overpower him. Adam positioned himself for a shot. Hannah was still wrestling against the boy, and Adam was afraid of shooting, for fear of hitting his sister. The boy exerted downward pressure on the knife. It inched towards Hannah's face. Using all available force, she pushed his hands to the side and sunk her teeth into his forearm, causing him to drop the knife. The boy grunted and tugged his arm. Using his free hand he grasped her hair and whipped his arm back. The pain caused Hannah to let up, and the boy punched her again.

The boy's knife rested in the dirt next to Hannah's head. He punched her two more times. Wet blood and dried tears enveloped Hannah's face. Her eyes glazed over. Her arms and legs lay rigid on the dirt. She moaned in despair. The boy, now facing Adam, lifted the knife above his head and gripped it in both hands as if preparing for a ritual sacrifice. The boy was in Adam's crosshair—just like the magpie. His heart was racing and he was breathing heavily. Killing the boy would make him a murderer, but so would letting the boy kill his sister. The bible was clear; the sixth commandment states thou shalt not kill. Would God forgive him? Could he forgive himself?

A deep echo permeated the orchard and a light smoke emerged from the end of the rifle barrel. Adam stood in awe. The boy flinched as the bullet struck him in the abdomen, then he grimaced. Hannah noticed the blood stain on the boy's shirt. She sighed and her muscles relaxed. Her eyes closed, as if that bullet were her almighty savior.

Then, as if the bullet merely caused an ephemeral time lapse, the boy resumed action—almost robotically. He drove the knife into Hannah's chest and she released a blood-curdling scream. Adam fired three more rounds. The boy flinched three times, then scrambled and fled, holding his abdomen in the process.

Adam dropped the rifle and rushed toward his sister. His feet skid through the dirt as he abruptly stopped by her side. She attempted to tilt her head, but almost immediately it fell back against the ground. Adam placed his hand under his sister's head. He screamed for help as loud as he could. Hannah lightly coughed, but the cough was muffled by a gurgle. The knife protruded from her chest. Underneath the bruises on her face the skin was pale. Her lips were dark. Adam screamed again for help. "You're going to be okay," he whimpered to Hannah. He stared at the knife wound. "Just hang in there." Tears slid down his cheeks and revealed his lies. He wanted to keep comforting her and convince her that everything would be okay—even if he could not convince himself. Hannah lifted her arm, reaching for his hand. Adam embraced her hand, and more tears emerged. He wanted to tell her that he loved her, even though they often fought. He wanted to tell her that they would fight again, but he could not form the words. Her eyes gazed directly into his eyes, then slowly closed. Her arm and hand went limp. Adam lightly shook her, trying to make her open her eyes again.

In the distance he heard a clamoring voice, "Adam? Hannah?" Adam looked up. It was their father, emerging from the front door with their mother and grandfather. Adam's father spotted them, and immediately sprinted in their direction. "Behind you!" he shouted, just a second too late.

Before Adam could turn, a sharp pain materialized in his right side. The pain was like nothing he ever experienced: an intense internal eruption redeemed only by its brevity. Adam fell forward. The surrounding environment blurred. In the corner of his eye stood a figure wearing a dark gray shirt and denim. Adam attempted to lift his head to see the figure's face, but lacked the strength. He blinked, and the figure was gone. His vision obscured into a dark haze as his final fragment of consciousness ceased operation.

3

Wednesday, October 12, 2067

A .22 caliber rifle rested in Adam's hands. Directly in front of him sat a wooden door. To the right he saw a stove and refrigerator. The only other person in the room was Hannah, and she was crying. Before he could ask her why she was crying, the door burst open. A six-foot tall figure paused in the doorway. His villainous face was identical to the boy in the orchard field, except his eyes were blood red. Fastened on each arm were short sword-like blades. He advanced straight towards Hannah, who cowered in a corner. Adam pointed the rifle at the boy, and fired repeatedly. The boy stood only ten feet away, but no bullets hit him or the surrounding area. Adam kept firing. He counted pulling the trigger fifteen times. The boy turned his head to look at Adam, smiled maniacally, then thrust his blade into Hannah's chest. Adam continued firing futilely. The boy laughed, and then casually walked out the door. Adam threw the rifle at the boy and cried. He looked down to find red fluid on his palms.

"Adam?" spoke a faint voice.

His eyes shot open and his heart pounded against his chest like a bass drum. He inhaled and exhaled rapidly and sporadically. His eyes darted around the room. Beige colored walls surrounded him. A small flat screen television hung from the high corner of the room. As he moved his arm he felt a pinch: embedded under his skin was a needle with a plastic tube protruding. A cotton ball was taped to his elbow pit. Several sticky pads adhered to his chest. A tangled mess of cords extended to a monitor.

"Are you okay?" He looked towards the voice and saw that it came from his mother. "Same nightmare?" she asked. Adam nodded while panting. It was the same nightmare reoccurring for the past ten days straight. The nightmare felt more real than anything he experienced in the last week. The memory of the boy stabbing Hannah was crystal clear, and he wished it were only a nightmare, but knew it was not.

"Adam," spoke Mrs. Carter. "The doctors think you're ready to start walking again. You've been bedridden for ten days and your muscles need to work." Two males and a female wearing scrubs approached.

"You haven't been out of the bed for over a week, so this may feel uncomfortable," said one of the men. The three adults removed the electrodes from his chest and disconnected his IV. "We're going to lift you up. Pretend you're a rag doll. This shouldn't hurt." Adults always said that immediately before something was about to hurt. The three adults slowly and deliberately lifted him from the bed. Adam screamed out in pain. His arms and legs were frozen in place, and his posture was unintentionally rigid. They stood him upright on the floor and supported his body. Pain continued flowing through his arms and legs.

"Try to take a step," said the woman. He pivoted, positioning his foot an inch forward while his whole body quivered. Tears slid down his cheek. Slowly, and painfully, he pivoted four more times.

"That's enough for now," said one of the men in scrubs. "Have him do this four times a day until he is able to fully walk again. The two other adults nodded, and then the three of them gently lifted Adam and placed him on the hospital bed. The pain ceased.

~

Adam continued that regimen for several days. Each day the pain was less intense than the previous day, and each day he could take several more steps. By Saturday he could walk the entire hospital wing. He had just returned from one of his walks when a female wearing scrubs entered the room. "Mrs. Carter," she spoke. "These two detectives would like to speak with Adam."

Two men wearing ties and jackets entered the room. "May we come in?" spoke one of the men.

"Yes, by all means," said Mrs. Carter. Adam closed his copy of *20,000 Leagues Under the Sea*, and set the book on his lap.

"I'm Detective Grimes, this is Detective Briggs." The detectives shook hands with Mrs. Carter. One of the officers sat next to Adam. "Adam, we have some difficult questions to ask, and every bit of information you can give us will help. Think you could do that?" Adam nodded. "Good. Now, can you explain to us what happened that day in the orchard?"

Adam recounted the entire story, starting with when he arrived at the orchard, and ending with the pain in his side.

"Do you remember anything else from that day?"

He paused and looked up. "I don't remember much else. I can remember throwing up blood... Then the next thing I remember is laying on my back while a bunch of people wearing gloves and masks looked at me."

The detective nodded. "The boy who hurt your sister," he said, "did you ever see him before?"

Adam shook his head.

"Think really hard. Someone at school? At the grocery store?"

"Sorry," said Adam. "I never saw him before."

The officers looked at each other, then one of them scribbled on his notepad. "What about the boy who stabbed you. Did you see his face?" Adam shook his head again. "What about any other markings such as tattoos or birth marks?"

"I didn't see him," responded Adam.

"Can you think of any reason why someone might want to hurt you or your sister?"

Adam pondered. People in Cammalot hurt each other for the sake of hurting each other—or so it seemed. Many kids at school made threats to one another and often brawled. But those fights were impulsive. As far as Adam could tell, none of them were capable of a well-planned, cold-blooded murder. Hannah had recently bumped another girl out of her starting position on the volleyball team, so of course the girl was upset, but not upset enough to kill. Adam explained this to the detectives.

"Did either of the boys say anything?"

Adam responded with a quiet and doleful, "No."

The detective stood. The other one placed his notepad in his jacket pocket. "Thank you for your help, Adam," spoke Officer Grimes. "Take care. If you recall any other details about that day, please give us a call."

"Wait, Mr. Grimes," said Adam. "What happened to the boy I shot?" The detectives looked at each other, then at Adam's mother. She nodded at them, thereby granting approval to tell Adam.

Grimes frowned then recounted the story. There were two boys in the field. One of them stabbed Adam and fled. There were no reported sightings of him, and police never apprehended him. Following the stabbing, Adam lost nearly three pints of blood. The other boy—the one who murdered Hannah—fled the scene. His body was found a quarter mile down the road. One of the .22 bullets punctured his lung, causing a slow death. Hannah died before paramedics arrived.

Nobody, including Adam, was able to identify the boys. The detectives scoured through yearbooks of all schools within a hundred mile radius, but never found matches. The only piece of discernible evidence was a small electronic device—about the size of an old cellular phone—found in the boy's pocket. Unfortunately, the device's purpose was ambiguous. The only set of fingerprints on it belonged to the dead boy. His prints were checked against every database, state and federal, but again, no matches. As far as anyone could tell, it was a random killing. It might well have been an unsolved murder; despite finding the killer, the motive was indiscernible.

"Thank you," said Mrs. Carter. The detectives left.

Adam shivered. It was the worst possible scenario for him: not only did he kill someone, but he also let his sister get killed. He had no intention of even killing a magpie, and now, he felt like a double-murderer. Adam's conscience was conflicted about the boy's death. Part of him wished the boy were alive so he could ask the boy why he killed Hannah. The other part of him was glad the boy was dead, but wished someone else had served the boy justice. Adam looked down and noticed his hands quivering. He turned his palms up and examined them closer, but they continued to tremble. His mother approached and softly grasped his hands. "Best to get some rest," she said.

~

Sunday, October 23, 2067

October 23 was the day of Hannah's funeral. Adam had only recently been released from the hospital. After the funeral, the family went home, along with some of their closest friends and relatives.

Before long the doorbell chimed. Mrs. Carter leisurely walked to the door, and slowly opened it. A tall man with broad shoulders and light blue eyes greeted her. His hair was short and dark with a hint of gray. "Mrs. Carter," spoke the man. "My name is Jeff Locke." His smile accentuated his chiseled jaw. Locke extended his hand to greet Mrs. Carter. "May I come in?"

Mrs. Carter stared blankly at the man. His gray suit was perfectly tailored to his shape. A Windsor-knotted tie completed the attire.

"Mrs. Carter?"

"Yes... yes, please come in."

Once inside, he again extended his hand and sternly, but gently shook her hand.

"I'm sorry..." trailed Mrs. Carter. "I was not expecting you."

"Don't be sorry. I'm the one who should be apologizing. I realize the timing of my visit is less than perfect. Timing was never my forte."

"Please, call me Andrea," said Mrs. Carter. "Follow me. I will introduce you to my husband."

As they proceeded to the dining room, Adam's uncle approached. "Do you know who that man is, Adam?" asked the uncle. Adam shook his head. "That's Jeff Locke, the owner of a successful technology company." Adam waited for his uncle to elaborate. "Not any technology company, Aegis Technology: the largest private enterprise in the world."

Adam looked at his uncle with a blank face, as if waiting for elaboration. "Is he the same 'Locke' who gave our schools the Locke Grant?"

The uncle nodded.

"What's he doing here?" Adam puzzled.

"Your guess is as good as mine, but I bet he saw your family's story on the news."

"What type of technology does he make?"

"Locke developed several prominent technologies. He's most famous for SSDs and predictive software." Adam's uncle proceeded to share the biography of Jeff Locke: a self-taught programmer who, in high school, adapted old traffic monitoring systems to enable them to discern speeding vehicles. In college, he created software that could accurately predict weather patterns, enabling him to make considerable fortune trading agricultural futures contracts. He completed his bachelor's degree in physics, then enrolled at Caltech to earn his PhD. Adam passively listened to his uncle's lengthy story, but perked up when his uncle began describing SSDs, or sonar surveillance drones.

"SSDs were intended to be used for military surveillance by mapping out enemy territory in explicit detail," he said. "The SSDs were systems of hubs and spokes. Several large drones—which were only the size of sparrows—would hover above enemy territory at an altitude where they could hardly be detected, much less shot down. The drones used various sound frequencies, inaudible to humans, to detail the surrounding territory and enemy movement."

"You lost me," muttered Adam, somewhat embarrassed by his merely inchoate knowledge of the topic.

"It's just echolocation, similar to how bats and whales navigate. Only, Locke used various sound frequencies. These drones could even see inside of buildings. This information would be relayed to a main station or computer where it was reassembled, thus providing real-time information."

"How is that any better than a video recording?"

"Video recording has limitations. You can only record a narrow angle, and it requires huge amounts of data. SSDs have a 360-degree view. A clever politician, Michael Cane, realized the potential of SSDs. If adapted properly, SSDs could create a massive surveillance system that could be used to prevent crime and catch criminals. Of course, there were practical issues with this massive surveillance. Surveilling a large metropolitan area would require storing huge amounts of data, and SSDs were not accurate enough to see individual faces. Locke developed an ingenious solution to each problem."

Adam focused intently on his uncle. The thought of using a massive surveillance system to catch criminals, specifically the one who stabbed him, provided motivation for Adam to listen to his uncle's technical jargon.

The uncle continued: "The data issue was overcome by looking for constants and variables. A drone hovering outside the empire state building will always observe the empire state building; the building is a constant. The people walking outside of the building are variables. Locke used a complicated computer algorithm to separate the constants from the variables. The main computer station would store a single copy of the empire state building, and if needed, recombine this "stage" with the people walking around, or variables. Think of it as multiple actors sharing the same stage, as opposed to having one stage per actor."

"How did they fix the clarity issue?" asked Adam, wondering if the system would be accurate enough to see the face of his assailant.

"The quality issue was overcome by creating sets of smaller drones (roughly the size of a butterfly), and piggybacking off of people's smart phones. Individually, a single small drone is useless. But collectively, they represent a formidable tool. Locke developed another innovative computer algorithm that could detect suspicious behavior—again, his software made strikingly accurate predictions. If suspicious behavior were detected, smaller drones would speed to the location of the suspect. These small drones also used sonar, and could get close enough to detect faces in high resolution. The algorithm then sent a message to nearby officers who could respond to the suspicious behavior. Within ten years of their founding, SSDs had been fully implemented in every major metropolitan area in the United States."

"People are okay with the government watching them?"

Adam's uncle replied. "Most citizens considered this surveillance system a massive breach of privacy, but they were willing to tolerate it because it significantly reduced crime. It also depends on who is in office. As long people trust those in charge, they're willing to live with marginally less freedom."

Adam tilted his head back slightly and looked up, as if trying to absorb all the new information. "Can the police use SSDs to find out where the boys in the orchard came from?" asked Adam.

"I suppose it's possible. Maybe that's why Mr. Locke is here." Adam's uncle finished the sentence just as his mother and father entered the room, followed by Jeff Locke.

"Adam, do you know who this gentleman is?" said Mr. Carter. Adam nodded his head.

"I just gave him the scuttlebutt," said the uncle.

"You're probably wondering why I'm here," spoke Locke.

"Yes, sir," replied Adam.

"I saw your story on national news. When I was younger, just like you, I lost a sibling to similar circumstances. I know how difficult it can be."

Adam thought of asking how Jeff Locke's sibling died, but did not like talking about his own sibling's death and assumed Locke would feel the same way. "I don't mean to sound rude Mr. Locke, but that still doesn't explain why you came all the way out here."

"Adam, I like helping people, and your story struck a chord. I've seen your academic record and test scores—I had to pull a few strings to see your scores, but it was necessary. I looked into your high school and noticed that it doesn't offer any AP classes."

"What are AP classes?" Adam impatiently asked, curious to know the answer, but even more eager for Jeff Locke to state his purpose.

"AP stands for Advanced Placement. They are classes for industrious students with the proclivity and ability to handle challenging tasks. In other words, students like you. Without AP classes, your chances of getting into a good college are slim. Have you thought much about what you want to do after high school?"

Adam shook his head. It was not entirely untrue. He considered what it would be like to work as a fireman, spy, and many other occupations, but he never gave it serious consideration. And given how miserable school was, the thought of completing four additional years never crossed his mind.

"Adam, I am here because I think you have a lot of potential and you remind me of myself at that age. I want to encourage you to apply to Arcadia."

Adam stared in astonishment at Jeff Locke. "You want me to apply to another school?"

Locke misread Adam's surprised look as a curious expression and responded, "Arcadia is boarding school for grades eight through twelve. Not just any boarding school, the best in the nation. They seek out the brightest students and train them to be future leaders. Every Arcadia graduate attends university, most of them at top tier schools. The alumni consists of CEOs of major corporations, governors, senators, Nobel laureates, military leaders, you name it. You sleep in the dorms, and you can still come home to visit each quarter. You'll be surrounded by people who want to work hard. It's a completely different environment than the Cammalot schools."

Adam sighed and looked at the floor. Upon hearing of SSD's he developed the unrealistic expectation that Mr. Locke had come to solve his sister's murder and catch the mystery boy who stabbed

Adam. Adam morosely looked at Jeff Locke, and then asked, "Then, I take it you didn't come here to tell us anything about Hannah's murder? You just want me to apply to a boarding school?"

"Adam!" scolded Mrs. Carter. "Mr. Locke has presented you with an amazing opportunity!" She looked to Jeff Locke. "Please, forgive my son Mr. Locke. He's had a difficult time."

"It's quite alright, really. I completely understand." Jeff Locke kneeled to Adam's level. "I'm sorry I misled you, Adam. Upon hearing of your sister's murder, I was disheartened to learn that neither boy was present on SSD footage. It's quite an anomaly. But that doesn't mean all hope is lost. I am certain that someone will find clues regarding the murder."

Adam frowned. "I'm sorry for being rude, Mr. Locke. Thank you for looking into the matter."

Locke stood and patted Adam on the back. "I'm no detective, but maybe, one day, you could be the one solving these types of crimes. The career opportunities for Arcadia graduates are immense. As long as you work hard, you'll be able to do anything you want to do." A momentary silence filled the space. "You don't have to decide today. At least fill out the application. Arcadia's school year is nontraditional; it starts at the beginning of January. You would technically be starting eighth grade. The application deadline is October 30, but your circumstances are different. I know the dean, and if your application arrives by November 15, I'll make sure it gets reviewed."

Adam was at a loss of words.

"Thank you Mr. Locke," said Mrs. Carter.

Mrs. Carter subtly nudged Adam. "Oh. Thank you Mr. Locke," said Adam.

"Mr. and Mrs. Carter, Adam," spoke Locke, as he tilted his head towards them. "It was a pleasure to meet you. If you ever need to contact me, here is my card." He reached into his suit jacket pocket and produced a contact card. "Farewell."

Mr. and Mrs. Carter returned farewells, walked Locke to the front door, and waved as he departed.

Adam turned towards his parents. "It doesn't make any sense." expressed Adam.

"What doesn't?" spoke Mr. Carter.

"Why Mr. Locke came all the way out here."

"I don't think it's so farfetched. He set up a grant for low-income schools, and the Cammalot School District is a recipient of that grant. He's familiar with the area, and as he said, he saw your story on the news."

"But there are millions of kids who have it far worse than me. Why did he target me?"

"That's an age old question Adam," Mrs. Carter kneeled to Adam's level. "It's been asked by people who are greatly blessed, and it's been asked repeatedly by those who suffer. But no matter what your circumstances are, you make the best of it."

Adam knew he would get no further questioning his parents. He smiled and said, "Thanks," and attempted to push the question to the back of his mind.

4

Monday, October 24, 2067

After weeks of recovering from his injury, Adam was finally healthy enough to return to school. Each day the students gathered in the downtrodden cafeteria prior to class. Adam had a few close friends he normally talked to, but he generally did not seek out new friends. Several students, older and younger, gave him cursory greetings. Many of them were students he recognized but never formally met. Gossip gallops in a small town such as Cammalot, and Adam earned two new reputations as "the boy who was stabbed" and "the boy whose sister died." A group of three older boys stumbled past Adam and his friends.

"I heard about your sister," one boy said. "Sorry."

Another boy from the group responded. "Your sister died? I wish I were that lucky. My little sister is annoying."

It was an appalling statement to Adam. Was it meant to be an expression of sympathy? Was the boy trying to place a positive spin on an abysmal situation? Or was it a simple expression of ignorance. Adam would gladly endure the brother-sister fights, common annoyances, and trivial arguments just to have his sister back. It was obvious that the boy's understanding of death was puerile, so Adam replied with the simplest and least awkward response he could think of: "Thanks." The older boys walked away, then the bell rang.

Upon arriving in the classroom, Adam was presented a card signed by his classmates. His presence in the room shocked a few students, one of who clamored, "Whoa! I thought you were dead!" A comment can be interpreted differently depending on who states it. This comment came from the same student who was once ardent that "the moon is bigger than the sun! Just look at it!" Adam knew the student was well intentioned, and tried his best to ignore the comment. Some students gave hugs, some waved, and others did nothing. It was an enlightening experience for Adam. He had never seen so many students at Cammalot Middle School act like civilized human beings. Students respected the teacher during class and completed the activities with minimal disruption and defiance. Students he never met offered condolences. One school bully offered to beat up anyone who "messed" with him. While he was in the hospital, his family even received gift baskets and a large pecuniary donation from the community. It was a rare occurrence in Cammalot—a town rife with poverty and void of civility somehow managed to pool resources to help a family in need. Adam failed to comprehend the situation. The people of Cammalot were outright antagonistic and never showed remorse. Why the change of heart? Had the family suddenly become "insiders?" For a short period of time, Cammalot was more than a starkly downtrodden town, it was a community. Adam wished Cammalot could be like that all the time. He even considered calling Jeff Locke to decline the offer and thank him for it, but his parents urged him not to be rash.

~

The following week Cammalot reverted to its roots. The empathy train departed on a one-way trip. Adam sat at his assigned table. The edges were marred by bored pencil holes. Doggerel and obscene drawings covered the top. A broken foot caused his hard chair to wobble. The teacher had drawn several rectangles and numbers on the board. She begged a question to the students, and Holly raised her hand to answer. Holly's answer was incorrect. She was a bright student (one of the few), and the mistake was a simple calculation error that any child or adult could have made. However, that did not stop her fellow classmate, Joseph, from laughing and shouting out, "What a retard!" The class laughed, which Joseph interpreted as a signal to continue lambasting. "It's like she's missing half a brain."

"Joseph!" admonished the teacher. "That's enough!"

Holly ran to the bathroom in tears, while Joseph and the other disruptive boys laughed. Adam always attempted to stay out of the trivial school politics, but he was growing tired of students like

Joseph. Joseph placed himself on the proverbial pedestal, and Adam decided that Joseph needed to be knocked down. Once the laughter ceased, Adam calmly stated, "Even if that's true, it's still half a brain more than you have."

"What did you say Carter?" blurted Joseph as he jumped to his feet. His assigned seat was at the same table as Adam, but on the opposite side. Adam smugly looked at Joseph. "I'll kick your ass!" threatened Joseph. Joseph kicked a chair and clenched his fists, attempting to evoke fear in Adam, but Adam remained seated, silent and calm, and continued staring Joseph in the eyes.

"Joseph, I said enough!" blared the teacher. "Report to the principal's office immediately!"

As Joseph left the room he turned, pointed at Adam, and glared.

Once Joseph was gone, the brown haired girl sitting next to Adam whispered, "I want to get him back for being mean to Holly. Do you want to help?"

Adam was unsure of how to react. He thought of his lessons in Sunday school. Romans 12:19 came to mind: "Avenge not yourselves, but rather give place unto wrath: for it is written, Vengeance is mine; I will repay, saith the Lord." But God's vengeance is slow, and Adam wanted swift justice.

"Sure," said Adam. "What do you have in mind?"

The girl produced a small thumb-tack. "One of us needs to distract Joseph, and the other person puts the thumb-tack on his seat."

"He will probably think it's me, so I should be the one to distract him," replied Adam.

The brown haired girl moved to the empty chair next to Joseph's seat and strategically placed the tack. When Joseph returned twenty minutes later, he proceeded to his seat and pulled the chair out. Adam, wishing to prevent Joseph from looking at his chair, nodded at Joseph and said, "Nice shirt." It was enough to get his attention.

"Go to hell," replied Joseph as he sat down. As soon as his bottom made contact with the chair he screamed like a five-year-old girl and grasped his rear-end. The entire class stopped what they were doing and stared at him. He looked at the chair and observed the brass thumbtack. He picked it up and held it in his hands. Realizing what happened, many students in class giggled.

"You did this! I know it was you!" he said, pointing at Adam.

"Did what?" Adam innocently said, placing his palms up.

"Don't play stupid Carter! You put a tack on my chair!"

"Did not," said Adam.

The teacher interrupted. "Joseph, no one put a tack on your chair. It probably fell from the table. Now sit down and get to work." As the teacher turned her head away, Adam noticed a thinly concealed smile. It was as if the teacher suspected foul play, but was willing to turn a blind eye.

~

Monday's tack incident satisfied Adam, but only infuriated Joseph. During Tuesday's lunch recess, Joseph and his friends challenged Adam and his friends to a game of touch football. Adam hesitated. He had not completely recovered from the injury, but the doctor said it was okay to resume physical activity. Adam had no intention of playing football, period—much less with Joseph. Despite his misgivings, he knew one thing for certain: in Cammalot, you never back down from a challenge. Doing so would signal physical weakness, the type of weakness that would transform Adam into an object of scorn and bullying. Adam looked up and scowled at Joseph. He always wondered how people like Joseph made friends. He wore the same sullied and fetid clothes each day. His greasy hair matched his grubby personality. It was that combination of traits that led Adam's best friend to coin the term "dirties" when referring to the Josephs of the school. Of course, they never called the students "dirties" to their faces—that would be distasteful. It was a term only used among friends. Before Adam had a chance to respond, he heard Peter say, "Game on! You guys are going down!"

A light mist sullied the air and caused the grass field to muddy. Within a few minutes of playing, the mist turned into a drizzle. Adam's team approached, but did not cross the invisible line of scrimmage. They spread out along the line. The center student bent over and placed his hands on the football. "Set," shouted the quarterback. Each student readied himself to sprint. "Hike!" The center snapped the ball. Adam ran a hook-route to distract the defense, while the quarterback tossed the ball to his friend, Peter. Once the dirties realized Peter had the ball, Adam attempted to screen the defense. Peter ran behind Adam, and Joseph was directly in front of Adam. Adam strategically positioned himself in Joseph's path, thereby successfully blocking Joseph and allowing Peter to score a touchdown. The new score stood six to eight, with the dirties in the lead. Adam despised the dirties, and the prospect of losing to such people antagonized him.

The makeshift field had no goal posts, so they did not kick field goals. Instead, after each touchdown, the team would attempt a two-point conversion. As Adam departed on his usual route, Joseph slyly struck him in the stomach. The rest of the team was covered, and the two-point conversion failed. All the boys were keeping track of the time, and they realized the whistle would blow in less than two minutes. Adam's team attempted an on-side kick. The ball awkwardly bounced to Joseph. Joseph struggled to catch it and lost possession of the ball to Peter.

Having missed a two point conversion earlier, Adam's team trailed the dirties by two points. They now possessed the football, but were at the opposite end of the makeshift football field. The group huddled together. "Way I see it," said the quarterback, "we only have one more chance to win."

"What should we do?" asked another boy.

The quarterback responded, "Hail Mary. Everyone run down field and I'll throw the ball as far as I can to whoever is open."

The boys put their hands in the center of the huddle and shouted, "Break!" in unison.

Everyone lined up. The quarterback stood five feet behind the center in shotgun formation. "Set!" shouted the quarterback. "Hike!" The center snapped the ball to the quarterback. Adam and most of the other players sprinted downfield for a pass. Joseph covered Adam, as he had the entire game. Adam was growing accustomed to Joseph's impish gambits, and suspected Joseph would try to push him down. Joseph, with his arms straight in front of him, lunged directly at Adam, but Adam sidestepped Joseph, causing Joseph to fall face-first into the sodden grass. Adam ran downfield uncontested and caught the football in his arms. He tagged the chain-link fence at the end of the field that represented the in-zone, thus scoring the winning touchdown. His friends cheered as he ran a few steps, then jumped and spiked the football.

Adam turned to find Joseph standing directly in front of him. "You cheated!" shouted Joseph, as he abruptly shoved Adam.

"You're just mad because we beat you!" snapped Adam as he shoved Joseph in a similar fashion. "Typical loser attitude."

Joseph cocked his right arm back and swung wide at Adam's face. Adam immediately noticed Joseph's clumsy attempt to cause bodily harm, and was able dodge the punch by leaning backwards. Joseph stumbled forward, allowing Adam to use Joseph's momentum against him, thereby slamming him into the chain link fence. Holding Joseph's face against the fence, Adam sternly stated, "Keep your dirty, slimy hands off of me. Try that again and it *will* be the last time you ever do."

The charades enraged Adam, though he attempted to remain calm. Never in his life had he threatened anyone, or treated anyone in that manner. It was antithetical to the way his parents raised him, and completely incompatible with his biblical teachings. Adam did not attenuate his grip on Joseph. Joseph struggled for a moment, then mumbled, "Fine." Adam gave Joseph a final shove and backed away, but as soon as Adam turned around, Joseph taunted, "Oh, look at the big man running away."

The taunt was the first strike to Adam's self control. He turned towards Joseph, clenched his fists, and gave Joseph a penetrating stare. "Just leave it be, Adam," said Peter. "He's just a loser and he's not worth getting in trouble over." For the second time, Adam attempted to leave. He took a deep breath.

Joseph kept taunting. "Wow, what a sissy. I bet if you weren't such a pansy your sister would still be alive."

That line reverberated through Adam's head. Only one person knew what truly happened that day and it was not Joseph. *This must stop*, thought Adam. *And there is only one way to stop people like Joseph.* He looked down at his palms and saw them trembling again. Once he clenched his fists the trembling ceased. Adam faced Joseph. Slowly and heavily he march in Joseph's direction. Joseph realized his miscalculation. He stepped back, but his shoe scraped the chain link fence. His eyes widened. His jaw lowered slightly. He cocked his right arm for another clumsy hook punch. Adam delivered a swift, straight blow to Joseph's nose, followed by an undercut to Joseph's belly. Joseph tipped back against the fence, and Adam grabbed Joseph's shirt and hurled him to the ground. Adam knew he was the victor of this fight, but it was not satisfying enough. He was intent to win every fight he would ever have with Joseph, and every fight Joseph might have with another person. He straddled Joseph and repeatedly connected his fists to Joseph's face.

Adam felt four hands grab his arms and lift him. He slowly blinked and glanced down to see Joseph in a bloody stupor. Blood imbrued Adam's knuckles. His hands shook dramatically and uncontrollably. Faint voices murmured in each of his ears, but his mind was in a catatonic state. Standing motionlessly, a hand waved in front of his face. He looked to the left and right and saw the faces of two of his friends. Two students huddled over Joseph. They were not friends of Joseph, but fellow schoolmates—Joseph's friends were nowhere to be seen.

"Adam, are you okay?" said one of the boys. "You looked like you were going to kill him."

"I don't think he'll mess with you again," said the other friend.

Once Adam realized that he had beaten Joseph to a bloody pulp, he started sobbing. Just like the day in the apple orchard, he felt like a monster. Every night he saw the face of the boy who killed Hannah. Every night he was reminded that he killed another human being. He told himself that he only resorted to violence to save Hannah's life, but there lay Joseph, bloody and unconscious. What would have happened if his friends did not restrain him? Would he have killed Joseph, too? Perhaps Joseph deserved retribution, but to what extent? Adam hated himself for what he did. His tears were drops of fear and remorse.

The next few minutes were a blur for Adam. It was not until he was seated in the principal's office that he regained his senses, though his hands never stopped trembling. He explained the entire story to the principal, starting with the comments made during math the previous day. But as soon as he reached the part about the fight, he sobbed uncontrollably and hyperventilated.

"Adam," spoke the principal, "I understand you're going through a rough time." Adam's sobs and breathing slowed. "But your actions sent Joseph to the hospital. He's been in my office many times before. There isn't a doubt in my mind that he was the aggressor, but I expect more from you. You're one of Cammalot's brightest. You may not realize it, but the other students admire you. Unfortunately, you set a terrible example today." Adam paused to absorb the information. The principal's sermon succeeded in making Adam even more remorseful. "Per school code, fighting results in suspension. I've already contacted your parents. You'll be suspended until Monday."

Adam's watery eyes widened. *Suspension is reserved for the worst kids at Cammalot Middle School,* thought Adam. *What will my friends and parents think?*

~

Adam sat hunched over in the main office, staring at the floor and twiddling his fingers. His mother and Henry walked through the door. Henry ran to Adam for a hug, and without making a sound, ran back to his mother. Mrs. Carter approached the counter and scribbled her signature on a piece of paper. She gave him a cursory glance and softly spoke, "Let's go Adam." She walked out the door, barely giving him time to gather his backpack and lunch sack. Never had he sensed such disappointment.

For the brief car ride home, they sat in silence.

When they arrived home Henry ran to the computer, and Adam went straight to his room. He lay in his bed and stared at the ceiling, thinking about the fight. He pictured himself striking Joseph in the face, over and over again. He flashed to the orchard and imagined the ragged boy beating his sister. Adam picked up the book, "10,000 Leagues Under the Sea." He had started reading it in the hospital and was nearly half way through it. After reading a single paragraph, his mind reverted to the fight. His eyes went through the motion of reading the words, but he failed to comprehend a single word he read. He attempted to nap, but could not shake the images from his mind.

At five-thirty he heard the front door open and close, followed by footsteps. The steps grew louder, then stopped. A light knock sounded on the door. It slowly opened. "Adam," said his father's voice. "Come downstairs. Your mother and I want to talk to you."

The family, minus Henry, gathered around the kitchen table. His father spoke and slowly shook his head: "What you did today..."

"I know," said Adam. His eyes moistened. He sniffled. "I didn't mean to..." Adam's eyes drifted down in shame.

"We're not mad that you got into a fight," said Mr. Carter. Adam looked at his father with wide eyes. "Sometimes people don't respond to words. And if someone swings at you, you need to be ready to stand up for yourself." Adam continued staring at his father. "You should always avoid violence if you can. But sometimes it's necessary—as a last resort."

"I'm not in trouble?" asked Adam, with a quiet, trembly voice.

"You're not in trouble. But there's something you need to understand." Adam waited patiently. "Your actions sent Joseph to the hospital."

"I know…"

"Fighting is one thing. Beating another kid senseless is entirely different. If they want to, Joseph's family could sue us for everything we have." Adam gulped and bowed his head in shame. "Have you thought about how your actions could affect our family?" Adam said nothing. "Have you thought about how much pain you caused Joseph?" Mr. Carter stood, and then spoke "I want you to think about this for a while." Mr. Carter exited the room.

Adam put his hands on the table and stood. "Wait," said Mrs. Carter. "There's something else you need to know." He sat down again. "Joseph has a rough life. The whole county knows about that family. The parents don't work, and the dad is an alcoholic. Half of the domestic disturbance calls in the county come from that house."

"What's domestic disturbance?"

"When there's a commotion, often neighbors will hear it and call the police. In that house, it means the dad is probably beating his wife and kids."

"Why don't they arrest the dad or take the kids away?"

"If the mom doesn't press charges, and there's no immediate evidence that he beat the kids, there's not much the police can do," said Mrs. Carter. Adam paused to absorb the information. "I know that doesn't give Joseph the right to be a bully, but it's probably all he knows."

A moment of silence passed.

"Mom," spoke Adam. "I don't want to go to Cammalot Middle School anymore…"

Mrs. Carter paused and exhaled. "You think you want to try Arcadia?"

Adam nodded.

"It's a big decision."

"I know."

"You can certainly fill out the application. But let's talk more about it later, when you feel better." Adam nodded, then stood and departed to his room. After he left, his father walked in.

Mr. Carter arched an eyebrow. "He wants to go to Arcadia?"

"It appears so," Mrs. Carter replied.

"What do you think of it?"

Mrs. Carter shrugged. "The selfish part of me doesn't want him to go, but ultimately, I want what's best for Adam. And I want him to be happy."

"Do you think Arcadia is best for him?" he asked.

"I don't know... but we're not doing him any favors here."

"I know... maybe Arcadia would be good for him."

The mother and father paused and thought. Then Mrs. Carter spoke, "Tomorrow I will help him complete his application."

~

Adam's suspension was finally over on Monday, November 3. When he returned to school his peers met him with awkward stares. A group of students looked at him and subtly pointed at him as their conversation became quiet. One classmate responded to his presence by saying, "I wish I could miss a week of school." But Adam's time away from school was dull and miserable. At least at school his mind was distracted. Not at home. His mother completed household chores and worked with Henry. When she was not working with Henry, Henry spent the remainder of his time on the computer. Adam had no company, no friends. The two scenes of violence, the day in the orchard, and the fight with Joseph, repeatedly flashed through his mind, as if his mind were stuck in an infinite loop. What other twelve year old could he relate to? No one else knew what it was like to kill a human being. Who could he talk to about savagely beating a fellow student? *No one*, he thought. *Civilized people do not do what I did.*

Adam found his own table at lunch. He felt unworthy to join his normal friends, and too isolated to seek out new ones. As he ate his lunch, another boy sat beside him. The boy reeked of stale cigarette smoke. Dark stains covered his shirt. Adam did not need to look up to see who it was; Joseph occupied the seat next to Adam. Neither boy spoke. Adam continued eating, waiting for Joseph to say something to antagonize him. Adam, though not finished with his food, stood to leave. "Wait," said Joseph. Adam paused and looked at Joseph. He wore a bandage across his nose. Several bruises still blemished his face. Joseph stuttered, "I... I..."

Adam turned to walk away.

"I'm sorry!" said Joseph.

Adam turned around and stared at Joseph in astonishment.

Joseph stumbled on his words. "What I said about your sister, it wasn't right. I'm sorry."

Several seconds passed while the two boys stared at each other in silence. In a soft voice, Adam spoke, "Thanks." Underneath Joseph's bruised face emerged a slight smile. "I'm sorry too." Joseph and Adam did not share any other words.

When Adam returned home his mother beckoned and said, "Come look what I have on the computer screen." So Adam peered at the screen:

Dear Adam Carter,

I am pleased to inform you that the Committee on Admissions has voted to offer you a place in the Arcadia Class of 2074. Please accept my personal congratulations for your outstanding achievements.

We are convinced that you will make important contributions during your time at Arcadia and beyond. Our faculty and students extend a special invitation for you to visit Arcadia over the next few weeks. We understand that choosing a school is a big decision. If you feel a visit will be helpful in making your final decision, we hope you will take advantage of this opportunity. When making your decision, please keep in mind that Arcadia is completely funded by alumni donations, allowing us to fully meet the financial needs of every admitted student.

Please inform us by December 1 whether you plan to accept our offer. If you accept admission for January 9, 2068, further information will be sent to you.

If you have any questions, feel free to contact us. I very much hope that you will decide to join us at Arcadia. Whatever your decision may be, you have my best wishes for every future success.

Sincerely,
Lawrence Kennedy

Adams eyes widened. "Congratulations," spoke Mrs. Carter with a soft smile. She patted Adam on the shoulder. "Your father and I are proud of you." She patted him again, and then left the room.

After his mother left, Adam re-read the message multiple times. He tried to remember how many times he read it. Ten? Twenty? Too many to count. For the first time since moving to Cammalot, Adam had something to look forward to. Though excited, he was also nervous. Included with his acceptance package was a list of prerequisite skills and online resources. Having spent several years at Cammalot Middle School, much of his prerequisite knowledge was lacking. Some of the math skills he learned the previous year in his gifted class, and he acquired some basic computer programming skills from building kit-robots with Henry, but his knowledge of current events and history were virtually non-existent.

When Adam's mother and father saw how thrilled he was to go to Arcadia, there was little need for a discussion. They knew he needed more than Cammalot could provide, and they were hopeful about the opportunities Arcadia could afford Adam. He accepted the offer that same day.

Because of the prerequisite skills Adam needed to obtain, his parents thought it best if Adam spent his time self-studying instead of attending Cammalot Middle School. Thus, November fourth marked his last day at that school. He shared the story with his friends. They congratulated him, said their goodbyes, and wished each other the best of luck.

Adam had one piece of unfinished business at school. Despite Joseph's apology the previous day, he felt that there was more to say. Then he heard through the grapevine that over the weekend, Joseph's older brother, fifteen, shot and killed himself. Adam wondered if that had something to do with Joseph's change in behavior. Did he have an epiphany and suddenly decide to become a better person? Or was it simply a fad that would pass in a few weeks? Unfortunately, Adam never found out, for Joseph was not in attendance that day.

After that incident, Adam had many lingering questions, not only about what happened to Joseph and his family, but about the uncertainties that lie in his future at Arcadia. Despite the many distractions bouncing around Adam's mind, he gave his best effort to ignore them and live out his final school day as a student of Cammalot Middle School.

5

Thursday, January 5, 2068

Adam stared in awe at the magnificent building. Thirty stories of unblemished ivory colored stone work. Four wings of Gothic design, each containing an uncountable number of columns. On top of each wing stood a small tower displaying a distinct sigil: wind, water, fire, and earth—a reference to the classical elements. On top of the main building rose a dome embellished with a shining emblem of the great blue heron; majestic, graceful, and powerful. In front of the building, a shallow pool reflected one thousand feet. Green grass graced all sides of the walkways, while shrubberies, oak trees, and barren cherry blossoms guarded the campus.

"Beautiful campus," said Mrs. Carter

"It certainly is," noted Mr. Carter. "It's quite the contrast to Cammalot's rusty vehicles and trash strewn yards."

"What do you think, Adam?" asked Mrs. Carter. Adam was too occupied gazing to realize his mother asked a question.

Adam paced towards the main entrance, several steps in front of his parents and Henry. With each step his eyes wandered in different directions, admiring the landscape. He strode up the stone steps, past the ornamental columns and through the main entrance. The columns continued inside the building, supporting a rib-vaulted ceiling. "May, I help you," sounded a voice. He turned left and saw a woman behind the counter. His parents followed behind him.

"Hello," said Mrs. Carter, "we're here to check in our son, Adam Carter."

The lady swiveled her chair around and fingered through some files while muttering inaudibly. "Ah, Carter," she pronounced. She handed him a folder containing many pieces of paper, as well as an electronic key. "Room 313 of the Water Hall. And here is a map of the campus."

"Thank you," said Mrs. Carter.

As they walked into the mostly empty foyer, Adam laid down his bag of clothes. "Why are you stopping here?" asked Mr. Carter. "We'll walk you to your room." Adam picked up his bag of clothes. "It looks like the Water Hall is that way." Mr. Carter pointed to the far right corner.

The family approached the door. Adam attempted to open it, but the door stuck. "I think you need to slide the key card," said his mother. She handed Adam the card. He looked at it, and then slid it through the electronic key slot, producing a low pitched "click." Adam opened the door. They climbed two stories, walked down the hall, and entered room 313. Inside was a small common area. A couch and two chairs furnished the open space. Two open doors on each side led to small rooms containing desks and twin sized beds. Adam set his bags next to one of the beds. He turned to say his goodbyes, but stopped abruptly when he saw his mother's damp eyes. She held a hand to her nose and sniffled, then wiped her eyes.

Mr. Carter kneeled next to Adam and clamped a hand on his shoulder. "Listen son," he solemnly said. "For the last thirteen years, your mother and I have been able to guide you in the right direction—to help you make wise choices." Adam looked his father in the eyes. His mother gently wept in the background. "You're going to have more freedom than ever before, but also more responsibility. Your mother and I won't be able to help you at every turn." Adam nodded. "There will be times when you are afraid. You might have to make difficult decisions." Mr. Carter took a deep breath. "When this happens, you can act courageously or cowardly. A courageous man will do what is right, even if it is difficult or unpopular. As your courage expands, so too will the depth of your character. Do you understand?"

Adam nodded. "Yes, sir."

Mr. Carter smiled. "Second," said Mr. Carter, "always work your hardest. It's not about doing your best at a single basketball game or a single test, it's about doing your best every single day. Your job, or school work, is not meant to make you happy. Happiness comes from a job well done. Take pride in your work."

Adam nodded again. "I will."

"Good," said Mr. Carter. "Finally, remember that every day matters. Everything we do has consequences. What you say, what you do, and how you treat others, will shape you into the person you are. Be careful of spending too much time with the wrong crowd. Friends lift each other up; they don't bring each other down. Afford people the same respect that you wish to receive." Adam nodded. "These traits, son, are the traits of a true man, and a true American. Make us proud."

"I will," Adam pensively stated.

"Good." Mr. Carter smiled and said, "Now give your old man a hug." Adam reached in and hugged his father. A hand patted him on the back. His father let go and stood, then patted him on the back again.

Adam's mother stepped forward and kneeled to his level. Her face was blush and her eyes teary. "We're so proud of the person you've become," she said as her voice trembled. "Keep making us proud." She embraced Adam in a tight hug that lasted several seconds longer than his father's hug. After several more seconds, she let go and stood. Henry ran to Adam, hugged him, said nothing, and ran back to his parents.

"Well," said Mr. Carter. "I suppose this is where we say goodbye." Adam hugged each of his family members again. They all said their goodbyes and wished him good luck. Adam promised to email his mother frequently.

Once the family departed, Adam slowly hovered around the empty room. He stared out the window and let his mind go blank. He scavenged around campus and whistled as he walked through the empty echoing halls. Few students had arrived on campus. Most would come over the next couple days. He was eager to be surrounded by people who valued education, but also nervous about what lie ahead. After a slow stroll around the campus, Adam returned to his room and sighed upon the realization that for the first time in his life, he was truly alone.

~

January sixth was Adam's thirteenth birthday, though he had no one to celebrate it with. More students trickled in, but none of his roommates were yet present. Less than twenty-four hours passed since he last saw his parents, but Adam was already left with a hollow feeling; it was the first time he had ever been truly away from his family. His mother sent him an electronic "happy birthday" card, but it was not the same. It was a nice gesture, but did not compare to spending the day with his family. He thought of sending an email to his mother, but wanted to wait. If he sent it too early, his mother may interpret it as a sign of loneliness and homesickness. The last thing he wanted to do was cause his mother more angst. She already had enough worries. As the economy had receded, his father was worried about being laid off, and Henry was always a handful. Not to mention how he seemingly abandoned his mother only months after his sister's premature demise. On top of that, his mother was assisting with the care of his grandparents. His grandpa had been terminally ill for several months, though Adam and Henry were not officially apprised until December. The doctors said he could pass any moment. Adam offered to rescind his acceptance to Arcadia so he could spend more time with his grandpa, but the grandpa said, "No way will I let you squander this once in a lifetime opportunity for me."

The illness baffled Adam because six months ago, his grandpa appeared healthy as could be. "Surely they can make you better?"

"Of course they can," said the grandpa, "but at what cost? The five-year survival rate of this cancer is less than two percent, and it costs hundreds of thousands of dollars. When healthcare is a shared resource, the public decides what should be treated, and they decided long ago that it's not worth the cost to treat people in my situation."

"Do you mean they won't cure someone who is old because they aren't likely to live very long after they're cured?" asked Adam.

The grandpa frowned and nodded.

"Can't you sell the orchard and pay for it yourself?"

"I could," said the grandpa, "but I want to leave something for my family. The way it is now, your grandma will have more than enough to live off of, with plenty remaining to pass on to my children and grandchildren. I survived eighty good years and have many things to be proud of. I can't ask for much more."

Despite his readiness to pass, the rest of the family was not ready. And despite the grandpa's wishes, Adam's conscience was burdened with the guilt of abandoning his terminally ill grandfather.

During solitude the mind has time to contemplate these issues. Adam needed a distraction, something to keep his mind from conjuring morose thoughts.

The distraction arrived that afternoon. Adam sat in his dorm room reading *20,000 Leagues Under the Sea*. There were fewer than thirty pages left to read, and he hoped to finish it before school started. He heard a soft noise at the door, and glanced over to see the doorknob turn. A dark haired, average looking boy, about the same size as Adam but slightly heavier and with wider shoulders, entered the room. "Hey," said the boy, "my name's Will. What's your name?"

Adam stood. "Adam Carter," he said, extending his arm for a handshake. The boys shook hands.

"Nice to meet you, Adam. Where did you come from?"

"A small, rainy, South Carolina town in the middle of nowhere. What about you?"

"Alexandria, Virginia. How come you don't have a southern accent?" asked Will.

Adam shrugged. "I only lived there for a couple years. I guess I never picked it up."

"So tell me," said Will, "what's small town living like? In the movies it's always such an idyllic picture."

"I can't speak for every small town," said Adam, "but Cammalot is white trash." Adam regaled Will with his personal narratives and many antics of Cammalot. He shared the awe he experienced upon arriving at Arcadia, a stark contrast to the financial situations of most Cammalot denizens. "I know I've only been here for a day, but I haven't seen any dirties yet!" Will arched an eyebrow, so Adam explained what a dirty was. Will laughed, and then shared some horrendous stories of his experience in Alexandria. At his mother's school, there was a paraplegic boy who participated in after-school drama. Unfortunately, he had difficulty ascending the stage. His parents insisted that a wheel chair elevator be installed. They argued their son was not receiving an appropriate education, so they sued the school district. The school was forced to spend nearly two million dollars installing the elevator (because a ramp would not suffice), and the family left a month after the elevator was installed.

"And that's not the worst of it!" said Will. "People have so much money that they make up new issues to worry about. We're seeing a renascence of TB and polio because people refuse to vaccinate."

"I remember seeing something about that on the news," Adam thoughtfully expressed. "It's happening in wealthy cities across the country. We never had any issues with it in Cammalot."

"Yeah!" scoffed Will. "Apparently, parents are worried that vaccines will make their kids autistic—even though there's no evidence to support that. They should be worried about these diseases killing their kids!"

"My mom used to be a nurse in the army," said Adam. "She said that when too many people don't vaccinate, it's likely to start harming the vaccinated people as well. She says you need over ninety percent of people to be vaccinated for most vaccines to be effective." Will and Adam could not help but chuckle at the situation.

After they finished chuckling, Will continued, "But that's not even the crux of it. My favorite is the most recent diet fad."

Adam shrugged. "We don't get too many diet fads in Cammalot. Most people just eat fried food, TV dinners, and chips."

"Wait until you hear this one," said Will with an eager smile. "People in Alexandria are hooked on the GC-free diet—or glycoalkaloid free."

"I've never heard of it," said Adam, with a puzzled expression. "What's a glycoalkaloid?"

"Most people probably couldn't tell you, but I was curious so I researched it," Will proudly proclaimed. "It's a natural pesticide produced in nightshade vegetables like tomatoes, eggplants, potatoes, and peppers, and it's produced in cherries and apples. GC-free people won't eat anything made from or containing nightshades, apples, or cherries. Supposedly, GC causes migraines, osteoporosis, and thyroid problems—but there's no evidence to back up the claims. But once a celebrity endorses the diet, everyone jumps onboard."

"I always thought people in the city were smarter than rural folk, but sometimes I wonder…"

"They're smarter about some things and dumber about others," said Will.

The conversation abruptly ended and an awkward silence passed. Adam twiddled his thumbs. Will scratched his head. A potential conversation starter came to mind causing Adam's eyes to widen. "Have you looked at your schedule yet?" he asked. "I wonder if we have any classes together."

The boys compared schedules. Physical training, or PT, began at 7:00a.m. Breakfast was served from 8:15 to 9:00. Next was math, then social studies, and music, followed by lunch from 12:00 p.m. to 1:00. Then computer programming, Mandarin, science, a half hour break, and self-defense. Dinner was served from 5:30 to 6:30 p.m. Lights out at 9:30 p.m., and free time for the three hours before that. "Looks like all of our classes are the same except for Mandarin," said Will. "I'm taking Russian instead."

"I don't know where anything is yet. Do you want to go explore and figure out where our classes are?" asked Adam.

"Sounds like a plan!" spoke Will.

Will and Adam explored the vast hallways of Arcadia, sharing stories of their childhood. Will was an only child. He lived in a suburb of Alexandria, where both of his parents were teachers. Through subtle clues, Will deduced that Adam was a Christian. "That's neat," said Will. "My family used to go to church, but we stopped when it shut down. Though, I usually don't tell people about it. We're probably the only two Christians on campus." They laughed, and agreed not to discuss it further—best not to draw any unwanted attention.

Despite their best attempts to avoid unwanted attention, it seemed to have a way of finding them. It happened around 6:00 p.m. Will and Adam sat at a cafeteria table where they had just finished eating supper. At the table in front of them sat two girls, one with fair skin and blonde hair, the other with a slightly darker complexion and straight dark hair. Three boys, dressed in expensive clothes, approached the girls. The school had uniforms, but since school was not yet in session, no one wore the uniforms. Two of the boys were burly, much bigger than Adam or Will. The one in the middle, with light brown and slick hair, was about the same size as Adam. The boy with light brown hair sat in the seat directly adjacent to the dark haired girl, despite the numerous empty seats nearby. The girls ignored him and quietly talked amongst themselves. "Excuse me, ladies," spoke the boy, "would one of you mind placing your hand on my shoulder?"

The girls stopped and stared at him with eyebrows raised.

"I want to tell my friends that I was touched by an angel." The boy smiled, but the girls scoffed. They turned away from him, and continued their conversation.

The boy's smile disappeared. "Maybe you don't know who I am," he said. "The name's Jett Holden." He paused, pompously waiting for one of them to respond to his name.

The dark haired girl turned, facing the boy. "Can't you see we're busy?" Again, the girls ignored him and continued talking. Jett stepped back in astonishment.

"Jett *Holden*," he said again, emphasizing his last name. "As in, the son of Governor Jack Holden of Massachusetts."

"Sorry, Jett," spoke the blonde haired girl, emphasizing every word. "But we're not interested." Adam and Will subtly observed the situation. It only took a few seconds for them to dislike Jett. Will met many people like Jett at his old school: spoiled, snobby, and conceited. They were all the same. There were few people of Jett's status at Cammalot, but many people with the same personality traits. At least Jett had something to be proud of. What did the people of Cammalot have?

"Look," said Jett, "maybe we got off to the wrong start." He placed his hand on the dark haired girl's shoulder.

She sternly and calmly spoke, "Get your hand off of me."

Jett slowly slid his hand down the girl's back. He opened his mouth to speak, but before a single word emerged, the girl grabbed his hand and twisted his fingers back. His shoulders hunkered and his body quailed. "I said keep your hands off of me!" she said through clenched teeth. Jett cringed.

"Okay, okay," he muttered in pain. The girl released Jett's hand. He stood up and shook his wrist, as if trying to fling away the pain. He looked at the girl again, and noticed her necklace. It was previously concealed by her shirt, but somehow became revealed during the commotion. Hanging at the bottom of the silver chain was a pendant formed by two triangles oriented in opposite directs. Jett brushed his shirt off and sneered, "If I would have known you were a Jew I would have kept my distance." He spat at the floor. "The way your provincial minded people treat Palestinians, you're worse than the Christians. Apparently they let anyone into Arcadia—even if they're feeble minded." Jett waved his arm. "Let's get out of here."

Will and Adam got up to clear their trays. Jett and his goons walked past Adam and Will, and then stopped. Jett turned towards Adam and said, "Watch out for those two. Wouldn't want to fall into the wrong crowd."

Adam eyed Jett. "I think I know the wrong crowd when I see it."

"Don't tell me you're one of those Jew-lovers," scorned Jett. "Or worse, one of those Jesus-freaks."

Adam and Will said nothing. They remained calm and stared at Jett and his two cronies.

"Whatever," Jett scoffed. "Not worth my time." Then Jett and his two cronies left.

Will and Adam cleared their trays. "Whew, my heart was racing," said Will. "I thought we were gonna fight—and they're way bigger than us. You ever been in a fight?" Adam shook his head. He was not pleased with the idea of starting a friendship with a lie, but it was more appealing than confessing to his only friend that he savagely beat another kid. "Maybe we'll learn some good moves in self defense. I wouldn't mind clocking that Jett kid."

They walked by the table where the two girls sat. Will happily commented, "That was pretty neat how you put Jett in his place. Where did you learn to do that?"

"From my father," said the dark haired girl. "He taught me most of what I know."

"Sounds like a great guy," said Will. "What does he do?"

The girl paused, and looked down. "He is dead."

"Oh," spoke Will with a solemn tone. "I'm sorry."

"If you came over here to pity me you can leave. I have no desire for your pity.

Adam interrupted, "We didn't come over to offer any pity. We're just trying to meet new people. We don't know anyone else yet. My name is Adam, and this my roommate, Will."

The light haired girl, who had not yet spoken a single word, said, "I'm Julie." She reached out her hand to greet Adam and Will.

"My name is Sahar," spoke the dark-haired girl.

"Which hall are you in?" asked Will.

"Water Hall, fifth floor," replied Julie.

"We're in the Water Hall too—third floor," said Will. "Maybe we'll see you around."

"Maybe," said Sahar.

After exchanging formalities, Will and Adam departed. They walked through the commons and foyer, and outside to the reflecting pool. They sat on the edge of the pool. Decorative lamps illuminated the otherwise dark campus. Stars twinkled in the clear black sky.

"What did you think of Sahar?" asked Will.

Adam shrugged his shoulders. "She seemed nice."

"And pretty," said Will, smiling, "but I wouldn't want to get on her bad side."

"I agree. We both saw how quickly she humbled Jett." Both of the boys chuckled. Before long they felt the cool air seep through their layers, and decided to go back inside. Despite school not being in session, there was still a 9:30 p.m. curfew. They left, retiring to their dorm.

Will seemed to have no trouble sleeping, but Adam lie awake with too many thoughts running through his head. He had naively hoped Arcadia would be free of people like Joseph, but then he met Jett. While Jett did not wear the same dirty clothes as Joseph, his personality was equally unpleasant. The situation baffled Adam; Joseph was a victim of abuse and neglect. His actions were the learned result of the way people treated him. Jett was obviously the benefactor of a more luxurious lifestyle. His father was a governor— one of the country's leaders. By every measure, society viewed that family as "better" and "more successful," but to Adam, the only apparent difference was the price of Jett's clothes. How could someone with everything still treat people like trash? What was his excuse? At least Jett momentarily got what he deserved, no matter how fleeting it was.

~

By Sunday afternoon the campus was swarming with students, new and old. The younger students dallied through the campus, while the older students chuckled at the new ones who got lost at every corner. Two new roommates, Jared and Nick, greeted Adam and Will. Nick's parents were professors, one at Georgetown and one at George Washington University. He was the youngest of three children and both of his older sisters attended Arcadia, as had the two parents. One sister recently graduated, and the other sister still had two years remaining. Similarly, Jared came from a well-to-do family. His father worked for Aegis Technology, and his mother was an accountant. His father and older brother were both legacies of Arcadia. The more people Adam met, the more he felt out of place. Almost everyone came from a wealthy family, and many had family members that were alumni of Arcadia. To the best of his knowledge, he and Will were the only ones who came from a modest, middle class upbringing. It was completely disparate from what Adam had grown accustomed to in Cammalot. Most of the students appeared healthy and fit, they wore unblemished upscale regalia, their word choices were more deliberate, and no one reeked of stale cigarettes. Adam wondered if students would silently condescend to his relative lower-class upbringing in the same way he disdained the savages in Cammalot.

At 6:45 p.m., the entire school gathered in the auditorium for the dean's commencement speech. Adam and his roommates attempted to enter the auditorium together, but were separated by the crowd. He surveyed the area and could not see Will, Jared, or Nick, but a few yards away sat Sahar and Julie. Adam slipped through the crowd and approached the girls. "Do you mind if I sit here?" he asked. With an open palm, Sahar pointed at the empty chair, and Adam sat.

"Where is your roommate?" she said with a hint of surprise.

"We got separated in the crowd." Despite the noise of the crowd, an awkward silence passed. Having spent the last two years in Cammalot, surrounded by people dissimilar to him, Adam rarely engaged in small talk. Failing to think of anything important to say, he asked, "Are you ready for classes?"

Sahar nodded. "I think so. I read my textbooks before I came here." A surprised look embodied Adam's face. The month before coming to Cammalot was the first time he voluntarily read textbooks, and even then, it was his mother's idea.

"Why?" said Adam. Sahar shrugged her shoulders.

"I want to be prepared," she replied. "Arcadia is known for the demanding workload. Nearly a quarter of first year students drop out within two years." The comment unsettled Adam.

"How do you know so much about Arcadia?" he asked, "is your father an Arcadia alumni?"

She shook her head. "No, he went to school in Tel Aviv. We didn't move to the United States until I was five."

"What made you move here?"

"My parents wanted an excuse to leave Tel Aviv. My father was Jewish, and my mother is Muslim. They always felt that people were judging them and watching them. That type of resentment is unsettling, so my father found a job in Boston as a computer programmer," said Sahar. "And my mother was accepted for a post-doc."

"What's a post-doc?"

"A post-doc is a short-term research project. My mother earned her PhD in chemistry, then worked on achieving citizenship while completing her post-doc."

Adam paused to absorb the information. Hesitantly, he asked, "Do you mind if I ask what happened to your father?"

Sahar looked away, considering whether to share. After a few seconds she spoke, "He was murdered a few years ago." Adam grimaced. He almost started to apologize, but remembered their earlier conversation where Sahar revealed a no-pity preference.

"My sister was murdered a few months ago," said Adam.

"Experiencing a family member's murder is an unfortunate event for us to have in common. I hope we have something more positive in common."

"Likewise," said Adam.

Before they could share another word, the auditorium lights dimmed and a man wearing a navy pinstriped suit approached the podium located center stage. "Greetings," he spoke. His voice bellowed through the speakers, filling every ounce of empty space. "My name is Lawrence Kennedy, Dean of Arcadia." Applause resounded. Adam found his mind reeling. Could he find enough commonalities to make new friends? Could he survive the academic rigor? He kept thinking of his family back home, hoping that they would forgive him for abandoning them. Occasionally, Adam caught himself sidetracking and he corrected himself. He caught some of the main points from Mr. Kennedy's speech. Mr. Kennedy reiterated his expectations of academic and professional excellence; in essence, students of Arcadia are "the best of the best" and are expected to work hard and abide by campus rules. He emphasized the culture of tolerance and open dialogue, as well as the need for academic integrity. The entire campus was monitored by SSDs, and all students were to adhere to the 9:30 p.m. curfew. He also confirmed Sahar's rumor: nearly one fourth of students fail to make it past year two. The speech was not markedly different than the welcome speech Adam heard at the Cammalot schools every year: have pride in your school, and strive to be an upstanding student and citizen.

After the opening ceremony, students gathered in the commons for a school social, though Adam decided to skip the social and study his textbooks. Sahar's comment about being prepared, and the dean's comment about the twenty five percent attrition rate, effectively scared Adam into studying.

The social concluded around 9:00 p.m., and Sahar left to her room. When she arrived on the fifth floor, a crowd was gathered in the middle of the hall. Inaudible chatter and whispers echoed down the corridor. She slowly approached the crowd, and realized they were gathered around her door. She squeezed through the standing bodies, and stared in awe at the door to her room. Etched in the door was a large swastika, about eighteen inches tall and wide. There were no words, but the message was clear: you are not welcome here.

6

Monday, January 9, 2068

Adam awoke from a restless night. Not only was he nervous about classes, the same reoccurring dream of the boy murdering Hannah haunted his mind. He quickly dressed into his gym clothes and left with his roommates to the gym.

There were two time periods during the day when students were not required to don the official school uniforms: physical training, and self-defense. Students were still required to wear Arcadia t-shirts and gym shorts or sweats, but it was still better than the dull navy blue uniforms.

They arrived at precisely 7:00a.m. At least twenty-five male students stood in line-formation. There were no female students in sight. A man stood center, calling out names for attendance. Adam, Will, Peter, and Jared, quickly realized that the students stood in alphabetical order. They hastily found their places. Once the man finished roll call, he spoke with a naturally loud voice that bellowed through the gymnasium, "Welcome to PT. My name is Dr. Rush, and yes, I am a real doctor. My undergraduate degree is in biology. I served as a marine in the Third Korean War, after which I earned my MD from Johns Hopkins. My goal is to make you faster and stronger." He paced back and forth, and continued talking. "You will sweat every day. You will push your body to exertion. I will break you down, only to build you back up. If your muscles do not ache, and you do not feel like kneeling to the porcelain god, then you have not worked hard enough." He paused, facing the class. "Questions?"

Each student stood completely still and silent. Dr. Rush shifted his eyes left and right, waiting for a response, but no student had the courage to speak. "We will meet in the gym on Mondays, Wednesdays, and Fridays. Tuesdays and Thursdays we will meet in the courtyard, by the reflecting pool. Rain, shine, snow, or blistering heat, we will be running. Mondays and Wednesdays are for cardio and strength training, and Fridays we will play my favorite game: dodge-ball." The boys cheered. "Let's get started!"

The students were then instructed to lightly jog for five minutes. Adam and Will ran next to each other. "I can't help but wonder if this will be our most demanding course," said Will.

"I have a feeling this is going to be our easiest course," replied Adam. Will quivered.

After the warm-up, Rush led the boys through ballistic stretches. For the next forty minutes, the boys completed several rounds of intense cardio, starting with suicides: sprinting to the opposite end of the gym as fast as possible. As soon as the last boy arrived at the opposite side, everyone sprinted again, back to where they started. Adam noticed that Jett always arrived at the opposite side first. Will always trailed slightly behind Adam, and Adam was neither the fastest nor slowest student. Push-ups followed suicides. Then floor-sprints, power jumps, and a myriad of other intense exercises. Forty-five minutes later, the workout ended.

"I think I'm going to blow chunks," grumbled Will, with his hands nurturing his stomach.

"My heart is about to jump out of my chest," groaned Adam.

A few yards away they saw Jett. His held his hands over his head. His face was red and he breathed heavily, but he seemed to be in much less discomfort than Adam and Will.

Adam showered, ate breakfast, and arrived at math. He had grown accustomed to the math lessons in Cammalot: dull, slow, easy, and many off-task students. There were no off-task students in Dr. DiPrima's class. He had gray hair and wrinkles, but perfect posture. His hoarse and stern voice could tame a banshee. When he moved across the room, he paced. Jett sat in the corner, completing a Sudoku puzzle while DiPrima introduced himself. DiPrima noticed Jett, and in a gravelly voice berated, "You! Get out of my classroom! Come back when you are ready to do some real math!" The class sat in astonishment—quiet enough to hear a pin drop.

Jett did not argue; he simply scoffed. "Whatever." When the door closed behind him, the entire class sat in silence.

DiPrima knew he was the smartest person in the room, and he had no problem making it known. He wrote as fast as he could talk while students scrambled to write down as many details as possible. The goal was not to learn everything in class, but to have a set of comprehensive notes that allowed one to piece together the details that evening. DiPrima could seamlessly recite physical constants to ten decimal places. The first day, he said, "I only have fifty minutes to give you a test, and I won't give you any test that I can't complete in less than a minute." Considering how fast DiPrima could write and mentally solve complex equations, no one doubted that statement.

Dr. DiPrima spent little time on introductions. The only tools he needed were chalk and a chalkboard (tools a few students recognized from old movies, but no one had ever seen in the real world). No modern technology. He spoke like a drill sergeant addressing new recruits. When he finished showing the class how to solve a problem he aggressively tapped the board with his chalk, dusted his hands, and stated, "That's how you solve that animal."

At the end of the lesson, DiPrima spoke, "Rarely will I ask you to memorize something—I always want you to be able to derive it by first principals. However, this is the exception. Commit this to your memory." He paced back and forth, pointing at the class. "Do you understand?" he asked rhetorically. "I want you to pretend that there is a man with a machete standing at the door." DiPrima pointed towards the door. "He is going to ask you to recite this formula, and if you fail to deliver, he will chop off your head! Memorize it!" Despite DiPrima's austere character, Adam enjoyed the math class. He understood the material, and was relieved to get through a math lesson without disruptions and complaints.

Social studies was next. Adam felt he would be more successful if he sat in the front of the room, but Will did not want to sit in the front row, so they sat in the second row. A slender, gray haired man of average height, wearing beige slacks and an argyle sweater vest stood at the front of the room. Projected on the screen were the words:

First Year Social Studies
Dr. Williams

The man waited patiently while the final group of students tread through the door. Adam noticed Sahar and Julie sitting on the opposite side of the room. "Welcome to social studies," spoke the man in the sweater vest. "I'm Dr. Williams." He slowly paced around the front of the class, utilizing the whole stage. "Can anyone tell me where the S&P 500 opened this morning?" The students looked around to see if anyone raised their hand. "Eleven thousand four hundred eighty nine points." He paused again. "Who can tell me the name of Napoleon Bonaparte's final battle?" Again, the class was silent. Then Sahar raised her hand. Dr. Williams pointed to her.

"The Battle of Waterloo."

"Good," said Professor Williams. He paced again. "Let us try another question. In what year did the United States enter World War Two?" After another brief pause, Sahar's hand was the only one raised. The professor pointed towards her with an open palm.

"December, 1941" she said.

"Excellent. What is your name?" said Dr. Williams. He looked at Sahar, and the rest of the class looked at her as well. They waited for her to respond.

"Sahar, sir."

Dr. Williams turned his attention back towards the entire class. "Let us try a more challenging question," he said. "Article One of the U.S. Constitution states 'The privilege of the writ of habeas corpus shall not be suspended, unless when in cases of rebellion or invasion the public safety may require it.' Which presidents have suspended habeas corpus? And for those who do not know, habeas corpus allows convicted persons the right to a court or judge."

Sahar did not need to raise her hand, for Dr. Williams was staring at her, waiting for an answer. She looked around the room and saw nothing but puzzled faces. She looked back to Dr. Williams and responded, "Officially, President Lincoln was the only president to suspend habeas corpus. He did so during the Civil War. Andrew Johnson later revoked the suspension. However, there have been several minor cases of martial law being instituted for short periods of time in the U.S., for example, during the Great Chicago Fire, and West Virginia Coal wars, to name a couple. The Posse Comitatus Act of 1878 forbids military involvement in domestic law enforcement without congressional approval, but the National Defense Authorization Act of 2012 essentially overrides that provision."

Dr. Williams smiled. "Very good," he said. "As a side note, the Defense Authorization Act also authorizes indefinite detention of persons suspected of terrorism." Williams slowly stepped to the other side of the room. "Let us see if someone other than Sahar can answer a question correctly. What resource did China place a full export embargo on in 2020?" The professor scanned the room. No students raised their hands. He pointed at a boy in the third row. "Young man, what is the resource?"

The boy stammered. "Umm... I'm not sure Professor Williams."

"Well go on, guess."

"Coal?" the boy asked.

The professor pompously replied, "Wrong." The boy slouched and turned red.

"How about you?" said the professor, pointing at Adam.

Adam's heart started racing. Everyone stared at him. He remembered reading something about it before school started. He searched through his mind. It was a material used in technology, and most of the world's supply was in China. He remembered reading that it was a strategic move intended to force firms to relocate production in China. Was it copper? Silver? Aluminum? He took a deep breath and guessed. "Is it silicon?"

Behind him he heard a student let out a low laugh. Adam turned his head, and saw Jett smugly smirking. Jett feigned a cough, as he not-so-subtly said, "neural implant malfunction," then coughed again. His two friends sitting next to him laughed. Adam had never heard of neural implants, and wondered what they were.

Dr. Williams peered towards Jett and said, "I suppose you know the answer?"

The comment startled Jett. He stuttered and said, "Gold."

"It appears your neural implant is also malfunctioning," stated the professor. The class laughed. Jett clenched his fists and scowled. The professor continued lecturing: "Surely someone's neural implant is functioning properly." Sahar raised her hand and Dr. Williams called on her.

"Rare earth elements," she stated calmly.

"Correct, indeed," said the professor.

In the corner of his ear, Adam heard Jett scoff.

"And what model is your neural implant?" asked Dr. Williams.

Sahar paused, then responded, "I don't have one sir."

"And her brain still trumped yours, even without a cognitive enhancement," said Williams, pointing at the class. He looked at Sahar and smiled. "Well done, young lady. Keep up the good work."

After the questions, which felt like an eternity, Williams lectured the students for the remainder of the class. He previewed the many topics they would learn about: economics, history, government, religion, and much more. When the class was dismissed, Adam could hear Jett complaining to his friends. "I don't even know why people without neural implants are allowed into Arcadia. When did our standards get so low?"

One of his friends laughed and said, "She still beat you."

Jett hit his friend and berated him. "Shut up, half-wit! She got lucky. It won't happen again. One day she'll get what she deserves." Will heard the conversation as well. He could not tell if Jett was venting, or if he had malicious intent.

"Mr. Holden," beckoned the professor. Jett halted. "I need to speak with you." Jett rolled his eyes and walked back into the classroom, while everyone else left. Adam and Will did not stick around to hear the conversation, but hoped for Jett to be reprimanded for his conduct.

Music came next. When they arrived at the classroom they saw a young attractive lady with dark hair and plastic-frame glasses, leaning against the wall. She welcomed and smiled at every single student that walked through the door. When everyone was seated she introduced herself as Dr. Kimberly Tait, but insisted that students feel free to call her Ms. Tait or Dr. Kim. Whenever a student asked a question, Dr. Kim sought to learn that student's name. Adam was not the first to notice that Ms. Tait was different than the other professors. Aside from being one of the few female teachers at Arcadia, Dr. Kim seemed genuinely nice and modest. She did not boast about her knowledge—though she her intelligence paralleled that of the other professors—and she did not need students to refer to her as "Dr." to validate her achievements or satisfy her ego. Students were more relaxed in her presence and less afraid of making mistakes. Judging from the syllabus, the class would be just as demanding as the other classes, but free of the pressure caused by rigid, egotistical professors.

During lunch break, Adam and Will spotted Jared and Nick, and joined them at the lunch table. The first thing Nick said was: "Did you here about the vandalism?" Adam and Will both looked at each other bewildered. "Someone etched a swastika on the door of some Jewish girl."

"Was it Sahar's room?" asked Will.

Nick shrugged his shoulders. "I don't know who's room it was, I just heard about it last class."

Will smacked his palm on the table. "I bet it was Jett!" he blurted. "We saw him harassing Sahar yesterday! I remember him saying that Jews and Christians shouldn't be allowed at Arcadia because they're too dumb."

"We should figure out a way to get him back," suggested Jared. "I met him in my English class today. My first thought was, 'what a jerk.' He thinks he's better than everyone because his dad is a governor."

Adam leaned forward and spoke quietly: "I don't like him either, but we don't even know for sure if it was him. Plus, if we get caught, we might get kicked out."

"How about this," started Nick. "We keep our ears open and eyes peeled for any evidence linking Jett to the swastika. If we find out it was him, we'll come up with a plan to get him quietly, so no one knows it was us. This place is monitored by SSDs twenty-four-seven."

"I'm in," said Will. He put his hand in the middle of the table. Jared and Nick followed suit. They all looked at Adam, waiting for his response. Adam hesitated. He thought about the last time he sought revenge; how it started with a pinprick and escalated until the perpetrator lay in a bloody stupor. Adam convinced himself that this would not escalate into something extreme.

"Only if we know for certain it was Jett, and nothing drastic," he said. Then he placed his hand in the middle. "No one else needs to know about this."

"I agree," said Will. "Let's keep this between the four of us."

~

Computer programming followed lunch. The first skill students studied was the binary number system. Having spent countless hours building robots with Henry, Adam was already familiar with binary. However, he never realized that he could use binary to count to one thousand twenty-three on his fingers. The computer programming class was mostly review. In Cammalot, Adam disliked that most of his classes were review; he wanted to assimilate new knowledge. But given the rigor of his previous classes, reviewing basic computer science was a relief.

After computer science, the Adam shuffled to Mandarin. The language looked difficult to learn, but the professor did not assign official homework. Instead, she simply encouraged the students to try to practice their new language skills outside of the classroom.

The final academic class was science. Similar to the other academic classes at Arcadia, it was fun, interesting, rigorous, and challenging. Adam recalled the comments from earlier in the day about neural implants, and thought the science teacher would be able to explain it. He stayed after class to ask the professor about it. The professor gave him a long-winded sermon. Adam did not understand every detail, but he understood the main points. For over fifty years, scientists across the world had been mapping the human brain. The "map" was still in development, but it was well known which regions of the brain were active for various functions. Every thought and emotional state is the result of neurons interacting, thereby creating minuscule electrical discharges. As the professor explained it, the neural implant, or NI, recognizes neural activity and stimulates the region of the brain where more neural activity is present, resulting in faster neural interactions. This leads to cognitive enhancements. For example, when a person is mentally solving a math problem, neural activity in the left supramarginal gyrus (part of the brain's parietal lobe) increases. The NI stimulates this area, allowing the subject to solve the problem faster. In general, the NI allows the user to read faster, memorize facts with less effort, and patterns become more apparent. Calculators become obsolete because it is quicker to perform the calculations mentally. Consequently, because NIs stimulated additional neural activity indiscriminately, they also caused subjects to experience a deeper, higher quality REM sleep, allowing the user to operate on fewer hours of rest.

The NI was not a panacea for doltishness. If the subject was not familiar with basic algebra, having an NI would not help them solve "three x plus seven equals 13." However, if the subject was trying to learn algebra, the neural implant could help him learn it quicker and make connections faster. The biggest drawback was a flaw with the first model. The original model could not differentiate between thoughts and emotions. It recognized neural activity in all regions, and stimulated that region indiscriminately. If the subject became angry, neural activity in the amygdala increased. The NI responded by further stimulating that area, causing the subject to experience extreme anger. When the amygdala is active, it overpowers the region of the brain responsible for thought and logic. If the subject was generally emotional or mercurial, the NI could potentially cause them to behave like a Neanderthal—opposite of the desired effect. In many cases, the subject would not revert to normal until they awoke from a deep sleep. Unfortunately, an NI was permanent, not to mention expensive.

The professor explained that the second generation NI mostly fixed the issue of exacerbating emotional states, but it still magnified personality traits. Nice people became nicer, mean people became meaner, and lazy people became lazier. The third and current generation model was not able to fix this, but it was built with the ability to receive software updates.

Adam thought about the implications of NIs. The professor said that nearly ninety percent of Arcadia students had either second or third generation NIs, and they had become increasingly popular for students from upper-middle class families. Yet, in small and rural areas such as Cammalot, NIs were virtually unheard of. Adam wondered what students at Arcadia would be like if they grew up in Cammalot. Were they inherently smarter than the average thirteen year old? Would they still have been accepted to Arcadia without neural implants? He questioned why he was accepted into Arcadia. Most of the other students seemed to have superior intellect and influential parents. Adam may have been the smartest thirteen-year-old in Cammalot, but the standards were low. Why did Jeff Locke recommend he apply to Arcadia? He had never heard of Arcadia before meeting Locke, but he wondered if Arcadia would have accepted him if he had applied without Locke's recommendation.

The conversation with his science professor took more time than he intended. Adam barely had enough time to change into gym clothes before going to self-defense. When he arrived at self-defense, he was surprised to see boys and girls in the same class, for boys and girls were segregated for PT. The idea of sparring with a girl was unsettling. His father taught him never to raise a hand against a female—it just was not right (unless, of course, his life was threatened). Even more dismaying was the fact that Jett was also in self-defense. Every time Adam thought about Jett, all he wanted to do was knock the smug grin from Jett's face. Luckily, he also had friends in class. His roommate, Will, was in self-defense, as was Sahar. Sahar was not exactly his friend per se, but aside from his other roommates, she was the closest thing to a friend. Plus, he respected her character and felt they were on the same side.

After the professor took attendance, a girl raised her hand. "Yes," said the instructor, pointing at her.

The girl asked, "I'm looking forward to learning how to defend myself, but it seems odd that this is one of our core classes. With all due respect, why do we need to learn this?"

"The short answer is politics. Some of our largest donors are prominent military families. As such, they expect a certain level of preparedness for those who will eventually enroll in officer school. It was during the Third Korean War, when there was talk of reinstating the draft, that combat training became a required course. Of course, certain people were appalled at the idea of teaching kids how to kill, so the academy renamed the class 'self-defense,' which appeased the yuppies, and everyone was happy. But truth be told, the U.S. is always firing at somebody, or is the target on someone else's radar, so it's best to be prepared for any and every situation you could potentially face." The instructor paused, paced, then asked, "Any more questions?"

No one raised a hand. The instructor started with a lesson about safety. Naturally, many students automatically droned-out of the dull safety lecture. Once the safety lesson was over, the professor reengaged everyone when he said, "You are all responsible students, otherwise you wouldn't be here. With that said, the first move I am going to show you is a type of chokehold. It can knock someone out in seven seconds, and it can kill someone in as little as ten seconds." Then he told everyone that the only acceptable time to use it is in a life and death situation.

One student volunteered to be the test dummy. While narrating, the professor stood behind the student. He pointed at the lower metacarpal bone of the thumb, just above the wrist. He then positioned his hand so that the bone was centered on the student's larynx. He reached his left arm under the student's left arm, then grabbed his right hand and exerted a light pressure on the larynx. The student felt a slight discomfort and coughed. "Once you are in this position, pull back with your left hand and step into a lunge position.

This will cause your opponent to fall back onto your knee, and he will not be able to escape this position before he is knocked unconscious." The students were then allowed to practice the move, but without exerting pressure.

After self defense, nearly every boy in the class, including Adam and Will, went back to their rooms to test the move on each other. When it was Adam's turn to be choked-out, he felt a slight discomfort, followed by a hysterical panic and intense pain. Then a dark haze enshrouded his vision. Before Adam completely lost consciousness, Will attenuated his grip. They had no desire to knock each other unconscious; they only wanted to make sure the move worked (and it did).

~

The rest of the evening, including the dinner hour, was free time for students, though "free time" was a relative phrase. It really meant, "Free to study your chosen topic." And even though curfew was 9:30 p.m., most students were in their rooms studying past that time. Some students chose to spend the evening socializing, but they would likely be the students who failed out within the first two years.

Adam returned to his room after dinner. When he arrived at the door, he noticed a large, but thin, hardcover book lying on the floor. He picked up the book, sat on his bed, and peered through it. The cover was the same color as Arcadia's school colors. It read 'Arcadia 2064.' There were pictures of students—all taken on the Arcadia campus. He browsed the yearbook, page by page. One particular picture caught his attention. There must have been over a hundred students in that picture, but a student in the back row looked conspicuous. To a casual observer, he was just another student, but Adam recognized the face. It glowed. It shouted at him, demanding his attention. It was a face he could never forget. The same face that had been haunting his dreams for several months. The face with an irreverent grin and murderous eyes: the face that killed Hannah.

7

Sunday, January 29, 2068

Nearly three weeks had passed since Adam saw Hannah's killer in the yearbook, and questions were rife in his mind. He had scanned through the yearbook dozens of times, but there was only one picture of the murderer. Every student had a standard mug shot with their name displayed below it, but not the murderer. Adam hoped the boy's name would be in the index. He used the standard photos to match each face to a name. Page by page he crossed out faces of named students. In the end, no names persisted, and the murderer remained a face without a name. Without the name of the killer, deciphering a motive was untenable.

Despite the unanswered questions, Adam had good reason to be optimistic. Whoever left the book for Adam to find knew something about the murder, and it stood to reason he or she would be willing to help Adam. Adam desperately wanted to talk to someone about the mystery. Maybe someone could approach the problem from a different angle, offer invaluable advice, or simply tell him he was paranoid. His mother often made the most trenchant observations, and during the past three weeks Adam sent weekly emails to his mother, but he purposefully neglected to mention the yearbook. He saw no justification for agitating settled emotions. Plus, his mother indicated that his grandpa had been in and out of the hospital multiple times over the past three weeks. She already had enough to worry about; she did not need to be bothered by Adam's conspiracy theories.

Adam finally decided that he needed to talk to someone. During lunch, he sat at an empty cafeteria table with Will. Adam fumbled with small talk while trying to summon the courage to share his thoughts. Naturally, the conversation shifted in a different direction.

"Did anyone get in trouble for the swastika?" said Will.

Adam replied, "Not that I know of." Will took a bite of his food.

After he finished chewing, Will remarked, "Something doesn't seem right. We're constantly being watched by SSDs, but they still don't know who carved the swastika on the door."

"Maybe the school is trying to downplay the incident," suggested Adam. "The school has a reputation to uphold. If they acknowledge that the event happened, they have to admit there is anti-Semitism here. If they ignore it, they can pretend that it didn't happen."

"Interesting idea," replied Will. "I was thinking that they might be testing us. Maybe they're waiting for someone to speak out against it, or at least do something about it." Adam scratched his chin. "Think about it. Jett hasn't gotten in trouble for any of his charades or comments. That wouldn't fly at any other school. This place is training our country's best leaders, and leaders take action."

"I don't know. That sort of thing happened all the time at Cammalot." said Adam.

"But we're not at Cammalot! We're at one of the best schools in the country!"

"By your logic, a school official could have drawn it just to give someone an opportunity to prove themselves," said Adam, "and I can't picture the school doing such a thing."

"But no one has gotten in trouble yet. We have to admit that either the school knows who did it and is refusing to act, or they truly have no idea."

"In other words, they are either cruel or incompetent."

"Exactly!" said Will. "And none of these people appear incompetent. They're some of the smartest people in the country. Why wouldn't they have figured it out by now?"

Adam scratched his head.

"You don't think I'm being paranoid, do you?" questioned Will.

Adam shook his head and said, "No."

The irony made him chuckle inside, because if anything, Adam was the paranoid one. After Will's conjecture, Adam became more comfortable about sharing the yearbook conspiracy. He deliberated for a moment, then said to Will: "I've been working on something. If I show you, can you promise not to judge?"

"Of course," said Will. Adam reached into his backpack and took out the yearbook. Will sat upright and looked at it. After seeing the front cover, he immediately recognized that it was a yearbook. "Where did you get that?"

"Three weeks ago someone left it in front of our door."

Will's eyes shifted. Adam followed Will's eyes and saw Julie and Sahar approach. "Do you mind if we sit here?" asked Julie. Adam preferred the privacy, but felt rude turning them away.

"No, go ahead," replied Adam.

"Where did you get the yearbook?" asked Sahar. She reached for it and opened the book. A strange look encompassed her face when she saw the faces crossed out.

"As I was telling Will, someone left it in front of our dorm room three weeks ago." Everyone stared at Adam, as if he was insane. "I know how it looks, so let me explain." He took a deep breath. "I never told you what happened to my sister."

"You said she was murdered," stated Sahar. Will and Julie gave each other surprised looks. It was the first they heard of Hannah.

"Almost four months ago, she was stabbed by an unidentified boy. He was probably thirteen or fourteen." Will bowed his head sorrowfully. Julie and Sahar reacted with solemn expressions. Adam took another deep breath. "The boy who killed her is in this yearbook."

A moment of silence passed. "I don't understand," said Will. "You said he was unidentified." Adam grabbed the yearbook, and opened it to the page with the boy's picture. Every face in the picture, except for one, was crossed out. The anonymous face was circled

"Police couldn't figure out who he was, but that's him," said Adam, pointing at the face. "It's the only picture of him in the entire yearbook, and it's the only picture without a name." Will, Julie, and Sahar stared at Adam. Their expressions indicated concern, but also a hint of fear. "You probably think I'm crazy..."

"Not exactly," said Will, "but it's hard to make out anyone's face in that photo." Adam's eyes grew moist. He did not want to cry in front of his friends, but was struggling to keep the tears at bay.

"I am sorry, Adam, but I agree with Will," spoke Sahar, in a quiet voice. "How do you even know that is the same boy?"

"Because I saw him kill her!" said Adam. "I watched him kick her in the ribs and pummel her face." Tears started to trickle. "I could see his face through the scope of my rifle. And after I shot him..." Adam sniffled and stuttered. His breathing grew heavy. Forming coherent words became difficult. "And after I shot him, I watched him stab her in the chest." Adam wiped the tears from his face. "I know that face, because it has haunted my dreams every night for the last four months."

Sahar gently touched his shoulder. He looked at her. In a soft voice, she spoke, "I am sorry." Adam never liked receiving pity, but those two words spoken in a melodious voice were like a gift from the sky. It was as if an angel recognized his pain and agony and promised to heal it.

"I'm sorry, too," said Will. "I didn't mean to doubt you."

"No," said Adam. "There's nothing to be sorry about." He wiped the dried tears from his face. "I didn't mean to—"

"It's okay," said Will. "No need to apologize." Adam faintly smiled. "Can I ask," started Will, "the boy who killed..."

"Hannah." said Adam.

"Right. The boy that killed Hannah. You shot him... did he..." Before Will could finish his question, Adam nodded his head. He knew exactly what Will wanted to ask. "You did what you had to do. I would have done the same thing in that situation."

"I know. But I wish it wasn't like that." Adam's voice trailed.

A moment of silence passed.

"I take it, you don't know who left the book for you to find?" asked Julie. Adam shook his head.

The conversation was abruptly interrupted by the sound of squeaking footsteps approaching. The scent of expensive cologne wafted in. Adam turned around to see Jett standing arrogantly behind him. Jett tilted his head to the side and offered a cocky smile. "Looks like I just missed the waterworks," said Jett with a caustic laugh.

"Buzz off," snarked Will.

Ignoring Will's request, Jett continued his lambast. "Wow, did someone die, or did you just scrape your knee?" Jett laughed again.

Will stood and shouted at Jett: "Are you deaf or stupid! I said go away!"

"And who's going to make me? You?" Jett's smile ceased when Will cocked his arm. Jett's eyes grew wide. Awash in the laughter from his own snide remark, he missed the opportunity to avoid Will's fist. Will's knuckles connected with Jett's nose, successfully knocking the grin from Jett's face. Jett stumbled and fell backwards. Everyone at the table gasped, then stood. They could not help but smile at the sight of Jett squirming on the floor, nursing his nose.

Jett quickly collected himself. He held his nose. Blood seeped between the cracks of his fingers. Tears greeted his eyes. With a slight whimper in his voice, Jett spoke, "You better watch your back!" He stormed away, and everyone congratulated Will.

Adam smiled and laughed. "I've been wanting to do that for three weeks," he said.

"You and the whole school," remarked Julie. Everyone laughed.

"I think I need some fresh air. I'll be outside if you need me," spoke Will.

"I could use a breather, too," said Julie. Will and Julie departed. Sahar reached into her pocket and pulled out a piece of paper.

"I was about to show this to everyone," she said, "but then Jett interrupted us." She handed the paper to Adam. He unfolded it, revealing a combination of letters:

ELERRLDEHIYHOKOTLNUADERF

Adam leaned in closer. "What is it?" he asked.

"I am not sure. But I found it in an envelope on the floor in front of my room—three weeks ago. At first I did not know what to think of it."

"But now you think it might be related to the yearbook someone left me?" Sahar nodded.

"Someone left you a message about your sister's murderer. Maybe this has to do with my father's murder." Adam gave the paper back to Sahar. She folded it and put it in her pocket.

"The police never found a killer?" asked Adam. Sahar shook her head. "I think Will may be right. Something sinister is happening at Arcadia."

~

The next day Adam's mind wandered while he was sitting in class. Nearly every trivial incident distracted him; the drop of a pencil and the turning of notebook pages quickly snagged his attention. He gazed out the window, only to be distracted by the piercing gaze of a crow perched in the cherry blossom tree. Despite his best attempts to stay engaged in class, he found it difficult to focus through the every day banalities while questions of his sister's murder were resurfacing. It perplexed him why someone with information about a murder, possibly two murders, would hide that information. Even though he found a picture of Hannah's killer, he still felt like he hit a dead end. After speaking with Will and Sahar, they concluded that the envelope Sahar received must be some sort of message. Unfortunately, they did not know if the letters represented a scrambled message or encoded message. If it were a scrambled message, they calculated that there would be at least two trillion, and possibly even six trillion ways to unscramble the message. Without some sort of key or cypher, the message was another dead end.

The only class that was able to take Adam's mind away from the murder was social studies, perhaps because it was equally depressing and interesting, or perhaps because Adam had been robbed of a formal study of the social sciences in Cammalot. Dr. Williams also had a unique ability to engage the class. He could talk the entire period, and his skillful orations and encyclopedic knowledge always guaranteed an interesting lesson. The class settled, and Dr. Williams spoke, "If I were to ask you to list the ten most important people, dead or alive, famous or infamous, how would you respond?" The class was silent. "Take a moment to ponder this query, then record your answers in your notebook."

The professor slowly paced while students wrote. After a couple minutes passed, the professor spoke again. "I am sure some of you listed the names of famous scientists. Surely Albert Einstein, Niels Bohr, and James Clerk Maxwell made important contributions to the way we understand the universe. Or perhaps, you listed famous musicians, for the music of John Sebastian Bach and Wolfgang Amadeus Mozart has touched millions, if not billions of souls. Maybe you listed some CEOs of Fortune 500 companies for their ability to manage trillions of dollars and provide tens of thousands of jobs to eager workers. For the record, let us see a show of hands. How many of you had a scientist listed in your top three?" The professor looked around the room. Every single student sat with a hand held high.

"Did anybody list a famous politician?" Most hands, except for a few, went down. "Interesting," he remarked. The professor pointed towards Sahar, who held her hand high. "And why did you list a famous politician?" he asked.

"Because politicians have the greatest influence over the greatest number of people. They can control the amount of money circulating in the economy; they can artificially set the value of a currency. They set policies that can generate wealth or leave millions in penury. Politicians execute laws and appropriate funds to protect a country and its environment. They can lead a country into prosperity or ruin."

"Excellent," said Dr. Williams. "I have no intention to disparage or downplay the innovations of the world's top scientists or entrepreneurs, but politicians are, unfortunately, the most important people on the planet. If you do not believe me, think back to the Second World War. One politician in Germany was responsible for the deaths of approximately twelve million people—and that does not include the casualties of the war he created. Then there was the Russian dictator whose policies resulted in the death of twenty million of his own people; that was before World War II started. Then, starting in 1958, a Chinese politician's 'Great Leap Forward' resulted in the death of forty-five million Chinese citizens. Each one of these politicians embarked on a morally misguided quest to transform their country into a utopia and dominant world power, but in the process, brought death and destruction to millions of people."

Adam paused for a moment to consider the professor's proposition. He then raised his hand. The professor pointed at him and said, "Yes, Adam."

"Professor Williams, who do you consider the five most important people alive today?"

"And if I told, I may rob you of the opportunity to reach that conclusion. However, I can tell you that certain positions wield a disproportionate amount of power. For example, the presidents of the United States, China, and International Monetary Foundation all wield unequivocal power. Of course, the list would not be complete, absent of yours truly." The class laughed. Then the professor smiled and said, "You laugh as if my proposition were a joke." The class chuckled again.

"One reason I broach this topic is because I would like us to start focusing more on national politics. Over the past couple weeks viral strains have been damaging crops and killing livestock. Thankfully, this force has been endemic in only two states. But scientists are studying the strain, attempting to find out how to eradicate it."

A student in the back raised his hand. The professor recognized him, and the student stated: "You said that politicians are the most important people in the country, but if this virus spreads, it will be scientists, not politicians, solving the problem."

"Indeed you are correct," said the professor. "The work of the scientists is indisputably important. But who appropriates the funds and resources for these scientists?"

The student pondered, and then responded. "Bureaucrats."

"Precisely," said Dr. Williams, with a smile. "Like it or not, the fate of our country rests in the hands of bureaucrats. Even the most renowned scientists are merely of ancillary importance."

The lecture struck a chord with Adam. Obviously politicians wielded power, but the sheer size and scope of the power was mind-boggling. Adam thought of the people in Cammalot who would say things like, "I don't concern myself with politics," as if engaging in conversation about current events was somehow beneath them. Naturally, these were the people who did not vote, but perhaps it was for the best. Democracy requires people to educate themselves. Even the best politician is only as good as the people who elect him. Without adequate participation, and without a populace willing to learn and use logic, is it any wonder that the most skillful orator with the most colorful lies gets elected? *Of course not*, thought Adam. It is the type of person America demands.

~

After social studies and music, Adam was scheduled to eat lunch with Will, Jared, Nick, Julie, and Sahar. As they walked out of the music room, Adam said to Will, "I'll meet everyone in the cafeteria. I need to stop and use the restroom first." Will nodded and they parted ways.

Students swarmed the halls, as they always did in between classes. Adam walked down the bustling hall and into the restroom. As he entered, another student exited. For privacy reasons, the restrooms were the only areas on campus not monitored by SSDs. Silence filled the empty room, save for faint echoes from the hall. Adam stood in front of the urinal, facing the wall. A moment later, two older boys entered the room. One went straight to the sink, behind Adam. Adam heard the water running, and paper towels being taken from the dispenser. The larger boy stood in front of the urinal next to Adam. Adam ignored the boy with the intent of avoiding an awkward bathroom conversation. The tone of the water stream in the sink ascended, indicating the sink was nearly full. Adam slowly approached the second sink to wash his hands. He heard the large boy follow behind him.

The water in the second sink had nearly risen to the brim. A paper towel wad clogged the drain. Adam ignored it, dispensed soap on his hands, and rubbed his hands together under the stream of water. From the corner of Adam's eye, he saw the boy standing near the sink eyeing him. Something felt awry. Several seconds passed before the boy spoke, "Your friend has much to learn." Adam gave the boy a confused expression. "Anyone who trifles with my little brother trifles with me."

Then he heard the burly boy standing behind him crack his knuckles and speak, "Jett sends his regards." The burly boy rushed Adam and grabbed the back of his shirt and head, while the second boy slugged him in the gut, then again in the nose. Together, they forced his head into the sink and held his face underwater. Adam's instinct was to inhale, but doing so only caused agony and allowed water to seep into his lungs. They pulled his head up allowing him a brief moment of air, then forced his face back into the water. The rapid exchange between agony and reprieve discombobulated his senses. He tried to think of an escape strategy, but *air* was the only word to cross his mind.

After his head had been dunked several times, the aggressors stopped and pushed him to the ground. Adam lay on his back stridently. Blood flowed from his nose, staining his shirt and dripping on the wet tiles. He rolled over and perched on his hands and knees in a pool of water and blood. His stomach ached. The coughing momentarily ceased when he vomited. Bile and water swept across the floor. The two boys laughed. "Had enough?" asked one of them in a mocking tone. Adam's violent cough continued. His muscles burned and his body felt weak. He expected the boys to continue their assault. They probably had someone guarding the door, thereby preventing anyone from assisting him.

No one is coming to help me, he thought. The two thugs could continue their batter unabridged. In his mind, there were only two viable options: accept another beating and let Jett win, or risk a more severe beating for the chance to escape. The latter option was worth the risk. Adam hurtled toward the larger boy, catching him by surprise. His shoulder struck the boy's midsection, causing the boy to stumble backwards and fall. Adam turned, only to see a fist on collision course with his face. The first connected to his face and stunned him. Then another, and another. He fell to the ground. Through his hazy vision he saw the large boy lying limp. His body was mostly flat. His head slouched against the wall beneath the urinal. Adam blinked, then felt a swift force batter his stomach repeatedly. The pain was too much. His eyes closed, but the beating continued.

After several more kicks, the beating ceased. Adam partially opened his eyes and saw the vague image of the aggressor squatting next to the unconscious boy. The door opened, and a voice shouted, "We need to get out of here." The boy stood and hastily left, leaving his fallen comrade behind. Adam groaned and shifted. The faint squeaking of the door's hinges sounded again. Feet scurried outside.

A minute later two people entered the bathroom. An adult voice muttered some obscenities and shouted, "Call an ambulance!" Adam heard footsteps nearby. He groaned and trembled. He slightly opened his eyes again and saw two adults huddled around the large boy on the floor. One of them muttered more obscenities before a despondent, shocked tone announced, "He doesn't have a pulse."

The other adult swore. "What the hell happened?"

"His head must've struck the urinal." The adults approached Adam and squatted over him. "Stay down until paramedics arrive." Tears rolled down his cheek, not because of the pain, but because of the guilt crushing his heart. He felt like he was back in the orchard. Another person died because of him. He knew it was an accident, that it was only self-defense, but he still made the choice to attack the burly boy. And that choice—the choice that resulted in the death of another human being—caused more agony than any of the physical abrasions. It did not matter that the boy attacked him first, or that the boy's barbarous disposition warranted some form of retribution. Adam's bruises would heal, but his soul was less mendable.

~

The arrival of paramedics warranted unsolicited attention. Every student tried to get as close as possible to the scene. The burly boy was hidden in a large black bag and transported to the ambulance. Paramedics gave Adam a cursory examination. They cleaned his cuts and bruises, and said there was no indication of a concussion, broken bones, or internal bleeding. Police documented and cleared the scene and interviewed Adam, but found no reason to take him into custody. They reviewed footage generated by the SSDs, but the surveillance footage did not show anyone other than Adam and the adults who discovered him enter the bathroom. It was perplexing even for the law enforcement officers. They attributed it to a glitch in the system. Police officers interviewed Jett's older brother. Several witnesses placed him at the opposite end of campus. Investigators completed a computerized search through the surveillance footage, looking for Jett's brother. He was found at the opposite side of campus several minutes before the attack, and then he disappeared completely from surveillance. The circumstances were suspect, but evidence was not strong enough to implicate Jett's brother in the attack or the death of the burly boy.

It was not until that evening that Adam was able to see his friends. Sahar gasped when she saw his bruised and battered face. "Is it that bad?" asked Adam, reaching up to touch his face. She shook her head. While focusing on himself, he almost failed to notice; something was different about Sahar. Instead of hair that flowed down to her waist, it barely scraped her shoulders. The edges were uneven.

Sahar noticed Adam staring at her hair. "I will get it fixed tomorrow," she said, referring to the choppy edges and rough cuts. "I was ambushed by three older boys. They held me down and cut my hair."

"Why?" asked Adam.

"Because of me," replied Will. "Because I punched Jett, they're trying to punish my friends."

"Why not just go after you?" asked Adam.

Sahar replied, "Is it not obvious? He wants to send a message. He wants us to know that bigger people are watching his back, and if we mess with him, he will come after our friends."

"I'm sorry," said Will, bowing his head remorsefully. "I didn't mean for this to happen."

Adam abruptly intruded, "Sorry for what? Were you the one who beat me? Did you cut Sahar's hair?"

"No," muttered Will, "but it feels like I did. If I hadn't punched Jett, none of this would have happened."

Sahar placed her hand on Will's shoulder. "That is exactly how Jett wants you to feel. Do not play into his game. It is not your fault."

"Thank you," said Will.

"Don't worry," said Adam. "We'll find a way to put an end to this. All three of us are shrewd and capable. It may not be today, or even this week, but we'll think of something."

Following the brief conversation, Sahar and Will provided Adam with the material he missed in class. At 9:00 p.m. he went outside. The cool breeze sent chills up and down his spine. A light snow dusted the ground. Alone, he stood in front of the reflecting pool. Other students were busy studying and avoiding the cold, but Adam rejoiced in solitude. The moment of silence gave him a sense of relief; a moment away from the bustling halls of overburdened students, and away from the vicious cycle of petulant politics. He walked over to a bench on the side of the walkway and brushed the snow off, then sat. Doleful images trickled into his mind. He thought of the day in the orchard. If he closed his eyes he could still feel the gun in his hands and smell the smoke after the shot fired. He could vicariously feel the visceral fear Hannah must have felt as she struggled for her life. Then he thought of Joseph laying on the ground, a scarlet mess, and finally, the semblance of the nameless burly boy, bleeding from the back of his head. Two people died because he acted; one was hospitalized, and one died because he acted too late. Adam again noticed the involuntary tremors in his hands. He focused solely on his hands, but they kept trembling uncontrollably.

A sudden twist perturbed his stomach. Adam keeled over to his hands and knees and hurled the food from his gut, then sobbed. He pleaded with God to make the pain go away and help him understand these tribulations. He begged for forgiveness, though he had yet to forgive himself. It did not matter that the most recent incident of violence was committed in self-defense, or that he killed Hannah's assailant attempting to protect her. The law might refer to these actions as "justifiable homicide," but that did not make killing two other humans any less abhorrent.

Pain is a construct the body creates to let the brain know something is awry. By necessity, it is an unpleasant sensation. If it were anything other than unpleasant, nearly every species would cease to exist, for pain could be replaced by ecstasy, and a mortally injured being would have no desire to cure its ailment. Adam realized that the soul serves the same purpose. The drums pounding in his mind and the piercing agony in his heart were signals, letting him know that his soul was being irreparably damaged. The incessant nightmares were merely reminders of Adam's incorporeal wounds. Injuries eventually heal. Even the grave wound that once marred his side eventually mended, but the scar tissue was a constant reminder of what happened.

8

Friday, February 24, 2068

Twice each semester students were given a temporary reprieve from classes: once during midterms and once during finals. Teachers did not hold classes with the presumption that students finished projects, solidified research papers, and studied for exams. However, students were still expected to attend physical training. With midterms fast approaching, Adam grew concerned with his grades. Every Friday at noon, grades were posted weekly on the electronic bulletin board in the main lobby. Names were not posted—only student ID numbers. The lobby was always crowded on Friday, as nearly everyone rushed to see their marks. At Cammalot, grades were something Adam never had to worry about. As long as he worked hard and tried hard, commanding the material and earning high marks was no challenge. Not at Arcadia. Adam typically studied and completed homework until 10:00 p.m. each night—sometimes later. Similarly, weekends were devoted to academic endeavors. But even with all the time and effort contributed to his studies, he was barely earning 'B' marks, and even had one 'C'. It was still on par with the average student—which should have felt like an accomplishment, given that the average student had the advantage of a neural implant—but it was still disheartening.

Other than Sahar, Adam did not know anyone without a neural implant that was earning mostly 'A's. Looking at the board, only a handful of students earned mostly 'A's. Jett was one of them. Every time grades were posted, Jett was always near the top of the class.

Adam and Will stood at the back of the crowd, waiting for people to leave so they could see the board. Then they heard Jett, cheering over his success, and disparaging everyone with lower marks. He pointed at his ID number, then Adam and Will heard his distinct arrogant voice shout, "Five 'A's! Beat that retards!" Jett performed this spectacle so often that Adam had memorized Jett's ID number. A football player may spike the ball to celebrate a touchdown. If that football player were Jett, he would spike the ball in his opponent's face, and then spit at him.

Will crossed his arms. "I don't think he earned those grades."

"You think he's lying?" asked Adam.

"No, I think he's cheating. Though I don't doubt he's a liar."

Adam scratched his chin.

"Think about it," continued Will, "he's always socializing. You can talk to anyone, and they never see him study in the library or commons, and he's never in his room."

"How do you think he's doing it?"

"Hard to say. But I've heard rumors that certain people in the Fire Hall have copies of tests, projects, and papers from previous years. And we know Jett has an older brother."

Adam thought for a moment, then spoke, "Given his character, I wouldn't put it past him to cheat."

Will nodded in agreement.

"I bet that if he got caught cheating, he would get kicked out of Arcadia," said Adam.

"So we need to figure out how he's cheating," said Will, "then make sure he gets caught." Will and Adam met with Sahar and Julie for lunch, and explained their hypothesis.

"I do not see how we can catch him cheating," said Sahar. "We cannot watch him twenty-four-seven."

"No," said Adam, "but SSDs watch everyone. What if we could get access to the surveillance footage?"

"You mean hacking into confidential files?" asked Sahar in astonishment. "We could be expelled for that."

"I agree with Sahar," said Julie. "This whole idea is a recipe for expulsion."

"What if we logon to the computer using Jett's account," suggested Will. "Everyone's username is last-name-first-initial, and the password is the student ID number. All we need is his ID number, and we can log on using his account. If we get caught, it gets traced back to him."

"I already know his ID number," said Adam. "He points at it during each weekly spectacle."

With a stern voice, Sahar interjected, "But we are breaking the rules; it is immoral."

Adam considered the proposition. "Would it really be that bad if he got caught? Wouldn't we be doing the school a favor?"

"The end does not justify the means!" declared Sahar.

Julie chimed in: "If we do that, we're no better than him! You might as well plant evidence, it wouldn't be any different."

Will laughed, and then said, "That's an even better idea!"

"I will not have any part of this," Sahar said firmly.

"Fine," said Will, waving her off. "Adam and I can handle it. If we have to get our hands dirty to catch a crook, so be it. You'll thank us for it later."

"Adam," pleaded Sahar, "are you seriously considering going through with this?"

Adam looked at Will, and then back at Sahar. Of all the people on campus, he respected her the most. She had a stern sense of right and wrong, a strong character, and an uncanny wisdom for a girl her age. She respected him too, and he wanted to keep her respect. But Jett was a snake that always seemed to slither his way out of trouble. If the traditional means fail to punish people like Jett, when does it become acceptable to use enhanced, or even questionable means? Adam continued pondering.

Sahar resumed her plead: "You are not a bad person. Jett will receive his punishment."

"And how much damage will he cause before he gets punished?" said Adam. "What if he succeeds at this school? What if he becomes a senator? What if he becomes the next Stalin? Would you look back at this and honestly say that we made the right decision if we could have prevented it, but decided not to?"

Sahar kindly replied, "You are speaking of things you cannot possibly know. It is all speculation. Have faith."

"God's justice is slow at best, and unfair at worst." Adam immediately regretted that statement. It was not his job to question God. His mother and father would be disappointed.

"Who are we to judge what is fair?" countered Sahar.

Adam thought of the Old Testament story of Pharaoh, and all the people God punished, ostensibly to persuade Pharaoh. "We may not have all the information, but in hindsight, we should be able to determine what is fair. Think about Exodus. Pharaoh was a cruel ruler who enslaved the Israelites. Moses asked Pharaoh to free his people, and Pharaoh refused. What did God do?"

Sahar answered, "He turned the Nile into blood, killing all the fish and preventing the Egyptians from drinking from the river."

"Why didn't he punish Pharaoh?" asked Adam. "Wouldn't that be more efficient?"

"It was not his intent to punish Pharaoh, only to show that the Israeli God was more powerful than the Egyptian gods."

"Fair enough," said Adam. "But Pharaoh still doubted God's power, so God plagued the entire country with frogs. Not Pharaoh's quarters or temple, but the entire country. Then, God plagued men and animals with lice. What else did he do?"

Sahar answered, "He sent swarms of flies upon Pharaoh and his officials, followed by a disease that killed the Egyptians' livestock."

"After he already sent three other plagues affecting an entire country, he finally punished Pharaoh, but not without punishing the rest of the Egyptians. Then he gives the Egyptians, but not Pharaoh, a skin disease. Followed by the most destructive hailstorm Egypt had ever seen, followed by locusts that cause further destruction. Then a plague of darkness that lasts three days. And what was the final plague?" Adam waited, and he knew Sahar knew the answer. She looked down.

Julie answered on Sahar's behalf. "He slew the first born child of every Egyptian."

"Exactly," said Adam. "He harmed Pharaoh by slaying his son, along with the rest of the first born children of Egypt."

"I suppose you will renounce your faith now?" mocked Sahar. "Given that you do not agree with God."

"I can't understand all of God's motives and reasoning," spoke Adam. "At face value, it doesn't seem fair, but my point is not to denounce God. The Israelites were eventually set free. But look what it took for the Israelites to get what they desired. An unfathomable amount of collateral damage happened before Pharaoh received any sort of punishment. Jett will eventually get what he deserves, but I can only speculate how much damage someone like Jett could do if given the opportunity. And with a father that's a governor, he will have ample opportunity."

"If I can add to that," said Will, "He's saying our situation isn't black and white, or right and wrong. It's somewhere in between. So I ask, what is intrinsically wrong with breaking some arbitrary rule in order to catch a bad person? We're not planting evidence."

"We don't even know if he is cheating. What if he's not cheating?" said Sahar with conviction. "Would you be willing to risk getting expelled, only to discover that Jett isn't cheating?" Will and Adam looked at each other.

"Do you think he is cheating?" asked Will.

"Of course. But I want him to be caught through traditional channels," said Sahar.

"Adam, Will, I think you're forgetting something," spoke Julie. "The rules are there as a safeguard. Students don't have access to SSD footage because no student should have that amount of power."

"In theory, I agree. But suppose those who wield the power fail to exercise it responsibly? Then what?" questioned Adam.

Then Julie retorted, "How do you know those with power are not acting or exercising it responsibly?"

"Because people like Jett are still acting the same!" replied Adam. "But even if the people with power are 'acting responsibly.'" Adam signaled quotation marks with his hands. "Suppose they still don't achieve any results. Don't we have an obligation to intervene?"

"I agree," spoke Will. "All that is necessary for the triumph of evil is that good men do nothing. I don't know if I would go as far as to call Jett evil, but his moral compass is certainly not pointing due North. We have to get access to the SSD footage. It's the right thing to do."

"That is what worries me," said Sahar. "Some of the worst atrocities known to mankind were committed by people who thought they were acting righteously."

"Now you're comparing me to Stalin?" joked Will. Adam and Julie laughed, but Sahar rolled her eyes.

"Listen Sahar," started Adam, "we will be careful and deliberate. We will only use the footage to see what Jett is doing. If we don't find anything, then so be it."

Sahar took a deep breath. "Fine," she said. "But please do not get caught. Arcadia will not be the same if you two were expelled."

Adam thought about Sahar's concerns. What would happen if someone like Jett were able to access SSD footage? What would he do with that knowledge and power? Adam cringed at the thought of Jett gaining additional power. He repeatedly questioned himself, wondering if his plan was morally sound. He tried to imagine what his mother or father would do, but the answer was ambiguous. Then he remembered what his uncle told him about SSDs: they were installed in every major city to reduce crime. In essence, they were meant to catch people breaking the rules. In order for the privacy invasions to be acceptable, SSDs have to be effective at catching crooks. This notion served to reaffirm Adam's original proclivity. Hacking into SSD footage was absolutely necessary. Jett had to be caught.

~

The next day Adam and Will visited the computer lab. "You sure about this?" asked Will. "Once we start, there's no 'undo' button."

Adam nodded.

"Good," said Will, "me, too."

"Let's hope we can find something useful." They sat down in front of one of the computers in the back of the room. The lab was mostly empty, save for a few students. Adam typed 'holdenj' for the username, and Jett's student ID number for the password. "We're in!" whispered Adam in an excited voice.

"Great!" said Will. Adam used the touchscreen and keyboard to pull up a command line interface. "Let me use the keyboard." Will typed some commands. "Wow, they're using a really old system. No one uses this anymore. It's full of vulnerabilities."

"Strange," said Adam. "I would think they would want to make it more difficult to exploit."

"All we need to do is overload the RPC buffer. Once it crashes, we navigate through the directory to find the footage."

"How do we overload the buffer?"

"First, we set the payload." He quickly typed a directive. "Done. Now, set the 'L-HOST' and 'R-HOST'..." His fingers moved like miniature lightning strikes across the keyboard. "And we're in!"

"Wait," said Adam. "We really need to be careful. Run the 'idle-time' to make sure no administrators are online." Will prompted the computer. A list appeared on the screen.

"Am I reading that correctly?" asked Will. "This can't be right."

Adam peered over the screen. "You're reading it correctly, but it's strange. The last administrator logged on several days ago. But look at some of the other users that have been in the system." They counted fifteen usernames. Most of them were unfamiliar and all had accessed the system within the last twenty-four hours. Two of the names were more familiar: 'holdene' and 'holdenj.'

"Jett already accessed the system yesterday," observed Will. "You think Holden-E is Jett's older brother?"

"Most likely," replied Adam. "It's too much of a coincidence for it to be otherwise."

Will scratched his head and spoke, "We don't even need to access the footage. We can take a screenshot of this, and send it to the proper authorities. It clearly shows Jett and fourteen other people accessed the file server."

"Something doesn't feel right," said Adam. "Fifteen people left a trail, and none of them have been caught." Adam paused. "Can we look back further to see if this was the first time they logged on?"

"Of course," said Will. He typed in another command. "Wow... these fifteen people have been busy. They're on here constantly!"

"Rumors spread quickly here. If anyone had gotten in trouble for hacking the system, we would have heard about it. But they left this obvious trail... so why have they not been caught?

"I don't know," said Will. "But I say we save a screen shot to my portable drive, and get out of here before we draw suspicions."

"Wait... Can we see what files they accessed?" asked Adam. Will typed in several more commands and pointed at the screen.

"It looks like they accessed folders for different classes. They most likely looked for test files."

Adam muttered to himself, then asked, "Can we look up the student ID numbers of the users who accessed the system?"

"What for?" asked Will.

"I have a suspicion," said Adam. "Can you do it?"

"Sure," said Will. "Since their ID numbers are their passwords, we just do a password dump and save it onto the portable drive." Will repeatedly and deliberately struck the proper keys. With a final tap he announced, "Done."

"Good," said Adam. "Now let's get out of here." Adam picked up his backpack and stood. Immediately before Will was about to log off, he paused. "What are you waiting for?"

Will twiddled his fingers. "Suppose we give this information to the proper authorities, and suppose Jett denies hacking the system."

"The system shows he accessed the server," replied Adam. "It will be obvious that he was lying."

"But what if he claims someone stole his password? Then the authorities look at the SSD footage and see us logging on at the same time and place Jett supposedly hacked the system."

"I see." Adam stopped to think. After a couple seconds of rumination, he said, "We need to get back on the server and delete the footage of us. We also need to temporarily halt recording, otherwise we will be caught leaving the room too."

After several minutes, Will was able to delete the footage and alter the time stamp, allowing them enough time to leave without being recorded.

As they walked, Will remarked, "That was too easy."

Adam grinned and said, "Now you're just being cocky."

"No," said Will. "I'm not bragging; I mean it was too easy. The server was not well protected. Anyone could have figured it out with a quick internet search."

"What are you suggesting?" asked Adam.

"I'm not exactly sure," said Will. "But something isn't right."

Adam paused to think about Will's comment. He thought about the incident with the swastika, and how no one was reprimanded. Jett's comments and gestures never landed him in the dean's office. One day Adam is attacked, a boy dies, and no one is punished. Not to mention the yearbook someone planted, and the encoded message left for Sahar. It was too much for mere coincidence. Adam shared this thought with Will, then said, "I have a hypothesis to test." They ran to the dorm, and opened the screenshot, then matched the passwords (student ID numbers) to the students who cheated. Adam recorded the information on a piece of paper, and then he and Will briskly walked to the electronic bulletin board where grades were posted. Their discovery was exactly what Adam expected to find: fifteen of the top twenty students matched the list of students who accessed the server. Jett, along with fourteen other "top" students achieved high marks not through intellect or industriousness, but through duplicity.

"What do you suppose happens if we share this with professors or administrators?" asked Will. Adam shrugged his shoulders.

"Most likely nothing. Worst case scenario, they get a wrist-slap."

"What if we make the information public, for the rest of the students," suggested Will. "Surely their outrage will provoke positive change."

Adam subtly frowned and said, "I doubt it. They'll just find another way to cheat."

"You're too young to be this cynical."

An awkward silence passed, then Adam snapped his fingers and blurted, "I have it!" Will became intrigued, and Adam continued: "We won't have time to do this for midterms, but I bet we can make it work for finals. Tell me what you think of this plan: we hack onto the server and partition a small section. We make the old files visible only to those who are supposed to have access, specifically, the professors. The professors will keep using these files, not noticing any difference. With the partition, we set up copies of original files. It will look exactly the same, but instead of having the original final exam, we change the questions."

"Brilliant!" blurted Will. "So Jett and the other cronies get the answers to the wrong exam."

"Final exams are worth fifty percent of the grade in every class. If they bomb the final, they will fail their courses and be kicked out."

"It will be a challenge," said Will. "But it's doable. We should start working on it now, and we'll put it together the week before finals. How much time does that leave us? Eight weeks?"

"Should be plenty of time," said Adam.

9

Wednesday, March 5, 2068

Midterm week passed, and Adam was back into his regular routine. All students had received their exam grades, and though Adam's marks were not as high as he wished, he was glad to be done with it. He missed the free time allotted during midterms, but ironically, the fast-paced and highly structured weekly schedules were less stressful.

He sat in Dr. DiPrima's math class, and Dr. DiPrima had just begun the lecture. "Our next unit is about cryptography. Does anyone know what cryptography is?" Several students raised their hands. DiPrima pointed at one of the students.

The student answered, "It's about making a message difficult to read for a third party."

"More or less correct," said Dr. DiPrima. His voice seemed to grow raspier each day, perhaps because of his exaggerated tone. "Cryptography is a Greek word. It means 'hidden, or secret writing.' Or, sometimes it is referred to as 'cryptology,' meaning the 'study of secret writing.' The question is, why would someone want to encode their message?" Several students again raised their hands. DiPrima paced back and forth. The lesson was atypical, for DiPrima usually lectured at students. Today, it felt more like a conversation.

DiPrima pointed at Adam, and Adam replied, "If you're at war and you send battle plans to troops, the enemy may intercept the plans. If the message is encoded, your plans have a better chance at succeeding."

"Good," said DiPrima. He pointed at another student.

"If you buy something with your credit card, the store sends that information to a bank. You wouldn't want hackers to intercept the message and see your credit card information, so the store encodes the message before sending it."

"Excellent," spoke DiPrima. "We're all on the right track. But there's an obvious problem: the party receiving the message has to know how to decode it. Naturally, if you send an encoded message, the party you send it to has to have a key. Otherwise, they won't be able to read a message. Further, the key has to decode the message so that you get the exact same message back. This is where mathematics can help us. We need to have a function for encoding the message, and the inverse of that function for decoding it." DiPrima continued pacing. "Similarly, if we were at war, and we intercepted a coded message, it would behoove us to decode the message as quickly and accurately as possible." In all capital letters, DiPrima wrote on the chalkboard:

WHAT IS ENCRYPTION

"We'll start with something simple," he said. "Below, you will see this message written five different ways. Four of them follow a pattern. See if you can figure out which one does not follow a pattern." He wrote five more strings.

```
(1) WHAT ISEN CRYP TION
(2) WHAT NESI CRYP NOIT
(3) WNCN HERO ASYI TIPT
(4) WINT OHIA SECR TNYP
(5) TAHW IITP SONY ENCR
```

Students were given several minutes to analyze the statements. Adam looked at the first one: it was obviously the same letters in the same order, but with different spacing. Add a space between the "S" and "E"; delete the next two spaces, and the message is the same. There appeared to be some sort of pattern to numbers two and three, but he could not figure out what the pattern was. Then the professor suggested: "Try stacking each quaternary sequence vertically." Adam rewrote the second sequence on his paper, stacking each four-letter sequence:

WHAT NESI CRYP NOIT

He soon noticed the pattern: read left to right, then down one line, right to left, and repeat. Almost like a switchback. He did this with the other sequences too:

```
WNCN        WINT        TAHW
HERO        OHIA        IITP
ASYI        SECR        SONY
TIPT        TNYP        ENCR
```

The patterns became more apparent. For number three, the message was vertical: start on the top left, then move down to the bottom row, then right one letter, then up, right, down, right, and up. He observed no apparent pattern in the fourth puzzle. The fifth one took him longer to decipher, but he eventually noticed that the message spiraled, starting from the top right. DiPrima continued lecturing, but his words did not connect to Adam, for another proposition occupied Adam's mind. Adam recalled several weeks ago, when someone left the yearbook in front of his dorm. The same person left another message for Sahar, possibly. He remembered twenty-four letters, but could not recall the specific letters or the order of the letters. He contemplated if Dr. DiPrima's lecture could help him decode the message. Sahar sat only two seats away, adjacent to Will. Adam considered passing a note to Sahar, but he knew better than pass notes in DiPrima's class.

After class Adam spoke to Sahar, "That note you showed me. The one someone left for you. Do you have it with you?"

"No," said Sahar, "it is in my room."

"Can you get it during lunch? I'd like to look at it again."

"You think it may be an encoded message?"

"I don't know, but it's worth looking at."

"Alright," said Sahar. "I will bring it to lunch."

"Thanks," said Adam.

The eagerness to analyze the message left a burning sensation inside Adam's gut—or so it felt. And that avidity made lunch feel like it was days away, even though it was less than an hour. Adam, Julie, Will, and Sahar still had to attend Dr. William's social studies lecture. They entered his class, sat down, and waited impatiently for the lecture to begin and end. Dr. Williams tapped his fingers.

Several students trickled in at the last moment. "Are we all met?" asked Dr. Williams, skimming the room for missing students. Two more scrambled through the door. Once they found their seats, the professor began, "A few noteworthy events occurred over the last week, but the three I am thinking of are perhaps the most significant. Anyone care to guess which events I speak of?"

No students raised their hands. They had grown used to the professor's Socratic method: beg a query, fish for a response, give false praise, then lambast the poor soul who was eager enough, and often, foolish enough, to have taken the bait. Whatever knowledge the student gained, he lost an equal amount of dignity. And the professor devoured the stolen dignity, using it to fortify his own ego. He paused for several seconds, hoping someone would take the bait, but his propensity for silence was unparalleled by that of his students.

Finally, he said, "I suppose there is no harm telling you. The first noteworthy event we have already been following: the viruses affecting livestock and crops have spread to two more states. Prices have not yet impacted the market, but in anticipation, speculators have bid up agricultural futures contracts."

The professor often failed to teach the necessary prerequisite knowledge, making some of his statements ambiguous and esoteric. A brave student raised his hand to ask what a futures contract was. The professor gave a long-winded explanation. As Adam understood the statement, a futures contract is a contract between two parties to buy or sell a certain asset at a set price. In January, a rancher may agree to sell his livestock for one hundred dollars per cattle, and the trade will be settled six months later (in June). The price could go up or down, causing the contract to become more or less valuable. Naturally, speculators will buy and sell contracts in anticipation of the volatile nature of the underlying assets. For this particular case, a virus will eventually cause a supply shortage, which means sellers can get more money for their products. This causes the price of the futures contract to increase, because people expect the underlying commodity to increase.

"Thank you for asking that question," stated the professor. "It is a perfect segue to our next topic. Have any of you heard of a derivative contract?" A few hands shot up. The professor pointed at a student.

"I've only heard it mentioned, I don't know what it is."

"I see," said the professor. "A futures contract is a type of derivative. The rancher can use a futures contract to mitigate risk. For example, if the price of his livestock declined to fifty dollars, but someone promised to pay one hundred dollars for the livestock, the contract prevents him from losing money. But someone else had to assume the risk. In this example, the person assuming the risk would have lost fifty dollars." Dr. Williams paced across the room and back. "Now consider, what would have happened if the price of livestock increased to a hundred and fifty dollars." A different student raised her hand, and the professor beckoned for her to speak.

"The rancher doesn't exactly lose money per se," she recited. "He still gets his hundred dollars, but without the contract, he could have gotten a hundred and fifty. But the person at the opposite end of the contract can buy the cattle for one hundred, then immediately sell it for a hundred and fifty."

"Precisely," said Dr. Williams. "The hypothetical rancher insures himself against losses, but misses the opportunity to make more money. Meanwhile, the second party assumes extra risk, and in this scenario, is rewarded for that risk. It is paramount to observe that risk never decreases; it merely shifts to the person most willing to assume it. And notice, this is a zero-sum game: in order for one person to win, the other person has to lose an equal amount." The professor paced again and scratched his chin. "Now, for our second event: the world's third largest investment bank, Myron Roberts, is facing insolvency and requesting a government bailout. As expected, the markets are panicking. The Dow Jones is down an additional ten percent this week, making that negative thirty percent year-to-date."

A student raised his hand. The professor called on him. "How does the world's third largest bank suddenly become insolvent?"

"Excellent question! To answer, let us return to the rancher example. Suppose a speculator buys a futures contract for ten dollars, with the intent to sell the contract before he has to buy the cattle. Despite only paying ten dollars, he is promising to pay one hundred dollars later. In essence, he is pledging money that he does not have. This is a form of leverage. Myron Roberts has trillions of dollars in outstanding derivatives contracts—derivatives much more exotic and complicated than the one I mentioned. One of their recent trades became a catastrophic blunder. They lost hundreds of billions of dollars, and because of their leverage ratios, losing just five or ten percent can cripple the firm." The students all appeared to be pondering, attempting to absorb the information. The professor continued: "It gets worse. Other banks fret that Myron Roberts will not be able to pay their debts, and they call back the borrowed money. Myron Roberts is forced to sell at fire-sale prices, resulting in further losses." Another student raised her hand.

The student asked, "Why does Myron Roberts need to be bailed out? If they make stupid decisions, shouldn't we let them fail?"

Dr. Williams responded: "The problem is that too many investment banks lent money to Myron Roberts. If Myron Roberts cannot pay their dues, then the other banks may also become insolvent. It is not Myron Roberts that is being bailed out, but the banks that lent money to Myron Roberts. These banks give short-term loans to virtually every major firm. Without the daily and weekly loans, many of these firms will not have adequate capital to continue operating. In essence, one large company, like Myron Roberts, can stop the flow of money in the economy. Economists refer to this phenomenon as systemic risk. This interconnectedness has been responsible for several economic crises. Following the savings and loan bailout of the 1980s, and the bailout of Long Term Capital Management in the late 90s, economic crises have become increase-ingly frequent. Some companies even plan for a bailout."

"It still doesn't sound fair," protested the student. "If a company knows they can get bailed out, what's to stop them from making irresponsible choices in the future? It's like parents never following through with threats."

"You are absolutely correct: saving an irresponsible firm, and the firms that enabled its reckless behavior, from ruin, is unfair. But imagine you live in an apartment complex. Your neighbor always leaves his space heater running, and he often falls asleep on the couch with a cigarette in his mouth. His apartment will inevitably catch fire, and maybe his negligence is reason not to call the fire department. After all, the fire department is a public resource; surely it can be used elsewhere. But what happens to the other apartments if the fire is not soon extinguished?" The professor paused for effect. "Several innocent families will lose their possessions, maybe even die. While the fire department may ostensibly be saving the negligent smoker, it is in sooth saving his neighbors."

The student crossed her arms, obviously displeased with the answer. Dr. Williams continued speaking: "Of course, there are ways to punish firms like Myron Roberts. Strings can be attached to the bailout money. Primary equity holders can be forced to sell to the government at pennies on the dollar, senior executives can be fired without compensation, new executives can be appointed, titular 'retention bonuses' and 'performance bonuses' can be halted. Debts can be adversely restructured, thereby punishing irresponsible lending practices. So long as the treasury does not repeat the 2008 bailout by writing blank checks with no strings attached, the moral hazard can be assuaged."

Adam paused to think about the scenario. It was not black and white, like so many scenarios often appear. Rather, one must take a calculated risk: do you risk the entire economy to punish a small group, or do you attempt to save everyone and risk reoccurrence of the crisis? What is the moral obligation?

"But enough about the burgeoning financial crisis," spoke Dr. Williams, "for we have yet to discover the third event. Massachusetts Senator Michael Cane announced his bid for presidency. As we approach the election, several months from now, we will be learning more about Mr. Cane and his opponents."

Michael Cane. The name was familiar to Adam, though he only heard the name once. It was when his uncle divulged the narrative of Jeff Locke, famous technology billionaire. Michael Cane was the clever senator who discerned the prodigious potential of SSDs. It was his idea to utilize their capacity as a surveillance system and to implement SSDs in every major city. He was partially responsible for the precipitous drop in crime. Adam wondered if the invasion of privacy was worth a lower crime rate. His experience with SSDs was distinctly negative, though limited. SSDs failed to catch Hannah's killer, failed to catch the anti-Semitic vandal, and failed to discern Adam's attacker. From Adam's experience, SSDs were questionable at best, and dangerous in the wrong hands. With little knowledge of Michael Cane, he could only hope that Cane was a man of probity.

~

After social studies and English, Adam met with Sahar, Will, and Julie. Sahar brought the note. It read:

ELERRLDEHIYHOKOTLNUADERF

Adam took a piece of paper and pencil from his backpack. He partitioned the letters into groups of four, then stacked each ternary sequence. Will peered over his shoulder to see what was written:

```
ELER
RLDE
HIYH
OKOT
LNUA
DERF
```

He positioned the paper so everyone could see, and all four students stared, searching for a pattern.

"Fat-here-d-you-ren-kill... Okay," said Will, "I don't think that's the pattern."

"Does anyone see a message?" asked Adam.

"I thought I did," said Will. "False alarm." Julie shook her head. Will looked at Sahar, and noticed a teardrop trickling down her cheek. He nudged Adam, who also noticed the tear drop.

"What is it?" asked Adam.

Sahar's eyes remained fixated on the paper.

"Look," said Julie. She pointed at the top left, and then outlined an invisible 'W'-like pattern. The message materialized before Adam and Will's eyes, and the cause of Sahar's tears became apparent. Adam rewrote the decoded message, adding spaces and punctuation to make it more coherent:

```
E.R. HOLDEN KILLED YOUR FATHER
```

"Let's go somewhere more private," suggested Adam. Adam put the note in his pocket, and led the group outside. Other students sat near the reflecting pool, eating lunch and basking in the sun's rays. Adam and his friends found a corner, away from the crowd. "Sahar, can you tell us more about your father's murder?"

Sahar sniffled and wiped her eyes. "I found him dead in our back yard. It was about three years ago on a Sunday afternoon. Police said he died from a stab wound in his lower back. No one witnessed or heard the crime. SSDs failed to find anything." The students started at Sahar, waiting for elaboration. "That is all," she said. "The case was unsolved."

"I don't know what's going on," said Adam, "but it has something to do with this place or the people here. It's too much of a coincidence. Someone gives me a picture of my sister's unnamed killer; someone leaves a message for you about your father's killer.

No one gets in trouble for cheating, fighting, or racism." Adam took a deep breath.

"Holden," said Will. "We suspected E. Holden might be Jett's brother. Do you think E.R. Holden is the same person?"

Adam shrugged his shoulders. "It's not a very common name. I'm sure we can figure out how many Holdens attend Arcadia."

Julie snapped her fingers. "The yearbook!" she proclaimed. "We can check the yearbook for anyone with the last name Holden."

"If he's not in there," said Adam, "we may be able to find old yearbooks in the library. Worst case scenario, we can hack on to the server again, though I would rather avoid it, if possible."

Sahar stood silent. A grave expression veiled her face. She had barely spoken a word since she decoded the message. The memory of her father's murder had been buried. She unwillingly learned to let go after realizing the hopeless prospect of catching the killer. There was nothing to be done, and she had no control over the situation. Then, along comes a message that reveals the scar tissue of a wound that never quite healed. A disturbing occurrence that plays tricks on the mind. If this person knew who killed Sahar's father, why not come forward? If this person could help lead police to Hannah's killer, why the secrecy? Each student sat in silence pondering the same queries. Finally, Will spoke: "Two people have been murdered. It would be in our best interest to keep this between the four of us, and maintain a low profile, lest we receive the same fate."

Adam concurred, "We should avoid any unwanted attention." Sahar and Julie both nodded in agreement. Adam continued: "I will look through the yearbook, and keep you informed about what I find."

With that, they finished lunch and attended their remaining classes of the day. Once classes culminated and supper settled, Adam returned to his room to search through the yearbook. The yearbook revealed exactly what Adam suspected: the audacious assailant from the bathroom, brother of the egregious Jett Holden, was none other than E. Holden. Or more precisely, Eric R. Holden, the only Holden listed in the three year old yearbook. Adam's blood boiled. The Holden family was more than a group of entitled, narcissistic, cruel, wannabe hegemons; they represented the embodiment of evil. Adam knew he could not boldly accuse Eric Holden of murder without substantial evidence, so he elected to find more. He had to be absolutely certain that there was only one E. Holden that ever attended Arcadia, and the answer could be found on the file server and in old yearbooks. But that would have to wait until the opportune moment presented itself.

Adam took a deep breath. He knew the proof could not be found overnight. It would require finesse and deliberation. And it would all have to be done without neglecting his studies. He decided to spend a few minutes with his personal computer (anything to distract him from the newfound obsession). In his email box was a message from his mother:

Dear Adam,

There is no easy way to say this, and it pains me to do so. Your grandfather passed away. He died peacefully in his sleep last night. We have not yet scheduled funeral arrangements. Please let us know when you may have an opportunity to come home. It would mean a great deal to your grandmother.

Henry is learning at a faster rate each day. He has already finished a course in differential equations, but he misses you. Your father's job still appears safe; we're one of the more fortunate families in Cammalot. We hope you are enjoying your time at Arcadia. Your father and I are looking forward to seeing you, though we wish it were under better circumstances. We are proud of you, and we love you.

Continue working hard, and please let us know when you can come home.

Love,

Mom and Dad

Normally a tear would meet Adam's cheek at this time, but for some reason, his eyes remained dry. Maybe it was the physical distance separating him from his loss, or maybe he had grown accustomed to the recent calamitous atmosphere. Death and sorrow were becoming rather trite. He loved his grandfather; the recent demise saddened him deeply, but he could not bring himself to cry. He clenched the desk, but his hands still trembled uncontrollably.

10

Friday, March 23, 2068
Over two weeks had passed since Adam read the unfortunate message. Of course, the school would have allowed Adam to travel to the funeral, but he would have quickly fallen behind in his studies. There were no foreseeable breaks in his schedule until the week of final exams ended: April 25. Then there was a one-week reprieve before classes resumed. Thus, it would be a delayed funeral, nearly two months after his grandfather's quietus. But the alternative was to miss the service entirely. Naturally, his parents and grandmother elected to hold a late service.

It seemed that lately Adam's mind was becoming more and more crowded with troublesome thoughts: his grandpa's death, his sister's death, and the unjust system that allowed people like Jett and Eric to garner evermore privilege. They escaped punishment for assaulting Adam, forcibly cutting Sahar's hair, and racial intimidation. Every night, the boy who killed Hannah haunted Adam's dreams, along with the boy he inadvertently killed in the bathroom. Then there was the ploy to end Jett's academic career, and he still had no idea where to find proof that Eric killed Sahar's father, though he knew it existed somewhere. Finally, despite all the tumultuous thoughts and events, he still had to maintain decent grade marks. After all, his primary objective was to learn and become a more capable human being. But learning is difficult when the mind is distracted. Adam learned this through experience. He thought of Cammalot, where one would be hard-pressed to find another student that came from a more adverse background. It was no wonder why Cammalot students had trouble learning: constantly struggling to keep life's primary necessities in the foreground naturally relegated education to the background.

Adam could always count on one class to keep his attention for the full fifty minutes: Dr. William's social studies. Perhaps because of the prevalent, relevant, and timely issues. At lunch, Adam, Will, Sahar, and Julie, often spoke further of the issues presented in Dr. Williams class. Adam and Will sat at the lunch table. Across the room, Adam could see his other roommates, Nick and Jared. As the year progressed, Nick and Jared slowly grew apart from Will and Adam, though in reality, they were never close. Their backgrounds presented an invisible barrier: Nick and Jared both had neural implants and older siblings that attended Arcadia, and prior to enrolling, they already had an established group of friends. Nothing prevented them from being friends with Adam and Will, but it would have taken substantially more effort. And with the heavy workload, none of the four boys needed an extra chore. So naturally, they remained friendly acquaintances, but mostly kept to themselves.

Will and Adam sat at an empty, round table in the cafeteria and were soon joined by Julie and Sahar. The students greeted each other. Then Julie asked, "What did you think of Dr. William's lecture?" She placed her food tray on the table and took a seat.

"Well, we're starting to see the effects of the food shortage," noted Will. "I don't know if you've noticed, but our servings have gotten smaller. Plus, we've been having less bread and more rice. And it's been two weeks since they served beef! I'm getting sick of chicken."

Adam replied, "I bet you'll think differently once we run out of chickens." Will grimaced.

"Boys," scolded Sahar, "there are more important things than our lunch menu. This affects the entire country. Food prices have nearly doubled. Millions of our own people can't afford to feed their children."

"Well I suppose that problem could be solved by eating the youngest child," cracked Will. Adam could not help but laugh. Julie and Sahar both rolled their eyes.

"You two are some of the best and brightest boys in the country," said Julie, "and sometimes that worries me."

"It was just a joke," said Will.

"Share it with one of the millions of breadwinners that lost his job in the financial crisis," said Sahar, bemoaning Will's joke, "I am sure he will find it hilarious."

"What do you think about the bailout?" asked Adam, shifting subjects. "Was passing it the right choice?"

"It is not appealing, but it is probably better than the alternative," said Sahar.

"But things are still looking pretty grim," said Julie. "Protests are happening across the country."

"I don't know what good protesting will do," said Adam. "Everyone knows food prices are skyrocketing. And picketing won't help you get a job."

"I think they are protesting for a policy change," said Julie. "They want the government to do something to help." Adam shrugged his shoulders.

"Let us speak of something other than politics," said Sahar. "It is such a depressing topic."

"Oh!" said Will. "I almost forgot to mention: I'm nearly done setting up fake files for the server. Now, all we need to do is wait until finals week approaches and change some links so the hackers get redirected to the fake files."

"Wow," said Adam. "I would have been happy to help."

"Sorry," replied Will. "I thought it would be quicker to work solo. But I might need some help when we transfer everything to the server." Will interlocked his fingers and stretched his hands, cracking his knuckles. Sahar smiled. She had criticized the original hacking plot, but as she learned of the Holdens' more despicable acts, turning their own immoral deeds against them felt less detestable.

~

After lunch, Adam and Will meandered to computer science. The professor gave students nearly the entire period to work on their projects. Adam and Will had been developing a computerized version of the old board game "Battleship." Creating a "dumb" version that randomly guessed where to fire was simple enough. It could be done using a large two-dimensional array, along with a series of "if" statements and "while" loops. The real trick was making the game intelligent. A human player would likely randomly guess where to fire until he hit one of the battleships, but once he hit a battleship, he would continue searching in that vicinity until he sunk the battleship.

Adam was working at making the artificial intelligence more human. He agreed to keep working on the class project, allowing Will to work on setting up the fake files.

While Adam was working, his screen flickered and turned black. A cursor flashed in the center of the screen. Adam clicked the mouse several times, but nothing happened. He repeatedly pressed CTRL +ALT+DELETE, the equivalent of swearing at one's computer. Nothing happened. He reached below to manually shut down the computer, but stopped when a message materialized on the screen:

ADAM CARTER

He tapped Will's shoulder and whispered, "Will, look."

"Hold on," mumbled Will. His eyes were locked on his screen. After a few seconds, he turned towards Adam. "What did you want to show me?" Adam pointed at his screen, but when he looked again, the screen was back to normal, as if nothing happened.

"My screen went blank," he said. "Then it displayed my name."

Will scratched his head. "Looks like it's fine now."

Adam shrugged his shoulders. "Never mind..."

He kept working on the battleship project. Several minutes later, the screen went blank again. He randomly struck various keys, waiting for something to happen. Then another message appeared:

TELL NO ONE. UNDERSTAND?

His first thought was *who is this?* Was it the same person that left the yearbook at his door? Or the encrypted message for Sahar? Even if it was the same person, he still had no idea who that person was. Adam pondered for a moment, and decided there was only one way to determine the identity of this person: play along. He slowly typed, "YES." The message disappeared, and another message materialized on the screen:

DID YOU RECEIVE THE CLUES?

Adam's heart rate increased. He was unsure if he should trust this person. What if it was someone with malicious intent? Someone perhaps, on the same side as Jett and Eric. His fingers hovered above the keyboard while his mind deliberated. Even if this was some sort of trap, it was worth the risk. Again, Adam typed, "YES." Almost immediately, another message appeared:

```
11:00 PM, ARCADIA GARDENS. COME ALONE.
            TELL NO ONE.
```

The message stayed on the screen for mere seconds before the screen reverted back to its original display.

The more Adam thought about the incident, the more suspect he became. What would happen if he told someone? Eleven p.m. was well beyond the school curfew. What would happen to him if someone caught him? Would he be expelled? Too many questions belabored his mind, and too few answers. In any case, he still had hours to make a decision.

~

Adam found it difficult to concentrate during his remaining classes. Conspiracy theories plagued his mind. All he wanted to do was rest. One final class remained: self-defense. Originally, the professor told students they would not be sparring until second semester. But in previous weeks, the professor was so pleased with the class's progress that he introduced them to sparring earlier than he originally intended. Normally, Adam partnered with Will, but this week there was a twist: students would not be allowed to choose a sparring partner. The professor insisted on randomly assigning partners because, in his words, "You don't have the luxury of choosing your enemies."

Thirty students formed a line with no particular order. The professor started at the beginning of the line, and counted out loud, pointing at a different student every time he said a number. At fifteen, the professor restarted the count at one. Adam kept his fingers crossed, hoping he would not have to spar with a girl. A female partner would present quite the quandary: if he won, then he would be a coward, and if he lost, then he would earn the reputation of "getting beat by a girl." His father always said it was wrong to raise your hand against a woman. There was no way to come out ahead.

Adam stood towards the end of the line. The professor pointed at him and said, "Thirteen." Once he finished counting, he instructed everyone to find his or her partner.

Everyone shouted their numbers and signaled with their fingers. Adam wandered around the mat, looking for the other 'lucky number thirteen.' Then he heard someone behind him shout "Thirteen!" He turned. To his dismay, the person shouting was Jett. He was unsure what was worse: having to spar with his mortal enemy, or having to spar with a girl. "Looks like I'm stuck with you," mocked Jett. "Go easy on me, killer." Jett laughed. Adam clenched his fists.

Once everyone had found their partner, the professor gave instructions: "Alright everybody. You know the rules: light contact only. Sweeps, throws, and holds are fair game, but keep it clean. I don't want to have to fill out any accident reports." The class laughed. "No joke, keep it clean!"

Jett and Adam found their places in the gym. All students wore padded gloves and shin guards, in case they accidentally struck each other. "So that Sahar girl," spoke Jett, in his normally arrogant tone. "She's pretty hot, even after the haircut." Adam ignored Jett. He would be lying if he claimed that he never noticed, but he refused to say anything because he did not fancy carrying on a conversation with Jett. "Too bad she's Jewish," Jett shook his head in faux sadness. "I just couldn't bring myself to date someone so... what's the word I'm looking for? Provincial."

Adam's mind was conflicted: he felt like he should stand up for his friend, but knew it would be futile, and may even make matters worse.

"You ever think of asking her out?" said Jett.

Adam said nothing.

"What? You think you're too good to talk to me?"

Adam shrugged his shoulders. "My mother always said, 'if you can't say something nice, then don't say anything at all.' Well, I don't have much to say," he calmly replied.

"Sounds like something a dumb housewife would say," snarked Jett. Jett rolled his eyes.

"Fine," said Adam. "If you must know: Sahar is much smarter than you'll ever be. Even if you were inclined to date her, she would have nothing to do with you. You may disparage my mother's social status, but she is loving, loyal, strong, intelligent, and she raised three great children, which is more than I can say about your parents. Anything else you wish to speak of?"

Jett sneered. "Whatever," he said. "Let's spar."

Adam and Jett assumed fighting stances. They slowly circled each other a few times. Jett teased with a few flimsy jabs. Adam jabbed straight towards Jett, but Jett deftly blocked the punch and landed a low kick to Adam's right leg. Jett lunged at Adam. Adam swept his arm downward, blocking the punch. He quickly returned a blow to Jett's nose. Jett swore and held his nose.

"Sorry," said Adam. "Didn't mean to hit you that hard." The last part was sincere, but Adam did not feel sorry. It felt surprisingly refreshing to hit Jett in the face. Will must have felt great when he punched Jett, for he hit Jett hard, and without a padded glove.

Jett scoffed and resumed his combat stance. His eyebrows tilted inward and his face reddened. Adam expected Jett to try something sly. Jett was obviously perturbed about being hit. Adam grew determined to land a preemptive blow, an attempt to mentally stun Jett to emphasize who was in charge. Adam feigned a left jab, then followed through with a right hook, expecting to land a blow to Jett's temple, but Jett ducked, kneeled, and shot towards Adam's leg. With great dexterity, he grabbed and pulled Adam's front leg, causing Adam to fall flat on his back. While Adam was momentarily stunned, Jett punched him in the face, then stood up and said, "Sorry, didn't mean to hit you that hard."

That type of blatant disregard for the rules could have, in theory, earned Jett a substantial punishment. But if Adam reported Jett's conduct, he would be acknowledging his own weakness, and by logical extension, Jett's superiority. Plus, if past events were any representation of future events, Jett would escape punishment. There was only one way to deal with people like Jett: the same way Adam dealt with people like Joseph. Fight fire with fire. Stand up for oneself. Jett stood, looking down towards Adam. Adam rolled to his side, and started to stand. While Jett smiled in his arrogant stupor, Adam swept his leg against Jett's ankles. The maneuver did not work as well as it did in the movies, but Adam produced enough force to cause Jett to lose his balance, and fall backwards. Jett landed on his back and a loud thud resounded. Adam hurled his fist towards Jett, but Jett rolled away, avoiding the strike. Adam's fist pounded the rubber mat, causing another loud echo that demanded everyone's attention.

Both boys sprang to their feet and found their bearings. Adam simultaneously stepped towards Jett while initiating a series of jabs, hooks, and cross-body blows. He struck Jett's midsection and face, but Jett blocked many of the moves. Adam planted his right foot and swung his left leg in roundhouse motion. Jett attempted to dodge the kick, but was struck in the shoulder. While Jett was momentarily recovering from the kick, Adam backhanded Jett's face, just enough to taunt him, but not enough to cause pain. Adam stepped back, appearing to be the obvious victor. Neither boy was hurt, but in a match, Adam would have earned far more points. From the opposite side of the room, the screeching sound of a whistle created a miniature cacophony. Adam turned his head to see the instructor meandering through the crowd of observing students. Adam turned his head back towards Jett and witnessed a blurred foot rapidly approaching. With no time to dodge or counter the attack, Jett's heal struck Adam in the chest, causing his lungs to abruptly empty of air. Adam stumbled, and then fell to his back.

Cheap shot, thought Adam. He climbed back to his feet, coughing in the process. The instructor witnessed the cheap shot, and Adam expected the instructor to scold Jett. The instructor spoke, "Students, what you just witnessed was a cheap, cowardly maneuver." Adam smiled. His one wish for Jett to be punished was finally coming true. "In this class, I expect everyone to fight fair. However, in the real world, you may find yourself in a rare life and death situation. Your enemy most certainly will not fight fair. He will kick you below the belt, throw dirt in your eyes, and pull your hair. There are two lessons to be learned from this: if your life is threatened, fight dirty. Do whatever you can to protect yourself and your loved ones. Second, never drop your guard. Mr. Carter dropped his guard, expecting his enemy to play by the rules, and you all saw what happened."

Adam was shocked. Some sleaze-ball cheap shots him, and he was the one who, apparently, did something wrong. The professor only mentioned two lessons learned from the example, but a third one could be found by reading between the lines: life is not fair. The lesson was plain and simple, which is perhaps why it is a common cliché. Sometimes nomenclature changes, but the message is always the same. Bad people often escape retribution. Do not count on the righteousness of your fellow man, you will be disappointed. It was not a message of solace, but a stark portrayal of reality.

~

For the remainder of the day, Adam contemplated whether to meet the mysterious hacker. Meeting the stranger could provide serious benefits, namely, a potential ally and information that may be used to solve the murders. There were also considerable risks: two people had already been murdered. A meeting in the middle of the night in an isolated area could provide the opportunity for a third murder. Adam was less worried about being caught and punished for leaving campus. No one seemed too concerned about the behavior of students. Rules appeared to be mere suggestions.

By 9:30 p.m., Adam decided meeting the stranger was worth the risk. He wrote a note, and hid it in his desk. The note contained every speculation and hypothesis Adam had developed, as well as where he planned to meet the stranger. His goal was to leave a trail of breadcrumbs, in case he disappeared. By 10:00 p.m., Adam's three roommates were asleep. Adam hid under his blanket with a flashlight, reading a book, ensuring he did not fall asleep.

At 10:30, he quietly stepped out of bed, grabbed a jacket and flashlight, stuffed a roll of clear tape in his pocket, and tiptoed towards the door. He heard a groan come from Will's bed. He looked back to see Will tossing and turning. Adam slowly opened the door, causing a loud creak. Will abruptly sat upright and rubbed his eyes. "What are you doing?" he asked.

Adam put finger to his lips and shushed Will. "I have to go."

"Where?" whispered Will.

"I can't say."

"Why not?"

Adam realized there was no quick path away from this conversation. He briefly summarized the scenario for Will. "I need to go," whispered Adam.

"By yourself? I'm coming too."

"No! He said come alone."

"Are you insane? This cloak and dagger routine is way too shady. How can you even think of going alone?"

"I don't have much of a choice, but trust me. I need to go alone. There's a note in my desk with all the details. If I'm not back in a couple hours, get help."

"I don't like this," whispered Will, "but if you need to go solo, I'll trust your judgment."

"Thanks," said Adam.

"Good luck."

Adam nodded to Will, and then slipped out the door and into the hallways. Everything was different at night. A delicate silence waited patiently to be shattered by the faintest sound. Each footstep produced a small echo that promised to give away his location, lest he tread lightly. Sheer traces of light from the single window at the end of the hall briefly interrupted the nearly perfect darkness. Adam reached the opposite end the hall, and slowly pushed on the crash bar of the heavy metal door. He gently closed the door behind him, but it still produced a noticeable sound. With no indication of any adults or students nearby, he treaded down the stairs. At the bottom of the stairs were two doors: one leading to more dorms and towards the lobby, another leading outside. With the utmost care, he pushed the crash bar of the door leading outside. The door would lock behind him, leaving him stranded until the morning. He reached into his pocket and pulled out the roll of tape. With his finger, he pressed the latch bolt of the door and used the tape to keep the bolt permanently depressed. He tested the door before exiting, and it appeared to open with ease.

Once outside, Adam was greeted by biting wind chills. Low street lights illuminated the walkways. Adam thought it safest to stay in the shadows. Even outside, there were no signs of adults. In the distance he could see lights from the surrounding city, and faintly hear the sound of cruising automobiles, but other than thick shadows and a biting wind, the campus felt deserted.

He approached the Arcadia gardens. Tall, pristinely trimmed shrubberies formed a series of incomplete circles. At their bases were flower beds containing fledgling perennials, and low light fixtures that embellished and brightened the landscape. He cautiously followed the stone walkway around the garden, looking for the mystery hacker. According to his watch, he was five minutes early. Adam strolled to the garden's center. An oversized byzantine fountain surrounded by four curved stone benches dominated the heart of the garden. He circled the fountain, admiring its intricacies. From the west entrance, a tall cloaked figure approached, seemingly materializing from the shadows. Adam stood still. His heart pounded.

A deep, harsh voice emitted from the cloaked figure: "Are you alone?"

Adam gulped. He quickly, but shakily nodded his head. His voice trembled and he answered, "Yes."

The clocked figure reached its arms towards its head, and pushed the hood back, revealing a face. Adam's eyes widened. He instantly recognized the face. The cloaked figure and mysterious hacker was none other than famous technology guru, Jeff Locke. In a more standard, less harsh voice, Locke spoke, "I must apologize for the cloak and dagger routine, but I place us both at great risk by meeting you." Adam was awe-struck. "Dozens of questions must be circulating your mind, and I will do my best to answer as many as I can. We have much to discuss. I assume you found the yearbook?"

"The book with the picture of the boy that killed Hannah."

"Were you able to decode the message for Sahar?"

Adam nodded, and then replied, "E.R. Holden killed your father."

"You may have deduced," spoke Locke, "those two murders are inextricably linked."

"Mr. Locke, if you know who killed Hannah, and you know who killed Sahar's father, why have you not informed the police?"

"I have been keeping tabs on Arcadia for years, and I still don't know exactly what happens, or how it happens. I will answer your question in a moment, but first, some background: does the word Agoge mean anything to you?" Adam shook his head. "Agoge was an ancient Greek training system for elite male Spartans. They were taught stealth, military tactics, hunting, social skills, any a myriad of other talents. They were taught to conform, to place the state above oneself, and they were subjected to trials meant to increase pain tolerance. The boys were purposefully given scant servings of food, and encouraged to steal to survive. Of course, those caught stealing were severely beaten."

"That sounds like our grading system," said Adam. "It seems like we have insufficient time to learn the material. The ones with the best grades have cheated."

"Precisely," said Locke. "Same game, different name. Those who survived the training became productive members of Spartan society. The crème of the crop—the most intelligent, strongest, cunning, and ruthless—were recruited to be members of government."

"Are you suggesting Arcadia is a modern day Agoge?"

"Similar," replied Locke, "but it's not sanctioned by the state." Adam stood in silence, attempting to absorb the information. "However, I don't believe the entire school is sinister—only a small faction: a secret society within Arcadia, known as *Erebus*. This society is even more connected than the general Arcadia academy. Some of our most well known senators, judges, governors, and CEOs are members of this society. Jack Holden, for example, is a member of Erebus."

"I'm not surprised," said Adam. "If Jett and Eric are anything like their father..."

"They learned by example," said Locke. "These people are extremely dangerous. Holden is bad, but he is only a single strand of the intricate network. As I said, I've been keeping tabs on Arcadia. My sources have only heard rumors, and they lack substantial and legal proof."

"Rumors of what? You think Erebus has something to do with Hannah's murder? And Sahar's father's murder?"

Locke nodded. "I believe so, but I don't know why. Keep in mind, these people are skilled at the art of deception. If we attempt to expose their crimes without any hard evidence, they brush it under the rug or divert blame to the most convenient person. That is why I need you."

Adam stuttered. "Me? Why me?"

"Many reasons," said Locke. His eyes constantly shifted as he spoke, searching for any sign of danger. "I have not been able to gather any substantial proof. I need someone on the inside to find that proof."

"If you couldn't find proof, what makes you think I can find it?"

"Because you are well on your way to gaining an invitation from the society. I need someone who can detail the inner-workings of Erebus's crimes. The problem is that Erebus only recruits children. They seek out a certain type of people, and some people bend easier than others. In their eyes, you have killed two people, and have thus far been willing take necessary steps to expose your enemies. For example, hacking on to the server."

"How did you—"

"Computer programming is my forte. I have undetectable bots keeping tabs on SSD footage and any attempts to illegally access the server. I saw what you and Will did." Adam looked down. This new revelation was slowly consuming his mind. "Most children do not go to such lengths to fight an enemy. Most people are not willing to kill another human. You must understand how Erebus sees you: tragedy struck you and your family. You've already killed another person— rightfully so—but still a difficult task. They see you as someone vulnerable and pliable. But before they're willing to take a risk by letting you in, they need to be absolutely certain that you're willing to bend your morals to accomplish your goals."

Adam scuffed his shoe against the stone and nervously twiddled his thumbs while pondering the situation. Could he follow through with Locke's request?

"Before you decline to help—" Adam looked up. It was as if Locke read his mind. "You may have heard Michael Cane is running for president."

"Was he a member of Erebus too?" asked Adam.

"Yes," said Locke. "His running mate was also a member. It has not been officially announced, but my sources tell me that Michael Cane has already selected Jack Holden as the vice presidential candidate. If elected, this will be the highest position ever held by a member of Erebus."

"Didn't you work with Michael Cane? Wasn't he the one that wanted to use SSDs to fight crime?"

"At the time, that is what I thought. But once SSDs were implemented nationwide, Cane dropped his facade. He is a master of manipulation. It shames me to admit, but he even fooled me." Locke took several steps to his left, and continued scanning the visible area. "After I was deluded, I recognized Cane for what he was: a crook bent on absolute authority. Cane doesn't care about the people, he only cares about himself. Everything he does is deliberate. He is well-calculated and patient. That man has been eyeing the presidency for decades, but even that is a means to an end."

"And what end is that?"

"The same end that men have been seeking for thousands of years. A desire that has engendered countless wars and unimaginable suffering."

"Power," said Adam, shaking his head in distaste.

"Not long after Cane implemented SSDs nationwide, he used the footage to analyze crime data. He bought real estate in high-crime areas and used several of his lower cronies to divert police resources to those areas. Once police cleaned up the area, he colluded with developers. They built new establishments, property values increased, and he made a killing. In return for their help, his cronies would be awarded positions with more authority. Holden was one of those cronies, and he is now the governor of Massachusetts. The more I worked with Cane, the less I trusted the man. So I kept close tabs on him. Call me paranoid, but something felt wrong. Once I discovered his ploy, I tried to expose his scheme, but he used his political muscle to attack me. He roused his comrades at the IRS to audit me. I've been audited every year for the last ten years, and I've spent millions of dollars fighting false charges brought against me."

"Audited for what?"

"The IRS does not need a reason to audit someone. It's an affront to the constitution. No laws prevent the IRS from searching and seizing records. There is no trial by jury and no due process. You are guilty until proven innocent. And with a federal tax code that spans over one hundred thousand pages, there is a high probability that everyone has inadvertently broken at least one tax law."

Adam shivered at the thought.

Locke continued speaking: "There's more. In the early stages of my company, I needed more capital to expand, so I issued a series of convertible bonds."

"What are those?" asked Adam.

"Essentially, I borrow money from people at a relatively low interest rate, and agree to pay them back. If my company makes significant money, which it did, the bondholders can convert their bonds into stocks."

"But I thought your company was private. I thought you never needed outside funding."

"The company is private, but that bit about never seeking outside funding is a myth from the Time magazine biography. I never approved it, and the author never consulted with me. Right now, I am still the majority shareholder, with fifty one percent. The convertible bonds considerably diluted my majority. Holden was a member of the board of directors of a rival company, Innovare. He is no longer officially a board member, but he is one of the largest shareholders. Innovare has been attempting a hostile takeover of my company, Aegis. Cane sent the IRS after the other shareholders of Aegis. One of the shareholders sold his shares, and the IRS left him alone. Then, Cane started accusing Aegis of using illegally imported materials, the same materials Innovare uses. Heavily armed SWAT teams raided our factories and offices, and confiscated the allegedly 'illegal' materials. The confiscation of those materials resulted in a halt in production, and cost the company billions of dollars. No criminal charges were ever filed. Our materials were eventually returned, several years later, but the result has been a nightmare for the company. Innovare offered a high premium for our shares, and the remaining shareholders sold their stakes. Innovare now owns the other forty nine percent of Aegis."

"What do they want with your company?"

"Well, I can think of two reasons they came after us. First, they want to intimidate and eliminate any perceived opponents. Second, Aegis holds some key pieces of technology, and the accompanying patents that could be disastrous in the wrong hands."

"It sounds like just about anything could be bad in the wrong hands of Cane and Holden," said Adam. "They can already use SSDs to spy on the entire population. But what are these key pieces of technology they seek?"

Locke frowned and shook his head. "I really cannot say, but trust me: it won't be good for anyone in the country except Erebus."

"Adam, your role is absolutely pivotal. Cane and Holden still have to be elected by the people. I have no doubts they will use the recent economic crisis and crop shortage as a platform for their campaign. If you can infiltrate Erebus and collect enough proof of their activities, it should be enough to discredit them. Right now, I only have hunches that can easily be dismissed as ludicrous conspiracy theories. We don't need any convictions, just enough proof to cast doubt. Cane and Holden cannot win."

Adam felt the pressure boiling inside of him. The dangers of getting caught could not be overstated. But what would happen if Cane and Holden were elected? Adam carefully pondered the situation. After several seconds of silence, he asked, "What would I have to do to get into Erebus?"

Locke hesitated and expressed discomfort. "I really can't say," he said. "You may have to point your moral compass in a different direction." Adam looked down. "You shouldn't have to do anything horrendous, and it's only temporary. Think like Jett, and you should be fine." Locke reached into his pocket and produced a small black, rectangular device, about the size of an old cell phone.

"What is that?" asked Adam.

"It's a disruptor," replied Locke. He took another one from his other pocket to show Adam, and then returned it to its original location. "Police officers found one on the boy who killed your sister." Adam's eyes remained fixated on the device. "SSDs work by bouncing high frequency waves off objects. This device determines the frequency of the wave, then returns the same frequency wave, but with the opposite amplitude, resulting in wave cancellation." Adam raised an eyebrow. "In other words," continued Locke, "it cancels the wave of the SSD, making you invisible to SSDs." Locke extended the object towards Adam. "Here, take it."

"Is this legal?" asked Adam.

"No," said Locke. "So don't get caught."

"Is this how Jett's brother was able to avoid detection when he assaulted me?"

"I would assume so."

"How do I use it?" asked Adam. Locke pointed to a small switch located on the devices side.

"Just turn that switch on or off. Only use it when you need to. The batteries don't last indefinitely." Adam held the device in his palm and carefully analyzed it. "I don't expect you to make a decision tonight," continued Locke. "But if you decide to infiltrate Erebus, you may find that tool useful."

"Thank you Mr. Locke."

"One last word: I am sorry that I put you in this position. It is more pressure than any thirteen year old should face. You have already suffered enough. And in all likelihood, succeeding with this mission will not result in any fame or fortune. No one will know of your contributions and sacrifices. But you have the opportunity to save lives and protect the freedom of millions. Please consider all the outcomes before making your decision." Adam looked down.

"I must be going now," said Locke. "Farewell."

Adam waved and Locke sunk into the shadows. Following Locke's departure, Adam briskly walked back towards the dorms, spending less time worrying about a stealthy return, and more time fretting about Locke's request. He wished someone else could make the difficult decisions. Most of his life had been spent acting more mature than fellow students, and assuming more responsibility. A part of him missed the simplicity of Cammalot. He arrived at the main campus building and seamlessly opened the door with the taped bolt. He crept up the stairs, slipped through the shadows, and quietly entered his dorm room. Will was still awake, eagerly waiting for Adam to return and divulge every detail of the meeting.

11

Wednesday, April 18, 2068

Final exams were fast approaching. It was the week before finals, or 'dead week,' as the professors called it. Per school policy, no assignments were supposed to be due during dead week, (though classes were still in session) with the expectation that students study for their final exams. Despite this guideline, professors still had assignments due. They exploited a small loophole: Wednesday before dead week, a project would be assigned, then the professor would say something like, "Well, technically the assignment is due tomorrow, but feel free to submit it next week." It was a cheap ploy, but effective.

Adam hoped his own ploy would be as effective. Three days earlier, Adam and Will sat in the computer lab. Adam watched the screen. Will's fingertips struck the keyboard with rapid succession. Will paused and said, "It's ready."

"Are you sure about this?" Adam said, hesitantly. "It doesn't feel right."

"We are trying to stop bad people from succeeding. Is that not moral?"

"Then why does it feel wrong?"

Will shrugged his shoulders. "Because we're breaking an arbitrary rule, and we were raised to abide by the law. I'll admit, it's not as clear-cut as 'thou shalt not steal.' By comparison, we are stealing from someone who stole from innocent people and returning their belongings."

Adam took a deep breath. "It's just that, this place is changing us." He paused. "And not for the better."

"I thought you were on board?" said Will in vexation.

"It's easy to be on board when we're frustrated. We don't see justice, and we picture ourselves serving justice. Now that we're actually following through, it feels more like revenge."

"Look, I spent months getting this ready. We already hacked the server."

"We could be expelled for this stunt," interrupted Adam.

"Exactly," said Will. "If we're going to risk expulsion, it better be for something good." Adam took another deep breath and pondered for a few seconds.

"I suppose you're correct."

"Thanks," said Will. "And here we go." Will struck several more keys. "It's done. When Jett and the other cronies attempt to hack the server, they will be redirected to the fake file folders."

"I hope it works," said Adam.

"Me too."

Though Adam hesitated at the moment of initiation, he convinced himself that it was necessary, even if it was not morally captivating. He had been thinking about their ploy since Sunday. What if the timing was wrong? What if Jett spotted the ruse? At least he would not be able to notify the authorities without exposing himself.

~

During self-defense, Adam was once again paired with Jett. He seemed to be paired with Jett too frequently. By the third or fourth time, Adam had discovered most of Jett's tricks. Perhaps that was why Jett ceased fighting dirty. Or, perhaps Adam had become so hyper-vigilant of Jett's tricks that he failed to predict the more obvious tactics, leading Jett to utilize more basic strategies. The third possibility, that Adam was not willing to admit, was that Jett was simply a better fighter. He fought dirty when he was losing, but no longer feared losing to Adam. Given that Adam had lost, albeit by a thin margin, six of the last eight matches, it was a distinct possibility.

Jett and Adam stood facing each other, assuming combat stances. Adam acted preemptively, stepping towards Jett while attempting a series of hooks, jabs, and cross-jabs. He landed a few effective hits and a kick to the leg, but Jett blocked most of the blows. Jett retaliated with a roundhouse. Rather than duck or block the kick, Adam leaned back, causing his balance to waver. Jett capitalized on the opportunity and followed through with a second kick. It was enough to cause Adam to fall, leaving Jett victorious. Adam huffed, justifying the defeat by convincing himself that he was mentally distracted by the recent ploy. He refused to admit that Jett was faster or stronger.

~

Two days later, Adam attended the final lecture for social studies, at least until next semester. Dr. Williams showed digital clips of recent events: protests were rampant, occurring in nearly every major city. The unemployment rate topped twelve percent. The Dow Jones and S&P trended upward after the bailout, but had since erased all gains, plus some. The S&P had lost forty-five percent year-to-date. Effects of the agricultural viruses were becoming apparent, with significantly higher food prices. Congress reached a stalemate, thereby implicitly guaranteeing inaction, and the president was visiting Martha's Vineyard. These were the issues the protesters were ostensibly protesting, though there was no indication about their endgame. Did they want the government to do something, or were they simply conveying their opprobrium? Adam remembered watching clips of protests over a month ago. Most of the people merely picketed. But deteriorating economic conditions coincided with escalating protests, which soon turned violent. Some were throwing Molotov cocktails, while others smashed windows.

The video clips showed brief interviews with multiple politicians. One said, "These dead-beats need to find a job." Dr. Williams pointed out how removed these politicians were from the middle class: jobs were becoming scarcer by the day. But Adam observed a particular irony in the protests: judging by the appearances and actions of the protestors, most of those people could not find a job even if jobs were in abundance. Would they continue protesting until someone offered them a job? The strategy seemed wildly ineffective.

~

The weekend passed seemingly quicker than normal, for Adam had spent eight hours per day studying and completing projects. Finals week passed equally as fast. Adam allowed himself time to socialize, but only after meeting his pre-designated study goals. Will followed a similar regime. Nick and Jared spent less time studying, utilizing one of the many benefits of neural implants. Will and Adam crossed paths with Julie on more than one occasion, but Sahar had nearly disappeared. She more or less lived in the library during finals week, leaving only for food, water, bathroom breaks, and, of course, the final exams. Adam's study regime paled in comparison to Sahar's. It would have felt like torture to most students, but to Sahar, it was discipline. It was this distinction that allowed her to earn the highest marks in the school, even higher than the cheaters and benefactors of neural implants. No one else possessed her discipline. Of course, to the outside observer, it appeared to be raw talent. They never looked behind the curtain to witness the grueling hours she committed to succeed.

Adam completed his last final exam on Thursday. On the morning of Friday, April 25, he packed a duffel bag with clothes, checked out at the front campus office, and departed towards the nearest train station. It was his first time off-campus since he arrived at Arcadia in January. The surrounding city was more desolate than he recalled. He remembered seeing a few homeless people, but they were ubiquitous along Campus Avenue. Most slept on benches or huddled in corners. Adam walked past a small group of homeless men and women standing on the sidewalk. He attempted not to make eye contact. One extended her hand and muttered, "Spare change?" Another rambled unintelligibly. Adam passed through the group. A homeless man stepped towards the shrubberies and urinated.

Tall buildings, offices, hotels, and apartments, crowded the blocks. Men and women in suits carrying lattes and briefcases briskly walked in all directions. An unfortunate observation crossed Adam's mind: he did not see a single white homeless person, they were all black. The only black men wearing suits were the ones standing by the hotel doors, holding the doors for the white men that were too busy talking on their mobile phones to acknowledge the doormen. Over eighty years after civil rights legislation passed, blacks were still disenfranchised. Adam recalled a comment from Professor Williams: the official unemployment rate was over twelve percent, but double that number for blacks.

He walked past a park containing clusters of tents. Garbage was strewn across the greens. Some of it littered the sidewalk. A few men and women in ragged clothes puffed their cigarettes. Picket signs lay on the ground and against the park fence. Across the street were shops with broken windows and vandalized doors. Adam suspected some unruly protestors might have been the culprits.

After thirty minutes of walking, Adam reached the train station. His mother had prepaid for a ticket; he only needed to present his student identification card to the ticket booth operator. He boarded the train, and for the first time since classes commenced, he read a book for pleasure: *I, Robot*, by Isaac Asimov. He knew he should be studying, or perhaps, reading ahead in his textbooks to prepare himself for second trimester classes, but he needed a break. Reading was the perfect release.

~

Several hours later he disembarked from the train. His mother and Henry were waiting. When Henry saw Adam, he ran to Adam, hugged him and ran back to his mother, without speaking a word. Adam's mother smiled and hugged him. They were still an hour's drive from Cammalot, and during the ride home, he told his mother all about the positive experiences at Arcadia, purposefully neglecting any details that could cause angst.

After an hour or so of driving, they arrived at Cammalot. It appeared unchanged: wet and dreary. Mildew still tarnished the houses. They drove past the same group of boys sitting on their undersized bicycles, smoking and chewing tobacco. Lawns of houses were still strewn with toys. It was the same Cammalot as it was three months ago, and probably three decades ago as well. A minor highway went straight through Cammalot, though a sleeping passenger could ride through the town without ever knowing the town existed. Not that anyone cared about the dismal town (Cammalot's feelings towards outsiders were mutual). Adam asked his mother about local events, and she was hard pressed to recall any notable ones. Just like the rest of the country, food prices increased. Apparently, food-stamp beneficiaries were protesting at the local grocery store. Adam tried to comprehend the situation. The grocery store had little control over prices, and people who were receiving free food still complained that it was too expensive. Some things are just nonsensical. In other local news, the unemployment rate ticked up by a couple points. It probably would have ticked higher, if more Cammalot citizens were originally in the workforce. But according to the Bureau of Labor and Statistics, those not looking for a job are not considered unemployed. By that definition, Cammalot may have had one of the lowest unemployment rates in the country (few people worked, but even fewer were inclined to).

When they arrived home, Henry went straight to his computer. Sitting next to the computer was a large, hardcover faded blue book with frayed edges, titled *Quantum Physics of Atoms, Molecules, Nuclei, and Solids*. Henry opened the book to the middle, and read. His attention periodically switched between the computer and the book. "That material is far beyond your father and me," said Mrs. Carter. "He's only been working at that book for two weeks, and he's already half way through."

"We're just starting trig-based physics," said Adam. Adam felt slightly jealous of Henry's intellect, but acknowledged that it came at a cost. Even though Henry was socially disabled, and may never cope independently, he always smiled. He seemed to love unconditionally, and his biggest worry was deviating from a routine. If only life at Arcadia was that simple.

Mrs. Carter worked on typical household chores, and Adam lost himself in his book. In the early evening he heard someone on the front porch. For a brief moment, he thought it was Hannah, but soon realized his preposterousness. Over the years he had spent many days reading in the living room, waiting for his sister to arrive, and had not grown accustomed to her absence, even though she had been gone for eight months. He could not imagine how his mother must have felt.

The door opened, and Adam's father entered. Henry ran to the door, and Adam rose to greet his father. "Both of my boys are here!" he said with a smile. He dropped his lunch pail and kneeled. "Well, what are you waiting for? Come give your old man a hug." Henry and Adam both hugged their father. "It's been a while. How are your studies?" Henry ran back to the computer. Mr. Carter unlaced his boots and proceeded to the kitchen. Adam followed.

"It's more challenging than Cammalot."

"Is your neck sore yet?" A puzzled look crossed Adam's face. "From walking like this." Mr. Carter tilted his chin upwards in mockery of the elitists always looking down on the lower classes. Adam gave his father a blank expression. "It's a joke—you know—snobby people looking down on others."

"Oh," replied Adam. After a few seconds, he understood the reference. "There's no shortage of snobbery at Arcadia. Almost everyone has neural implants, and they think that makes them better and smarter than everyone else."

"Just remember, it's not the size of a man's wallet that makes him a man, but the scope of his character."

"If we think we're better than someone," said Adam, "then doesn't that make us worse? Isn't that why you have so much disdain for elitists?"

Mr. Carter chuckled. "It's a complicated situation," he said. "Some people have weak character. Able bodied people who refuse to work, men who beat their children."

"But acting like we're better than people is one reason people dislike Christians so much. They say we act 'holier than thou,' and we become alienated."

"Son, many of the Christians who act 'holier than thou' are not living the lives they preach. Matthew 7:5 says "first cast out the beam out of thine own eye; and then shalt thou see clearly to cast out the mote out of thy brother's eye." The point is, many Christians act is if their religion makes them better people. Being a Christian does not make you better than an atheist. I've met atheists who were finer people than many Christians." Mr. Carter paused. Adam scuffed his foot against the ground. "Maybe this analogy will help: when the U.S. entered World War Two, Nazi Germany was in the process of murdering and enslaving entire groups of people. Jews, Gypsies, blacks, the mentally disabled, homosexuals; the list goes on. I would argue that the U.S. was culturally and morally superior. We committed atrocities in the past, but had since become more civilized and aware. This gave us justification to intervene. But imagine if the U.S. was attempting the genocide of Hispanics. How could we denounce the actions of Nazi Germany if our actions were nearly identical?"

"We would be hypocrites. And no one likes a hypocrite."

"Exactly. Our actions were consistent with our words."

Adam pondered for a moment, then asked, "So, as long as we're not flawed, we can critique the flaws of others?"

"Everyone is flawed, but some people are consistently trying to fix their flaws and become better people."

"So those people can look down on others?"

"You're twisting my words, son. We shouldn't act superior to others. Doing so only yields animosity, and is often dangerous. We should set good examples, and not be afraid to denounce certain actions."

"What do you mean when you say it's dangerous?"

"Look son, it would be asinine to say that no culture is superior to another. The Aztecs reportedly sacrificed up to twenty thousand people per year. People need to censure activities such as that. But, if one group internalizes its alleged superiority, it can lead to horrific abuses of human rights. Whites used their alleged superiority as justification for slavery. Nazi Germany used their alleged superiority as justification for genocide."

Adam pondered for another moment. "I think I understand," he replied, nodding his head.

After the conversation, Adam went back to the couch to read, but was distracted. He thought about the fake test he and Will rigged to catch the cheaters. Cheating was wrong, but was cheating to stop cheating wrong? He must have internally debated this issue hundreds of times, yet he still had not reached a conclusion. Could he still claim moral superiority over Jett? He did not mention the acts to his father, partly because he did not want anyone to worry about him, but also because he was ashamed.

Failing to focus, he decided to watch television. Not counting the news clips watched in class, it was his first time watching television in months. Once on, the television displayed the previous channel viewed: the news station. What Adam saw caused chills. Across the entire country were massive, violent protests. Images of burning buildings and smashed windows flashed across the screen. The news anchors kept referring to people as 'protestors,' but Adam hesitated to call them protestors. Police officers in full armor do not wield 'protest shields.' The National Guard is not summoned to squelch disgruntled citizens. These people were rioters. They were unhappy, and willing to face significant bodily harm and risk arrest to make the world aware of their pain. According to the news report, thousands of people had been injured, and nearly a hundred were dead. There were even cases of reported gang rapes. The incident was disheartening, but Adam was glad to be in isolated Cammalot, as opposed to a major city.

12

Sunday, April 30, 2068

It was the day after Adam's grandfather's memorial service. That was the second time Adam ever saw his father cry, the first being Hannah's funeral. Adam shed a few tears at the funeral, but felt like he should have shed more. He loved his grandpa, and missed his grandpa's company. So why did he not sob at the funeral? He felt like there was something wrong with him. So many adults were sobbing, even his father, who rarely sobbed. *But why not me?* he thought. Had he become inured to death, after losing a sister and killing two boys? Was it even possible?

That Sunday afternoon, Adam's father was walking out the door when Adam asked, "Where are you going?"

"To pick up your grandma," replied Mr. Carter. "She will be joining us for an early supper. Care to join me?" Adam shrugged his shoulders, grabbed a jacket, and followed his father at the door. They climbed into the truck.

As they drove through Cammalot, Adam noticed an unusual number of people walking the streets and congregating on main road. "What's everyone doing?" asked Adam.

"Someone's probably giving away free food stamps," said Mr. Carter, with a chuckle. Adam cocked an eyebrow towards his father. "Sorry, that slipped out."

"That's okay," said Adam, "it's probably true. Either that, or someone's giving away free beer." Mr. Carter laughed, and Adam smiled.

Thirty minutes later, they arrived at the orchard. As soon as Adam's father turned off the car engine, they saw his grandmother exit the house. Adam exited the vehicle, and opened the front passenger door for his grandmother.

Another thirty minutes later, they were back in Cammalot, but it was different. Crowds of people flooded the streets and sidewalks. A short line of cars rolled slower than people were walking. Adam questioned why so many people flooded the streets. During his entire time spent in Cammalot, he had never seen even half as many people outside at once, not even during the annual Fourth of July parade. A white sedan, three cars ahead, honked its horn. A couple people turned towards the car, extended their middle fingers at the driver, then nonchalantly continued wandering.

"We're taking a detour," said Mr. Carter. The vehicle turned and Adam looked back. A couple people were smashing windows. Another person threw his drink at the white sedan. The side road was not nearly as crowded, but still contained an abnormal number of people.

"The riots were on the news recently. Maybe this is related?"

"Must be," said his grandmother. "But I've never seen the town like this."

"The whole town must be in the streets," said Mr. Carter.

They arrived at the Carter's house and exited the vehicle. Adam's grandmother stood and stretched her back. Four crows perched on the rail of the front porch. Adam turned his attention to the crows. In unison, they turned their heads towards him. The foremost crow cawed, and the others followed suit. Adam approached the door. Two of the crows flew away. The other two hopped in the opposite direction.

Once inside, Henry warmly greeted Adam and his father and grandmother. Henry ran to the door, hugged his grandmother and ran back to the computer. Mrs. Carter's eyes fixated on the news, broadcasting from the television. She turned, and solemnly said, "Last night, protestors took up arms. They fired on the National Guard. Congress held an emergency session. The military is authorized to detain political prisoners indefinitely. The entire country is under an 11:00 p.m. curfew, and the second amendment has been suspended until further notice."

"The president can't do that!" shouted Mr. Carter.

"It wasn't the president, it was congress. The house and senate both passed the bill. Democrats, Republicans, and Independents voted almost unanimously."

"The Constitution is supposed to protect our rights!"

"But those rights can be suspended under national emergencies," said Adam. "Or in the interest of national security."

"There's more," said Mrs. Carter. "Anyone convicted of a felony can have their assets seized by the state."

Mr. Carter turned and kicked the door. He clenched his fists. His face exuded red shades of anger. Adam's father had always been calm and collected. He never let his anger show. "Just because it can happen doesn't mean it should! That means the only thing upholding freedom is the good faith of our elected officials!"

"But—" Adam felt a hand on his shoulder. He turned, and saw his mother's hand. He recognized the signal: nothing he could say would calm his father. The man had spent his entire life believing in freedom. The freedom to speak freely, to take his son shooting for sport, to engage in commerce, and most importantly, the freedom to live without fear. Adam looked closely at his father. Beneath the indignant facade was a man trembling in fear and disappointment. The unspoken corollary of 'a government for the people, by the people,' is that the government is only as good as its people. When people abuse their freedoms, the freedoms are seized. Eventually, the only remnants of freedom exist as fragments of distant memories. Adam's father could see the freedom fading. The fundamental dream every American hopes for is a better life for his children and grand-children. In that brief moment, the dreams of Adam's father were crushed. Mr. Carter stormed out of the room with a tear in the corner of his eye.

Henry sat at the computer, oblivious to the environment. Adam wished he could have Henry's insouciance. He walked towards Henry, curious about what Henry was studying. "What—" he began to say, but was interrupted by a loud crash from behind. Mrs. Carter screamed. Adam turned to see shards of glass litter the floor. Three ragged men wielding bricks and bats approached the house. Mr. Carter marched into the room wielding a pump-action shotgun. He opened the front door. The men stood on the front porch.

"Out of our way, old man!" threatened the white thug, brand-ishing his baseball bat.

Mr. Carter cocked the shotgun, and pointed it at the thug. Sternly, yet calmly, Mr. Carter stated: "Get the hell off my property you filthy troglodytes."

"Look at this gringo," said one of the thugs. He chuckled. He leaned to the right, peering inside. "That your wife in there, gringo? She's a fine piece of meat."

Mr. Carter shouldered the shotgun. "Mind your tongue, swine."

"Swine?" said the third thug. Then the thug, with his limited vocabulary and vulgarities, threatened Mr. Carter with a severe beating. "And after we're done with you..." He continued, threatening explicit, vulgar, sexual acts against Mrs. Carter while the kids watched.

"Take one step and I—" one of the men stepped forward. Adam heard what sounded like a blast from a cannon. Mr. Carter pumped the shotgun again. Through the window, Adam saw one of the thugs fall backwards. The one with the bat raised his bat and lunged towards Mr. Carter. Another shot fired. Mr. Carter stepped left. The thug fell face first on the porch. The final thug yelled some curse words and fled.

Adam curiously stepped outside. His father turned, pointed at the house, and sternly stated, "Go inside!"

Adam sulked, and stepped inside. He sneakily peered through the window. His father kneeled next to one of the downed thugs, and placed his finger against the thug's neck. He stood, shaking his head. He walked down the steps and kneeled next to the second thug. Again, he placed his fingers on the thug's neck, checking for a pulse. Mr. Carter walked back inside. Adam heard footsteps, and saw his mother enter the room, carrying a rifle.

The door slowly opened. Adam's father looked at his mother and said, "Is everyone okay?"

"Henry is upstairs with your mother. They're both a bit shaken, but they're fine. I tried calling 9-1-1 multiple times, but I kept hearing the busy signal."

"I'm not surprised," said Mr. Carter. "It's chaos outside."

"Are you okay?" asked Mrs. Carter, embracing her husband.

He lifted his arms, gave himself a cursory exam. "I'm not injured."

"But are you okay?"

"My family is safe. I will be fine."

~

After the incident, Mr. Carter kept dialing 9-1-1, and was finally able to reach someone. Several hours later, authorities arrived and questioned the family. Given the circumstances, they saw no reason to press charges, but advised Mr. Carter to stay close, in case further contact was required. They confiscated the shotgun involved in the homicide, but never mentioned anything about relinquishing additional firearms. The officers revealed that most of the violence was isolated in the vicinity of the protests, but there were a few reports of small groups of thugs looting vulnerable houses. Some of the nearby houses had been looted, but thankfully, no one was home.

That evening, the family established a new plan: the grandmother and Henry would leave for the orchard. Mr. and Mrs. Carter would accompany Adam back to Arcadia. Until he could ensure everyone was safe, Mr. Carter opted to stay home from work.

~

Monday morning was calm. After a tumultuous night, many of the protestors were arrested or returned home. Henry was the only one who slept well. Emergency sirens blaring throughout the night kept anyone else from sleeping adequately. When Adam went downstairs, his parents and grandmother were all awake. His father stood in the kitchen, cooking breakfast, while his mother and grandmother watched the news. Throughout the entire country, thousands of protestors had been arrested. At least they took a break in the morning. Even the small town of Cammalot was mentioned on the news. It seemed that high-poverty cities and neighborhoods like Cammalot were laden with looters. There was little logic to the situation. High-poverty cities had few valuables to loot, but violence and random destruction of property was how those people dealt with their problems. Knowing that police officers were occupied with the protests, certain people seized the opportunity to pillage with little risk of being caught.

After breakfast, everyone piled into the truck and drove thirty minutes to the rural orchard. It felt safer than being in the center of town. Mrs. Carter carried a suitcase for Henry, while the grandmother carried a box containing Henry's robot. Henry carried some books. Adam and his father followed, carrying guns and ammunition. Even though guns had recently been outlawed, everyone felt safer having the guns nearby, especially after the attempted robbery. Adam's mother gave the grandmother a hug, then kneeled to Henry's level. "Goodbye Henry," she said. "Stay on good behavior for grandma. We will return in a few days." Henry hugged his mother and father, and then ran to the computer. Once everyone said their goodbyes, Adam and his parents departed towards Cammalot.

During the ride home, Adam asked, "Why aren't we staying at the orchard?"

His father responded: "You've been given a once in a lifetime opportunity to study at Arcadia. We're all aware of the great things Arcadia students have done. I don't want this opportunity squandered because of some protestors. If you quit now, you'll regret it the rest of your life. Once you're back at Arcadia, your mother and I will stay at the orchard with Henry and grandma." Adam looked down and twiddled his thumbs. "Did I ever tell you that I was accepted into Yale?" Adam gave his father a surprised look.

"No," said Adam. "Why didn't you go?"

"I didn't want to graduate with debt. I was able to defer my admission for one year, while I saved money working. You see, during the summers I worked construction. One of the guys I worked with, a friend from high school, decided to quit and start a business renovating and flipping houses. He asked if I wanted to join. I figured, why not? We would buy a house using the bank's money. Then, we would renovate the house and resell it. The housing market was hot. I made more than enough money to pay my tuition at Yale. I even bought a Lexus. Given how much money I was making without a college degree, the thought of paying an exorbitant sum for tuition and spending four years broke, only to get a job making less money, seemed asinine. So, I kept flipping houses. Then the market crashed, and we lost most of the extra money we made. By that time, my admission offer expired. I didn't know what to do, so I joined the army."

"And you still regret the decision to defer admission?"

"The only reason I don't regret it is because otherwise, I would not have met your mother. But I always wondered how different my life would have been if I had gone to Yale."

"I see," Adam solemnly said.

"Our country is in pretty bad shape," said Mr. Carter. "We need smart people with integrity making decisions. And who knows, maybe you could be one of those people."

"I thought integrity excludes one from politics," said Adam.

His father laughed. "Unfortunately, that seems to be the case."

When they arrived home, his mother went upstairs. Adam started upstairs, but Mr. Carter stopped him. "Wait," he said. "There's something I need to show you. Follow me." Adam followed his father outside, and to the backside of the house. He bent over and opened a small wooden door leading to the crawlspace under the house. They crawled under the house, on the soft damp dirt. Next to one of the walls was a garbage bag. Mr. Carter pointed at the bag. "Inside that garbage bag is a wooden box containing an old thirty-eight special revolver, and twelve rounds. It's old enough that it isn't registered to anyone. In fact, it's our only gun that isn't registered."

"Why are you showing me?" asked Adam.

"In case you need it."

~

Two days later, Adam began packing. It was Wednesday, and on Thursday, he was to take the train back to Arcadia. While he packed, he thought of the story his father told him. He walked downstairs. His father sat on the couch, reading the news, while his mother was in the kitchen. She always seemed to have something to do. At that moment, she stood at the counter kneading bread dough. "Mom," said Adam. Mrs. Carter turned her head.

"How did you and dad meet?" asked Adam.

She paused for a moment, then answered while continuing to knead the bread dough. "We met during the Third Korean War. I was a nurse in the Army, and your father was an Army soldier. He came in with a piece of shrapnel in his arm, and I tended his wounds. He asked me on a date, and I said 'no.'"

"Why did you say no; didn't you like him?"

"No, it wasn't that. I just had too much on my mind at the time," she said while continuing to knead the bread dough. "I didn't want to have more to worry about. Anyway, a couple weeks later, he came back with a broken leg. He said he broke it on purpose, because it was the only way he could see me. Sometimes, I still wonder if he wasn't joking."

"Then what happened?"

"He was sent back to Fort McNair in Virginia, and I was sent there a couple months later. His leg healed, and we ran into each other on the base. He asked me on a date again, and I couldn't think of any good reasons to say no. So we went on a date, and a few more... and a year and a half later, we married."

"Why did you say yes?" asked Adam.

"Well, he seemed like a nice guy, and he was persistent. I thought I should give him a chance. And I'm glad I did."

A loud knock from the front door permeated the house. In the front room, Adam heard his father's voice shout, "I'll get it." There was no hint of fear or concern in his voice. Criminals generally do not knock.

"I'm going to finish packing," said Adam. He walked out of the kitchen and dashed upstairs.

His father opened the door. Several men wearing camouflage gear, ballistic helmets, and Kevlar vests stood in the door. Each one carried an automatic rifle. One of the men spoke with a twang, "Captain Jeffery Dunn. On behalf of the United States government, and as required by the Public Safety and Firearms Protection act, we are authorized to search the premise for firearms."

"You're here to take our guns?" asked Mr. Carter, angrily.

"We are authorized to confiscate all privately owned firearms."

"Ruthless thugs are roaming the streets, and you mean to tell me that you're taking away my only means to defend my family?"

"Do you own any firearms?"

"Yes I do!" Mr. Carter firmly stated. "And I intend to keep them to protect my family. Now please get off my property."

"If you do not comply, we are authorized to use force."

Mrs. Carter entered from the kitchen, just as her husband was closing the door. Before it was completely closed, it burst open. Men with M16s held tightly against their shoulders entered.

"Search the premises," commanded Sergeant Dunn.

"Hey!" shouted Mr. Carter. He stepped towards Dunn.

Dunn pointed at two men and ordered, "Restrain him." Two soldiers grabbed Mr. Carter's arms and shoulders. He squirmed and jerked, trying to break free.

"Get your hands off me!" He pulled one arm free, but Dunn rammed the father in the gut with the butt of his rifle. Mr. Carter fell to his knees and the men let go of him. The mother attempted to run to his aid, but was restrained by two more soldiers.

"Don't you touch her!" shouted Mr. Carter. He attempted to stand, but Dunn pointed his rifle at Mr. Carter.

"Stay down!" commanded Dunn. Mr. Carter raised his hands in the air and remained kneeled. Facing the stairs, he looked up and saw Adam watching the incident. The soldiers had not yet noticed the boy.

Two soldiers entered. One spoke, "Found this in one of the bedrooms."

"That's a fancy rifle," said Dunn.

"Careful with that! That's a family heirloom—my great-great grandfather's Thompson from World War Two."

"We'll hold on to it for safekeeping," replied Dunn.

"I want a receipt for that!" demanded Mr. Carter.

"I don't have time to spend all day fillin' out paperwork." He tossed the gun on the floor. "Oops."

One of the other soldiers spoke: "There's also a safe in the other room, sir."

Dunn squatted in front of Mr. Carter and sardonically said, "Now, how about you tell me how I get into that safe." Mr. Carter looked into Dunn's eyes.

In an equally mocking tone, he replied, "You turn the dial, clockwise and counterclockwise, to the appropriate numbers. Then you turn the wheel, and open the door. Did they not teach you how to open doors in basic training?" Dunn stood, turned away, and scoffed. Then, with a swift pivot on his right foot, he turned and hammered his fist into Mr. Carter's face. Adam's father grunted. Mrs. Carter whimpered empathetically. Tears of fear glazed her eyes.

Mr. Carter looked up at Dunn, and excoriated: "When I was in the army, we were fighting for Americans, not against them."

Dunn scoffed. "You gonna tell me how to unlock the safe or not?"

Mr. Carter ignored Dunn's question and continued his lambaste: "Have you forgotten who the real enemy is? Iran is pointing nuclear missiles at us! China is forcefully annexing new territories! Muslim extremists have promised to eradicate the West. Russia has massive totalitarian, anti-U.S. government, and you're bullwhipping American citizens!" Mr. Carter understood that confiscating firearms was a larger issue than it appeared; it was about more than ostensibly improving public safety. It was about freedom. Unfortunately, Dunn could not comprehend this.

"I didn't think so," replied Dunn.

Dunn calmly walked over to Mrs. Carter and grabbed a fistful of hair. The other men stepped aside. She let out a short, high-pitched shriek. "House by house, street by street, city by city, we are confiscating all firearms. Those are our orders. We don't need your cooperation, but it sure would make our job easier." Dunn un-holstered his sidearm, then slowly moved it in the direction of Mrs. Carter.

Even during war, the lives of women and children were always sacred. Adam's father understood this. It was a tacit concept to most, but to Dunn, it was foreign. Mr. Carter had served in the army. He fought to uphold the freedoms of his fellow countrymen. Defend your country. Defend the vulnerable. Adam's father did not need to be reminded of this. His wife was vulnerable, and Dunn had broken a primordial code of conduct. Maybe it was an empty threat and Dunn had no intention of harming anyone. It was conceivable that Dunn did not want to confiscate firearms, that he was simply following orders. Perhaps, in light of recent events, he was equally as stressed as Adam's father, and not acting rationally.

Whatever his motives were, they did not matter. As soon as Dunn motioned his weapon towards Mrs. Carter, the father sprung free and charged Dunn, tackling him in the process. Dunn's firearm discharged. The bullet struck the wall, a couple feet from Adam. Adam grew tense. His father punched Dunn in the face multiple times. Adam watched the other two soldiers grab his father, and ply him off of Dunn.

Dunn stood and wiped the blood from his lip. He forcefully spit on the floor and muttered some obscenities. He took three steps, bent down, and retrieved his sidearm. He marched over to Adam's father and pistol-whipped him in the back of the head. Mrs. Carter screamed and sobbed uncontrollably. Adam leaned against the wall. His hands trembled uncontrollably. His breaths grew shallow and sporadic. Silent tears rolled down his cheeks. Mr. Carter's head fell forward and hung limp. His body became a rag doll. The soldiers released him and he fell to the floor, producing a low thud.

"Sir!" shouted one of the soldiers.

Dunn looked at the soldier. "This man attacked me. He attacked us. It was self-defense." Dunn paced nervously. "Damn-it! Why can't these people let us do our jobs?"

The soldier kneeled to check on Mr. Carter.

Dunn continued, "Well, now that he's unconscious, we can continue searching the house." He wiped the blood from his lip.

The kneeling soldier placed his finger against Mr. Carter's neck. Another soldier entered the room. "Sir," he said. "I found this hanging underneath the stairwell." The soldier extended his hand. In his palm were two small keys on a ring.

"See if it opens the safe," ordered Dunn. Two soldiers left the room.

The kneeling soldier turned towards Dunn and with great concern said, "Sir, we have a problem." Dunn made eye contact with the soldier. "He's dead." Adam's mother sobbed harder. More tears rolled down Adam's cheek. Dunn muttered some obscenities and kicked a piece of furniture. "Sir, what should we do?" Dunn rested his hand on his helmet and continued pacing anxiously.

The two soldiers came back a few seconds later. "Looks like we hit the jackpot."

Dunn stopped pacing and relaxed. "Good," he replied. "Search the rest of the house."

"Sir, what about..." started one of the soldiers, pointing at Adam's mother.

"She's a witness," said Dunn, hesitantly. "And we can't have any witnesses. Take care of it."

"But we can't just—"

"That's an order soldier! Take care of her, or I'll take care of you!" Dunn opened the front door, and exited the house.

Adam just lost one parent, and was about to lose another. Every instinct told him to help his mother, but fear and logic prevented him from doing so. They killed his father in a heated argument. They were ordered to kill the mother because she was a witness. If they knew he was a witness, he would surely die as well. He was outnumbered by several armed men, each one nearly twice his size. Attempting to save his mother would be suicide. For a moment, that thought seemed appealing. He could die, protecting his mother, and be freed of the burdens life handed him. No more guilt from killing two people. No nightmares haunting his sleep. No more tough decisions. Erebus could continue killing; let someone else deal with it. Michael Cane and Jack Holden could have the world; Adam would not be around to see it. Surely, there was someone more capable than a thirteen-year-old boy to uphold the country's freedom. But then,

Adam thought of Henry and his grandmother. Henry's only blood relative remaining would be his grandmother. Nearly the entire family would be slaughtered. He thought of his father, who had just given his life in a feeble attempt to protect the freedom of people he neither knew nor liked. It was the ultimate sacrifice. If his father could die for a noble cause, surely Adam could live for one. Let no sacrifice be in vain.

Mrs. Carter looked up and saw Adam at the top of the stairs. He stared into her eyes, hoping that she would send him a signal, some indication of what to do. A thunderous sound bellowed through the house. Mrs. Carter fell face down into the floor. Behind her head was a smoking pistol. More tears spilled from Adam's eyes. A voice from downstairs shouted, "We'll cover the garage. You check upstairs."

Adam's heart pounded even faster. He looked left and right. The stairs creaked. Adam scrambled to the nearest bedroom, and hid behind the door. Each of the bedrooms had a window, but beneath each window was a large drop. He would surely injure his leg. A small window in the bathroom led to the roof. If he could get to the roof, then he could hang on the ledge, and quietly slip out without injury. Adam peered into the hall. No soldiers in sight, only sounds of rummaging from the other bedrooms. He took a deep breath, and darted towards the bathroom. Unlike the soldiers, he was barefoot, thus allowing him to walk without producing audible footsteps.

He slowly closed the bathroom door. The back yard was visible from the window. It appeared empty, but the overhang of the roof blocked the entire view. Adam lifted the bottom of the window. Once it was open, he climbed through it and peered over the ledge. No soldiers in sight. He gripped the ledge and lowered himself. When he dropped to the ground, he immediately felt the cold damp dirt on his bare feet.

Adam dashed to the opening of the crawlspace and hid under the house. He crawled over to the garbage bag and tore it open, revealing an aged box. Inside the box rested a blued revolver. A large 'S' and 'W' emblem was embedded in the hilt. Adam opened the cylinder. Six rounds filled each slot. Six more rounds sat in the box. Adam placed the revolver in his left pocket and the rounds in his right pocket. He sobbed and shivered in the cold moist air, wishing there was something he could have done. For two hours, he waited under the house until there were no signs of harm.

13

Monday, May 7, 2068

It was Monday, and Adam was back at Arcadia. Classes were in full swing. Adam's friends were quick to notice his somberness. Bizarre and nightmarish dreams incessantly plagued his sleep. His friends pried and pried, in a considerate manner, until after dinner, when they all gathered in the commons. Coincidentally, he yearned to tell someone what happened. He never told his grandmother what really happened, he was too ashamed to bear witness without making an attempt to stop the soldiers. Against his better judgment, he finally divulged the story to Will, Sahar, and Julie, though he neglected to tell them about the revolver, which was now stored in his dorm room.

When it finally ended, Will and Julie were awestruck. Sahar's only response was, "I am so sorry."

Will adjusted his posture. "You should tell the police about it," he suggested. Adam looked at the table, then back at Will.

"I thought about it," said Adam, "but it's not worth the risk. Besides, habeas corpus has been suspended."

"What risk?" blurted Will, tightly gripping the edge of the table. "They killed your parents! They need to be brought to justice." Adam inhaled deeply, and then slowly released the air.

"I wish I could see them pay for their crimes," he said, "but it's not that simple." Each of his friends looked at him in silence, waiting for elaboration. "They gave my grandma the flimsy but 'official' report: two members of an extremist antigovernment group refused to relinquish their weapons and were fatally injured resisting arrest."

"Sad," said Sahar. She looked Adam directly in the eyes with the utmost sincerity. "I wish I could have had the privilege to know your parents. They sound like wonderful people."

Adam dolefully bowed his head. "Instead, their deaths have been relegated to the slew of unnamed protestors who died in vain. They were posthumously labeled 'enemies of the state.' If I attempt to share what happened, my grandma and I could be labeled enemies of the state and held indefinitely, without due process. My parents' assets have been seized. They can do the same to my grandma. It's part of the new law!"

"And Henry would be placed for adoption," said Julie.

"Exactly," said Adam. "I might never see him again."

"When is the memorial service?" asked Sahar.

"We're not having one." Everyone looked at Adam in astonishment. "I told my grandmother it was too stressful, after already losing two family members this year. Maybe, if this whole mess is ever sorted. If I can ever share what really happened, then we will hold a memorial service. Until then, we have work to do."

Will raised an eyebrow. "And she's okay with that?"

"She respected the request. I think she knows the story of their death was fabricated, but she didn't push me for details. Instead, she suggested I promptly return to Arcadia. And that's what my father wanted as well."

"If you need anything," said Sahar, softly touching Adam's hands, "we are here for you." Will and Julie both nodded.

"Thanks," said Adam. "I can't do everything alone. I still don't know how I'm going to infiltrate Erebus. That should be our priority."

"I agree," said Will. "If we're going to expose Erebus for their crimes, and stop Cane and Holden, we need someone on the inside."

"While I agree with the cause," started Julie, "doesn't this lead to the same conundrum? Namely, that you could be labeled an enemy of the state?"

"It's a possibility," said Adam. "But if Cane and Holden are able to seize the presidency, what will stop them from labeling any opponent an enemy of the state? The current president and our congress passed a law that allows for political detention, but it's mostly been applied to rioters. The problem is that this law gives the president unequivocal power. I still believe our current president is attempting, albeit, misguidedly, to restore peace and prosperity. Unfortunately, the only thing standing between our freedom and a complete totalitarian regime is the faith of our elected officials. And I have little faith in Cane or Holden. The president's approval rating is at an all-time low of twenty percent. Chances are, Cane and Holden will easily sweep the election, unless someone stops them. So yes, we're still in the same conundrum, but the stakes are higher. My father died at the hands of men like Cane and Holden, and more will likely follow. We must fight for the good of our country—for freedom!"

"You would risk indefinite detainment to protect the freedom of all citizens," stated Sahar. She smiled. "That is very noble of you Adam. I will do whatever I can to assist."

"I know I need help, but I can't ask anyone to sacrifice themselves for this cause. It's not my right."

"If succeeding means upholding America freedom, the freedom of three hundred fifty million people, then no price is too great to pay," said Sahar. "My father was also a casualty of people who wished to subjugate our freedom. There is more at stake than I ever imagined. I will help any way I can."

Adam smiled and replied, "Thank you, Sahar. I will make sure your father did not die in vain."

"I can't imagine a country ruled by people like that twerp Jett," said Will. "Count me in."

"Thank you, Will." Adam nodded, and Will nodded in return.

Julie bowed her head, and with a slight stammer, said: "Adam, Sahar, Will: I will always consider you my dearest friends. And your goal is laudable. But..." She took a deep breath. "If these people are as bad as you say, then we're all putting our entire families at risk. I have two younger brothers, and a younger sister. I would gladly sacrifice my safety for this cause, but I can't sacrifice their safety. It's not my choice to make."

"I understand," said Adam.

"If something were to happen to them, I couldn't live with myself, knowing that I may have been partly responsible."

"You do not have to explain yourself," said Sahar. "We are friends, and always will be."

A tear slid down Julie's cheek. She sniffled. "I'll still study with you, and socialize, but when you're discussing tactics, I will be somewhere else." Julie sniffled again. "I'm thirteen years old. This is too much." Will placed his hand on Julie's shoulder.

"Let's make a deal," said Will. "At least once every week, we all get together, and promise not to discuss these issues. We can talk about classes, events, and people, whatever, as long as it's not depressing. We'll put all of our issues aside, and just enjoy each other's company."

Julie smiled weakly. "I like that idea."

"So do I," said Adam.

"Me too," said Sahar.

Julie stood, picked up her backpack, and swung it around her shoulder. "I need to go study. But before I go, I will leave you with one last idea." She slipped her arm through the other strap on the backpack. "Locke said you need to infiltrate Erebus, and you need to think like Jett. Well, school elections are approaching. If you could devise a way to 'shift' the results, maybe Erebus would be more likely to extend an invitation."

Adam stood. "Thank you," he said. Will and Sahar also stood to bid farewell to Julie. She hugged Sahar.

"I will see you later this evening," said Sahar. Julie nodded, and then hugged Will.

"Why don't we get together Friday evening?" suggested Will.

"I'll look for you in the rec room," she replied with a smile. Lastly, she hugged Adam.

"I'm so sorry about your family," she said.

"Me too," said Adam. "Take care. I'll see you in class tomorrow." Julie pulled on her backpack's straps to adjust it, then turned and walked towards the library. Adam, Will, and Sahar sat, and continued their discussion.

"Does anyone else feel bad?" asked Will. "Like we just lost a friend."

"I got the impression that she feels that way," said Adam. "We just need to make sure that we don't discuss our plans when she is present; we have to make her feel welcome. She deserves as much."

"If I were in her situation," stated Sahar, "I would probably act accordingly. Julie is of the highest probity, but the truth is, she has much more to lose than any of us." Adam and Will nodded in concurrence. "We cannot ask her to join our battle, knowing what could happen."

Will sat straight, and cracked his knuckles. "On a different note, I have some moderately positive news." Adam and Sahar looked to Will, waiting for him to divulge the specifics. "I looked at the posted grades, and I didn't see Jett's student ID number at the top of the list. In fact, none of the people who hacked the server were at the top of the list."

"So it worked?" asked Sahar, partially astonished.

"Well, it worked, but not enough. Only two of the people on the list did bad enough to fail their classes. Jett and Eric still passed with 'C' marks."

"At least we took care of two cronies," said Adam, shrugging his shoulders.

"Like I said, moderately positive. Now, I highly doubt that the trick will work again, so I instituted some adjustments to the server. Every time someone attempts to hack the portion of the server with test keys, a message will be sent to every professor, administrator, and student." Before anyone could ask the question, Will pre-emptively answered: "I know you're going to ask how, so let me answer: I piggybacked off the emergency response system. The server records every user who accesses it. Every time an entry is created, it links to the emergency response system, and sends a message to everyone."

"That's brilliant!" said Adam.

"Well done," said Sahar.

"Just a thought," offered Adam, "hypothetically, could someone log on as Jett and hack the server, with the intention of landing him in trouble?"

"I already thought about that," replied Will. "If we want them to get in trouble, we need good evidence. The system will also broadcast their location, which can be cross-checked against SSD footage."

"Probably for the best," said Adam. "So we will patiently wait for someone culpable, like Jett, to attempt to cheat."

"Exactly," replied Will.

An awkward pause passed before Adam asked, "The idea Julie mentioned about swinging an election; what do you think about it?"

Will and Sahar looked at each other. Then Sahar spoke, "I know it is not right." Will nodded in agreement. "But given that you need to do something questionable to gain access to Erebus, this could be one of the more benign acts."

"I don't even know what responsibilities the class officers have," said Will. "I know the president is some sort of liaison between the students and administrators."

"Students usually run for vice president when they want a job title on their college resume, but they do not want to do the work that comes with president," replied Sahar.

Adam nodded, and continued elaborating: "The secretary is a pretty similar position, but requires more organization skills."

"Sounds simple enough," said Will, nodding in comprehension. "Maybe we should run for office." Adam and Sahar both raised an eyebrow.

"I need to stay out of the general spotlight," said Adam. "But you two can run."

"I do not think it is a good idea," said Sahar. "Suppose we are implicated for fixing the election. It is much easier to deny if we are fixing it for someone we do not know, as opposed to fixing it for ourselves."

"True," replied Will. "But it's more audacious for us to fix the election for ourselves. And we need audacious."

"You don't have to decide today," said Adam.

"I will consider it," said Sahar.

"Great!" said Will. "Because when I'm president, I could use a good secretary!"

Sahar's eyes perked. She straightened her posture. "Are you implying that girls make better secretaries than presidents?"

Adam laughed. "Not sure how you're going to talk your way out of this one, Will."

Will quickly backed away. "Oh no, I wasn't implying anything." He coughed. Sahar relaxed. "Rather," continued Will, "I was stating a pretty well known truth."

Sahar scowled at Will, then sternly stated, "Then it is settled. I will run for president. If you are lucky, I might even let you be my running mate for vice president." Will smirked. Sahar continued, "We can discuss this more at a later time. I need to retreat to my studies." Sahar stood and grabbed her backpack. "Good bye Adam."

"Good night," replied Adam. Sahar departed. Will offered a customary farewell, but Sahar promptly ignored it.

Once Sahar was out of sight, Will said, "I think I'm finally starting to understand the opposite sex. And I think that went well."

Adam chuckled. "How do you figure?"

"We needed audacious, and from the looks of it, she had no intention of running for office. Well, I seem to have fixed that problem."

Adam's jaw dropped. "That was your plan, the whole time? To trick Sahar into running for office?" Will nodded and grinned cheekily. Adam shook his head and laughed.

With a hint of laughter and a dash of self-importance in his voice, Will spoke: "Next time you need advice with girls, just let me know. I would be happy to offer my wisdom."

Adam laughed again. "Sure, next time I need to know how to make a girl angry, I'll find you."

"It's easier than you might think," replied Will. Adam stood and grabbed his backpack. "You leaving too?"

"I also need to study before I go to sleep." Adam waved, and Will waved back. Adam started his departure, but turned back towards Will and said: "You might be the self-proclaimed expert, but at least she will still speak with me tomorrow."

"I suppose I didn't think that through all the way."

"I guess not," said Adam.

14

Wednesday, May 23, 2068
Adam stood towards the back of what appeared to be an infinite line
of students. Or rather, the line felt infinite because of his incessantly
growling stomach; any amount of waiting feels like eternity when one
is hungry. Beyond the cacophony of gregarious, hungry students,
Adam heard a subtle screech behind him. He turned to see Will. Will
raised a hand and held his index finger while panting heavily. "I just
saw—"

"A ghost?"

"No," said Will, continuing to breath heavily. "Jack Holden!"

Adam arced an eyebrow. "Jack Holden?"

"Yes!" said Will. "Massachusetts Governor, Jack Holden!"

A keen curiosity instantly trumped Adam's insatiable hunger.
"What's he doing here?"

"I don't know," replied Will. "But he was walking towards Mr.
Kennedy's office."

"We're going to find out why, aren't we?" asked Adam with a
tone that was equally as inquisitive as it was ebullient.

Will proudly replied, "Of course. Are we not obligated to
uncover every detail?"

Adam nodded. "Lunch can wait."

The two boys dashed as fast as they could, just short of running,
through the crowded lunchroom, down the hall, and up the central
staircase. By the time they reached the top of the staircase, both boys
were panting. Neither boy knew how many flights of stairs they

climbed. Adam stopped counting after twelve. Will stopped counting after fifteen. They slowed their pace and walked past the registrar. At the end of the hall was the lobby to the dean's office. Will and Adam peered inside. A receptionist sat at an immaculate rosewood desk. Several plush chairs, chairs that looked much more comfortable than classroom chairs, lined the wall. In the background was a large window overlooking the campus.

"Look," whispered Will, pointing at a man pacing in the lobby. Will kept panting. "That's him."

"Mr. Holden," said the receptionist, "you're welcome to take a seat. Mr. Kennedy will be with you in a few minutes."

Holden scowled at the receptionist. In an irritable tone he replied, "I prefer to stand." Holden continued pacing, periodically glancing at his watch.

"What do you think he's doing here?" whispered Adam.

"I don't know, but he's obviously not happy to be here." Will and Adam kept watching intently, waiting for something to happen.

A few minutes later, Dean Kennedy emerged from the door on the left. He started to introduce himself, but was cut off by Holden.

"Kennedy!" blurted Holden.

"Yes, Mr. Holden," the dean calmly replied.

"Care to tell me why my son is on the short list for expulsion?"

"Perhaps you would like to speak in my office?" The dean held the office door open for Holden. Holden marched into the office.

"Shoot!" said Will. "We can't hear them now! And we can't just wait in the office." Adam checked his surroundings.

"The restroom!" Adam pointed to the door adjacent to the office. "It looks like it shares a wall with Kennedy's office."

The restroom was much fancier than the student rooms; countertops constructed from granite, the faucets were polished, and stalls were made of oak. A nearly perfect silence filled the room. When the boys stood absolutely still, they could faintly hear the conversation emanating from the dean's office.

"Your son was caught illegally accessing test materials from the server. Arcadia has a strict and explicit policy with regards to academic dishonesty."

"The way I understand it, your academy is funded completely by alumni donations. It is in the academy's best interest to maintain positive relationships—especially with prominent donors."

"Your status in no way changes your son's actions."

"What proof do you have that my son committed these acts?"

"More than enough. Your son, and several other students, can be seen on SSD footage accessing the server at the same time and place the server indicated they accessed it. Looking back through the data, this wasn't even his first offense."

"My lawyers would take issue with that story. It sounds like Jett was coerced. It would be a shame to have to involve lawyers."

"Despite your threats, I still have an image to uphold."

"Is that image more important than the contributions I make to the academy?"

"Be blunt Mr. Holden. What do you propose?"

"Suppose Jett comes forward. He indicts the other perpetrators and receives a lesser punishment because of his honesty. Meanwhile, you maintain your image, and the major donor remains content."

"And if word of this leaks?"

"It won't."

"Humor me. Hypothetically, if someone were to discover this discrepancy—"

"What evidence is there to refute it? The donor has long made contributions, and Jett will give you the name of every student involved. It's based mostly on the truth."

"I must admit: a career in politics has made you well versed at the art of deceit."

"And you think that is a vice?"

"Is it not?"

"It comes with the territory, Kennedy. Despite the many grumblings you may hear, the voters demand leaders with supple tongues—eloquent speakers who can artfully blend duplicity with facts. Honest politicians don't get elected. They tell people exactly what they hate to hear."

"And what do voters hate to hear?"

"The truth. They're too stubborn and stupid to accept the truth. They need people like me to make decisions for them."

"You should leave, now."

"Yes, I should. I am needed elsewhere."

Adam turned towards Will. "I can't believe it!"

"I can," replied Will, "though I don't want to."

~

Wednesday, May 30, 2068

One week following the incident, the school was in campaign mode. Sahar was running against Jett for the office of president, and Will was running against a formerly unknown classmate for vice president. Campaign posters plastered every wall and column on campus. Students would vote Friday, during social studies. That left Thursday for the final campaign speeches.

For the first time in the academy's history, Dr. Williams volunteered to schedule a presidential debate after dinner. He reasoned that students needed to make informed decisions, and allowing each candidate a single speech amounted to, in many cases, students voting based solely on popularity. A debate would force students to think more about the "fundamental issues," referred to by Dr. Williams. During lunch, Will, Adam, and Sahar contemplated what these "issues" could possibly be.

Adam gave the blanket inquiry to Will and Sahar: "What exactly do you intend to change? Are there even any issues that student representatives can influence?"

"It doesn't matter," said Will. "As long as people think we have influence, they'll vote for us."

"Let me rephrase." Adam cleared his throat. "What issues do you purportedly intend to change?"

After a brief pause, Sahar spoke: "Well, academic dishonesty is an obvious issue."

Adam gave a slight wince. "I heard that Jett's already capitalizing on that issue. He's painting himself as a maverick who revealed a ubiquitous network of cheaters."

Will scoffed. Adam looked to Will. "You're serious?" questioned Will. "He's at the apex of that network! We should expose him."

"It is not feasible," stated Sahar. "Any evidence we give also implicates us. That leaves us with baseless slander."

In a laughably innocent fashion, Will asked, "Would attacking his character be so terrible?" He paused, waiting for a response. Adam and Sahar looked at each other, then at Will. "Let's be honest, his character is sinister."

Sahar eloquently replied, "I refuse to succumb to the barbarism of politics, even if Jett is an ignoble putz." She crossed her arms.

"Rest assured that Jett has an arsenal of aspersions aimed at you. And, if I may play the devil's advocate, have we not already yielded to the barbarism of politics? Are you two not running for the purpose of allowing us to fix the election? So that I can infiltrate Erebus? Does this not boil down to the quest for power?"

"That may be," said Sahar. "But I will at least maintain dignity. And I intend use whatever power I acquire to make the campus better." Adam shrugged.

Will raised his index finger and tilted his head. "If we are fixing the election," he spoke, "why bother wooing voters?"

"We still need to uphold the appearance of truth. If Jett is the favorite, people will wonder how Sahar took the election. It needs to be a subtle victory." Adam paused. "The system I used to fix the election—everyone votes from their own computer. All the votes coming from IP addresses from Fire Hall, where Jett resides, are diverted. I predict that they are more likely to vote for Jett, so those are the votes we need to steal. Anyway, I set up a proxy that diverts those votes, recasts every third 'Jett' vote as a 'Sahar' vote, then sends the votes to the main server, where the remaining votes are electronically tallied."

"I see," said Will. "So we steal enough that it doesn't draw suspicion."

"And it still requires me to obtain a large share of the votes."

"Exactly," said Adam.

Will looked at his watch. "I think we need to get to class."

Adam looked at his watch and concurred. "I hope you think of something by this evening."

~

That evening, first-year students gathered in the auditorium. Towards the back of the stage, Dr. Williams stood at a podium. Two more podiums had been purposely planted left and right stage, respectively. The stage lights dimmed, and the clamor of hundreds of student conversations waned. A light static from the speakers, and the occasional crackling sound could be heard. Dr. Williams took center stage. "You are in the midst of Arcadian history. Never before, have we been blessed with the opportunity to stage a live presidential debate." A roaring applause resounded, then quickly faded. Dr. Williams stepped forward. "I have prepared a series of questions. Each candidate will be allocated one minute to respond to each question, and an additional minute to state their rebuttal. Neither candidate has seen the questions, but they have been informed of the rules. Once all questions have been answered, each candidate will have one minute for closing remarks. A coin flip will determine who gets to respond first. With that said, please welcome Jett Holden and Sahar Rosen."

The crowd applauded and cheered when Sahar and Jett entered the stage. Both smiled and waved at the audience. Each stopped next to Dr. Williams. The professor reached into his pocket and produced a large silver coin. He looked at Sahar and spoke, "Sahar, call the coin while it is in the air." Dr. Williams flipped the coin several feet into the air.

"Tails," called Sahar. The coin landed in the professor's hand. He opened his palm.

"Heads," he spoke. He turned to Jett. "Jett, you won the coin toss. Do you prefer to speak first or second?"

"I'll go first, Dr. Williams." Each candidate walked to their podiums, and Dr. Williams walked back to his.

"Our first question:" spoke Dr. Williams, "if elected president, what items will be on the forefront of your agenda? Jett, your stage, one minute."

Jett stepped away from his podium, to center stage, and responded, "Excellent question, Dr. Williams. And before I respond, let me say thank you for granting us this privilege, and let me thank the audience for attending."

"Sycophant," Will whispered to Adam.

Adam frowned distastefully.

"I have two major items on my agenda," continued Jett. "The first is our entrance standards, or lack thereof."

"He must be referring to Jews and Christians entering Arcadia," whispered Adam.

Will shrugged and whispered back: "Probably, but he will shroud it with charming rhetoric."

"For years, this academy his been considered the most rigorous and prominent secondary school in the nation. Arcadian alumni are overly represented in the most prestigious colleges and universities, and many become CEOs of Fortune 500 companies, or join the ranks of prominent Nobel laureates. They have become political leaders: state governors and U.S. senators. In the last decade, the admissions committee has dramatically expanded the number of accepted applicants. Similarly, in the last ten years, our reputation has lost ground to competing prep schools. As the number of new enrollees has increased, our standards for entrance have declined. It's no surprise that our reputation is suffering. If this pattern continues, Arcadia risks losing its dominance, which directly harms the prospects of Arcadian graduates. If we wish to remain competitive, we must increase our admissions standards. I will work with the admissions committee, redefining our mission and standards so that Arcadian graduates do not suffer." Jett paced across the stage.

"Second," he continued in a strong, eloquent voice, "and likely a direct result of lowering admissions standards, is the ubiquity of academic dishonesty. We are admitting students who do not have the requisite skills to succeed, and naturally, in order to maintain an adequate GPA, they cheat. I recently discovered and exposed a wide network of students gaining illegal access to exams. Some of these students were friends of mine. This presented me with quite the quandary, but I decided that those who would ask me to remain silent were not true friends, and their actions ultimately diminish the prestige of an Arcadian degree. I, therefore, chose to expose the network. Academic dishonesty is still prevalent, so I will use my power to expose these cheaters, and have them expelled from the university. This elected position will require many difficult decisions, and if my recent experiences are telltale, the Arcadian students need someone like me."

Jett smiled, nodded his head, and returned to the podium. The audience clapped with enthusiasm. Adam turned to Will and grimaced. He spoke with revulsion, "I can't believe people are buying this garbage!

"I know!" replied Will, equally disgusted. "His audacity is sickening."

Once the cheering faded, Dr. Williams beckoned to Sahar and spoke, "The floor is yours."

"Thank you, Dr. Williams," spoke Sahar. She approached center stage. "It is true that Arcadia has lost ground to other institutions, but not because of our admission standards. The admission standards have actually increased in the last decade, and our applicant pool grows stronger each year. We are accepting students from all over the country, of different socioeconomic backgrounds, and they have all met higher admissions standards than students from decades past. The reason our reputation has declined is because our dominance has made us myopic. At other institutions, students spend less time in the classroom, and more time gaining real world experience. The rising academies have student-run dining halls, they encourage community outreach and service projects, and require students to complete internships in research and business. Our curriculum has not changed in over ten years. If we are to remain competitive, we must be more adaptive and innovative. We must update our curriculum to reflect new dynamics."

Sahar walked closer to the front of the stage, and continued speaking. "Second, is the lack of enforcement of rules. Officials have turned a blind eye. Students have been assaulted on campus, while others get away with hate crimes and cheating. Our security system is more than adequate enough to detect these transgressions, yet they seem to go unnoticed. As president, I will form an independent task force to investigate claims of assault, cheating, and vandalism, so that transgressors are held accountable. There is no room at Arcadia for people who do not abide by our civil rules." She subtly glanced at Jett. "And there is no reason why justice should go unserved." Sahar returned to her podium, and again, the crowd cheered.

Once they ceased, Dr. Williams spoke. "Folks, please refrain from applause until the end of the debate." Dr. Williams beckoned Jett. "Your rebuttal Mr. Holden."

Jett stepped forward. "Ms. Rosen would like you to believe that retaining our prestige is as simple as putting on make-up in the morning. But truth be told, minor cosmetic adjustments to the curriculum will do little to make our academy more competitive. If we are to be competitive, we need exactly that—competition. This can be achieved through higher entrance standards. I find it dis-heartening that a cognitive enhancement is not a prerequisite for admission, given the rigor required to survive at Arcadia. Perhaps that is why my opponent is opposed to higher entrance standards; because she otherwise would not have been admitted." He smiled as if victorious.

Sahar stood at her podium and immediately responded. "Unlike my opponent, I do not require a cognitive enhancement to achieve high marks. But I will not hold it against him." The audience laughed. Even Dr. Williams struggled to conceal his smile. "I must partially agree with Mr. Holden: our entrance requirements need to be reexamined. I think what Mr. Holden means to say is that if we are to remain competitive, the requirements must be purely meritocratic. In other words, the academy needs to stop favoring children of alumni."

"She's good," whispered Will, in admiration.

"Too good," replied Adam. "That last statement was bold, but I think it worked. She didn't directly slander him, but she turned his comments against him."

"Everyone knows his father is a wealthy alumni. Now he really looks like a hypocrite."

The onslaught continued for another thirty minutes. Every attempt Jett made to smear Sahar was flung back at him. Sahar never took a hardline stance on any issue. She later argued that the debate was not about crafting an eloquent and appealing opinion; opinions can be neither correct nor incorrect. The goal of any debate is to make your opponent appear wrong. If your opponent is wrong, then by default, you win. She did not require aspersions and character attacks to make Jett appear wrong, just a supple tongue capable of twisting his words.

By the next morning, the opinions about the debate were nearly unanimous: Sahar had slaughtered Jett. Two days later when the votes were electronically tallied, Sahar had won by a twenty-point margin.

15

Tuesday, July 5, 2068

Adam returned from physical training, dripping in sweat and flush. He briefly checked his email. One new message from his grandmother read:

Dear Adam,

I hope all is well at Arcadia, and that you occasionally find time to step away from your studies to enjoy yourself. I've enjoyed spending time with Henry. Even though he is not a conversationalist, I still appreciate his company. His learning is progressing at an amazing rate; he is reading graduate level physics textbooks. It's far beyond my skill set. He alternates between studying and programming his robots. He no longer uses robotics kits, but rather builds them from scratch. I wish he could articulate his thought process, but regardless, he seems content.

Have you been paying attention to recent events? The protests in Cammalot have ceased, but nationally, the protests still hold strong. Similarly, the battalions have left Cammalot. I suppose they're moving on to other cities to confiscate firearms and keep the peace.

We miss you, and look forward to your next visit.

Love,

Grandma and Henry.

A thin smile appeared on Adam's face. After the deaths and destruction that plagued his family, positive news about his little brother warmed his heart. The many restless nights spent dreaming of his sister's and parents' deaths, and the chilling apparitions of the people he killed were, for a fleeting moment, trivial. Waking up drenched in sweat and habitually crying himself to sleep were insignificant issues. As long as his brother was safe and happy, he could continue enduring the multitude of challenges thrown at him.

~

Over a month had passed since Adam helped steal the election for Sahar and Will, but Erebus never contacted him. With little direction, he proceeded through his regime of rigorous, but mundane tasks. He sat through another math lecture by Dr. DiPrima. Adam had grown accustomed to DiPrima's drill instructor persona. The eccentric professor spoke as if each lesson was a life or death situation. And at least once per week, DiPrima would end an example by emphatically tapping the chalk against the board, and turning towards the class. Then, with great pride, he would state his mathematically poetic catchphrase (or some variation of it): "That's how you solve that animal!" That was when Adam could drop his pen and nurse his cramped wrist—it never became inured to the rapid note taking required in DiPrima's class. Adam was certain he would develop carpal tunnel by the end of the year.

Dr. Williams's class had also grown stale, not because the topics lacked any flare, but because the topics were predominantly dismal. The conversation always gravitated towards politics and current events: the economy was morose, the job market was anemic, food was in short supply, prices were rising, schools were failing to educate, and income and wealth disparities were a mile wide. Naturally, people turned to the government to solve their problems, but elected officials were more focused on protecting special interests. Of course, this gave Michael Cane an excellent platform to run with. As predicted by Jeff Locke, Cane had announced Jack Holden as his vice presidential candidate. Together, Cane and Holden promised price controls for food, a stimulus package for creating jobs, and cognitive enhancing neural implants for all school-age children. Unless the current president and his party could think of even more outlandish promises, a second term seemed unlikely.

Supper finally disrupted Adam's seemingly mundane activities. Like most other suppers, he sat with Will and Sahar.

"How was the ASB meeting yesterday?" asked Adam. "Did you accomplish anything noteworthy?" Each bimonthly ASB (associated student body) meeting included student officers from every grade level, along with student representatives that voted on issues. Student representatives were elected for each of the four halls. It was intended to simulate congressional meetings.

"The meeting was a waste of time," replied Sahar.

"I agree," said Will. "Fire hall representatives seem to vote against everything unless it directly benefits them, and only them."

"So you're saying it's comparable to congress?" said Adam, somewhat provokingly.

"More or less," bemoaned Sahar. She rolled her eyes.

"Those pinheads in Fire Hall are still upset Jett lost. For years, they've controlled the executive branch of our school," grumbled Will. "Who knows how long they'll continue harboring resentment against us."

A proverbial light bulb flickered in Adam's mind. "I have a thought," he said. Will and Sahar eagerly waited for elaboration. "The school population has swelled in the last few years, but each hall still gets the same number of representatives. Even though Fire Hall supported Jett, there were plenty of people in Fire Hall that voted for you—not a majority, but a nontrivial amount."

"What are you hinting at?" said Will.

"Normally, each hall, as a whole, elects representatives. But what if representatives were elected from each floor?"

"What difference does that make?" said Sahar. "There is still the same number of voters in the hall."

"Recently, I was looking at election data." Adam took a piece of paper and a pen from his backpack and sketched a profile of Fire Hall. "People who voted for Jett resided almost entirely on the top floors. The remaining floors favored you by the slightest majority." He drew labels on the diagram.

Sahar analyzed it for a moment. Will peered over to see the diagram, while Sahar tapped her fingers on the table. Her eyes widened and she then responded, "Which means, if representatives were elected by floor, Fire Hall representatives would go from unanimously supporting Jett, to mostly supporting Will and me."

"Exactly!" said Adam. "We redraw the boundaries to garnish more representatives." Unbeknownst to the three students, Adam was describing a phenomenon that is common practice among politicians at the state, local, and federal levels. A process practiced by all political parties, known as gerrymandering.

Will cleared his throat. "I don't mean to be a Debbie downer," he insisted, "but where will you get the support to redraw boundaries? Wouldn't the representatives need to approve it? And of course, there is the questionable morality of the situation."

"Adam will do it," said Sahar.

Adam arched an eyebrow. "Me? I don't hold an office. How? And why me?"

"Two reasons," Sahar replied. "First, until you infiltrate Erebus, morally questionable is your repertoire. And as president, I can issue an executive order to create and appoint a committee, headed by you, and designated to analyzing demographics. I'll throw in some small print that allows you to redraw the boundary lines. Of course, the representatives still need to approve your appointment, but if I tell them that the study could result in more representatives from their hall, I am sure they will vote yes."

"I'll start redrawing the boundaries tonight," Adam said with great enthusiasm. "When's the next election for representatives?"

"Not until after the trimester ends," replied Sahar.

Hesitantly, Will spoke, "The Sahar from a few months ago would have considered this abhorrent."

"It is abhorrent," said Sahar. "So was stealing the election. But the U.S. presidential election is less than five months away. Like you have said before, we may need to get our hands dirty to stop Holden and Cane."

"I suppose you're right," acknowledged Will.

Will tapped his fingers. An awkward silence passed before Sahar finally spoke. "Adam, I had a revelation yesterday, and I have been meaning to share." Adam fidgeted and sat up straight. "We may need to expedite the infiltration, and I have an idea." Adam and Will stared at Sahar waiting for her to expatiate.

"Let's hear it!" said Will. "The suspense is killing me!"

"We are fairly certain Eric Holden is a member, yes?" Adam and Will both nodded. "And surely, Erebus has to meet occasionally." Adam and Will nodded again. Sahar continued: "Can you track him using SSD footage?"

"We thought of this before," said Will. "He never showed up on SSD footage when he attacked Adam in the bathroom."

"He most likely has a disruptor," stated Adam. "As long as he's using the disruptor, we have no idea where he could be."

"But the disruptor will not be perpetually running," said Sahar. "When, do you suppose, he would likely want to disappear from SSD footage?"

Adam and Will paused, looking at each other. Adam looked back to Sahar. His face lit up and he raised his index finger. After his "ah-hah" moment he proclaimed, "When he's engaged in activities with Erebus!"

Then Will had his "ah-hah" moment. Ebulliently he proclaimed, "I can run the built-in algorithm to search his whereabouts on the SSD footage! I will look at old data and find out when he disappears. Once we know when the meetings are, you can follow him. I can have the information by Friday!"

"Why didn't we think of this earlier?" said Adam.

"Is that rhetorical?" Will asked with a hint of sarcasm. "Or do you really want an answer?" Before Adam could entertain Will's query, Will continued, "I suppose it's because we're not as smart as we thought we were."

"Speak for yourself," said Sahar.

Sardonically, Will said, "Oh please!" Sahar glared at Will. "I was trying to be modest, but we all know I'm the brains of this operation."

"In what bizarre reality are you the brains of the operation?" Sahar mockingly replied. "The one with leprechauns and unicorns?"

Will took a deep breath and calmly stated, "I'll give you credit: you're the smartest girl I know."

"And what's that supposed to mean?"

With a subtle and pompous laugh Will continued, "Well, it's common knowledge that boys are smarter than girls." Adam looked at Sahar, who was glaring at Will. "I mean, we're all familiar with the rhyme: 'Boys go to college to get more knowledge, girls go to Jupiter to get more stupider.'"

Sahar crossed her arms and responded, "How many babbling buffoons does it take to compile a sentence rife with grammatical errors and logical inconsistencies? Apparently, just one."

"I think it's about time for me to leave." Adam stood and nodded his head at Will, then Sahar.

Will extended his arm to halt Adam from leaving. "Wait," he said, "you can't go until you settle the debate. Which one of us do you think is smarter: me, or Sahar?"

"What debate? Everyone knows Sahar is smarter than us."

"Adam!"

Sahar smiled and victoriously proclaimed, "Hah!"

"She's not smarter," countered Will, "she just works harder!"

"Because she's smarter," remarked Adam. "People who choose not to work hard are dumb. If they were smart, they would realize that working hard leads to success."

"Speaking of working hard," said Sahar, "I have homework to complete."

"Likewise," said Adam.

Will crossed his arms and rolled his eyes. "I suppose we will have to settle this another time."

With that said, the students departed to their quarters and attacked their assignments. Similar to the other banalities of life, it was never-ending. By Friday evening, just as Will promised, he had analyzed SSD footage. Eric Holden disappeared from the footage the second Friday of every month at 9:00 p.m. The next meeting would be held in nine days.

16

Friday, July 11, 2068

At nine fifteen p.m., Adam cautiously followed Eric Holden. It had been several months since he crossed Eric in the restroom. Holden approached the main entrance to Fire Hall and reached into his pocket, producing a small piece of plastic. It looked identical to the electronic key Adam used to obtain entrance to his own hall. Eric swiped the key in front of the keypad and flung the door open. The door slowly swung back. Adam jogged to the door, barely catching it before it latched. He continued following Holden up to the sixth floor and down the hall. In the distance he could see Holden pause before entering a dorm room. Adam ducked into the bathroom and waited patiently in a bathroom stall. According to Will, Eric Holden habitually entered his dorm between 9:15 p.m. and 9:30 p.m. He would then walk into the bathroom across the hall before disappearing from SSD footage for several hours. It happened the second Friday of each month. Holden was precisely on schedule.

Nine forty. The bathroom door swung open. From under the stall, Adam could see the same colored sneakers Eric Holden wore a few minutes ago. A minute later, an older boy, presumably Eric Holden, turned on the faucet. Shortly thereafter, the sound of water ceased and the door swung open. Adam counted to ten, and then followed.

Several thoughts flowed through Adam's mind. *What if I'm caught? What will they do?* He inhaled deeply, attempting to calm himself. He peaked his head outside of the stall and could see Holden walking away. It was ten minutes past curfew, and everyone had vacated the halls and retired to their rooms. Once Holden was out of sight, Adam trotted down the hall. He carefully opened the metal door to the stairs, and closed it even more carefully, ensuring it would not make a sound. A few flights down he could see the top of Holden's head, covered by a hooded sweatshirt. Adam treaded lightly down the stairwell, hugging the wall to stay concealed. A clunky sound echoed through the empty stairwell as Eric pushed the large door's crash bar. Adam hurriedly descended the stairs and exited through the same door.

Adam looked left and right. Holden was rounding the corner of the building. Once Holden was out of sight, Adam jogged in an attempt to narrow the gap between them. He rounded the same corner. A momentous force struck his gut, causing him to bend over and cough. Staring at the ground, he saw the same gray sneakers from the bathroom stall. He shifted his eyes upwards and saw Holden's face. Two other boys occupied his peripheral view. Holden socked the left side of Adam's face. The pain was sharp, but not the worst he had ever felt. It was, however, enough to disrupt Adam's train of thought. Holden and one of the other boys grasped Adam's arms, while the third boy stuck tape across Adam's mouth. Adam squirmed and struggled futilely. The third boy pulled a black cloth bag, about half the size of a pillowcase, from his pocket, and then placed it over Adam's head. Adam's heart pounded. As if the ambush did not cause enough angst, losing his vision made matters worse. The bag obstructed his access to fresh air, causing his breaths to grow heavier. The boys forced his hands behind his back. He heard a ripping sound before a tight adhesive material locked his hands in place. Holden and the two cronies used the same roll of tape to bind Adam's feet then tilted him horizontal and carried him away.

Several minutes later, after being carried across unknown terrain, through doors, and down stairs, Adam was forcibly placed in a hard wooden chair. He felt a hand rip the hood away, unveiling his face while simultaneously plucking some hairs from his scalp. Adam squinted and blinked several times in an attempt to focus his eyes. Several people wearing denim and hooded sweatshirts surrounded Adam, though hoods concealed their faces. Eric Holden and his two cronies were the only ones with visible faces. Holden leaned towards Adam and delicately pinched the tape covering Adam's mouth, then harshly and quickly ripped it away.

Holden stepped back. "Why were you following me?" he commanded with a stentorian tone.

"Following you? Don't flatter yourself."

Holden scoffed, and then backhanded Adam's face. "I'll ask you again you trivial little fly. Why were you following me?"

"Just doing what flies do: following the stench."

Eric Holden raised his hand again to backhand Adam a second time, but a hooded figure stepped forward and commanded, "Stop."

Holden lowered his hand, glowered towards Adam, and stepped back.

"We have been keeping tabs on you, Mr. Carter," spoke the hooded figure.

Adam instantly recognized the voice. "Professor Williams?" he questioned.

The hooded figure removed his hood revealing a face that matched the voice. Professor Williams. "Mr. Carter," spoke the professor, "no doubt your mind is rife with questions. And as much as you may desire answers, you are not yet privy to the information." Adam stared blankly at the professor, waiting for elaboration. "I will tell you all that you need to know." The professor paced, just like he did during class. "You have stumbled upon one of history's greatest organizations. We call our organization *Erebus*, after one of the primordial Greek deities. Each year, we select a handful of students from the academy to join our ranks. I say we, but ultimately, the decision is mine. This year was an especially difficult year. I winnowed the pool down to ten candidates, but received permission from the board to induct only two first-year students. Needless to say, you were on the short list. Thus far, have I made myself clear?"

Adam nodded and replied, "Yes, sir."

The professor continued, "I must say, your ambition is impressive, and I am tempted to offer you an invitation." Adam's eyes grew wide. "If you accept, we will tell you more. However, before you may become a full-fledged member, you must pass a trial."

"What does the trial consist of?" asked Adam.

"I cannot tell you," said the professor. "It will not be easy. Many have tried and failed. The consequences for failing are considerable, but the rewards are infinite. If you choose to decline our offer, you will be given a light dose of a drug that will place you in a deep slumber and cause you to forget the last several hours. You will awaken tomorrow morning with no memory of tonight's events."

"Am I privy to any additional information before making a decision?"

"No," replied the professor. "You have thirty seconds to make a decision based solely on the information I provided."

Adam's heart raced. These people were responsible for killing Hannah and Sahar's father, and God knows who else. But what did Dr. Williams mean by "the consequences for failing are considerable?" And what would the trial entail? Was it worth the risk? What would happen if he failed? Then he recalled his prior meeting with Jeff Locke, when Locke told him he could save lives and uphold the freedom of millions. *If I stop now*, he thought, *Hannah died for nothing. My mother and father died for nothing. Michael Cane and Jack Holden assume the presidency and usurp the freedom of millions of Americans. What difference does it make if I die fighting, if the alternative is not worth living?*

He looked into the eyes of the professor and solemnly stated, "I accept your invitation."

"Good," said Dr. Williams. The professor stepped behind Adam and peeled away the tape that was restraining his hands. One of the hooded members drew a knife and cut the tape binding Adam's legs. Adam stood and stretched. He wiggled his fingers and nursed his wrists.

The professor continued: "Your test will come soon, but first, there is much for you to see. We leave immediately for Chicago."

"Should I pack a bag?" asked Adam.

The professor shook his head. "We have not sufficient time. A driverless TTR is waiting for us."

"TTR?" questioned Adam.

"Twin-engined tilt rotor. It's a dual-purpose aircraft: helicopter and airplane. It is a neat device. You will enjoy the ride." The professor stepped towards a door that appeared to lead out of the small dark room. He turned back towards Adam and said, "Follow me."

Adam followed the professor out of the room.

After he left, one of the hooded figures spoke to the others, "Why is Williams so confident in this kid?"

Another responded, "I wish I knew. Thus far, Williams has delivered only the highest quality recruits. However, I must express certain qualms about this new recruit. How will he react if he discovers why his sister died? He's a smart kid."

"He is a bright student, but we covered our tracks well."

"You don't think he will connect the dots?"

A third hooded figure responded: "I can see no reason why he would make that discovery. I have to agree: our trail is concealed. As far as anyone is concerned, Hannah Carter was in the wrong place at the wrong time. End of story."

"Do you think he will accept that story?"

"If he asks too many questions..." The figure looked at Eric Holden. "Mr. Holden will find a solution."

Eric nodded, and then cracked his knuckles. He smiled grimly and said, "With pleasure."

~

Late that night, perhaps even early the next morning, Adam and Professor Williams had arrived in Chicago. They departed the twin-engined tilt rotor, and boarded an autonomous luxury sedan.

"I've never been in a self-driving car," said Adam.

"Do not worry," said the professor. He smiled. "They are safer than human operated vehicles."

They rode from the downtrodden airport through similarly blighted suburban neighborhoods. An array of dark clouds prevented the moonlight from shining. Sparse streetlights cast scant amounts of light on the sidewalks. Shady characters lurked in the shadows. Many of the lights flickered on and off. The buildings, sidewalks, and streets had withered and rotted from years of neglected maintenance.

"Would you believe that this city used to be one of the greatest cities in the country?" asked the professor.

Adam looked at the professor in consternation.

"Chicago has been declining for ninety years," said Professor Williams.

"What happened?"

"Many things happened. The economy evolved, but Chicago did not. Jobs disappeared. The city attempted to fill the void. Unions grew too powerful and demanded lavish, unsustainable benefits. Politicians protected their own skin and created sinecures for their pals. This city is the epicenter of corruption and despair. In the last century, three of every four mayors have been indicted. Four of every five state governors see a similar fate. Tax revenue has seemingly vanished. Eventually, the system collapsed on itself, and Chicago became the largest municipality in the country to declare bankruptcy. Detroit saw the same fate."

"It's interesting, and sad," commented Adam, "but why are you showing me this?"

"Just wait," replied Dr. Williams.

The car drove past buildings covered in graffiti so dense that the original color of the bricks was no longer visible. The car stopped at an intersection. Adam gazed out the window. Old vehicles missing their wheels rested on cinder blocks. Shattered glass and fast food wrappers littered the streets and sidewalks.

"Look over there," said the professor, pointing at a group of boys. Adam saw a group of three boys dressed in baggy clothes. "Adam, do you know what time it is?"

Adam shrugged. "Two?"

"Almost three." The professor lowered his watch. "Would your parents have let you roam this time of night?" Adam shook his head. The car continued driving. "It makes one wonder, where are the parents?" The professor paused for several seconds to allow Adam time to ponder the question. "Can you see the fundamental problem? If left to their own devices, people make bad choices. The people least able to care for themselves propagate. In turn, they raise children that are even more unfit." Adam looked down. "Let me ask you this, Adam: suppose you are a parent working a low-wage job and living paycheck to paycheck. You barely have enough money to feed your children, but one day, you are gifted one hundred dollars. What would you do with the money?"

Adam scratched his chin, then answered: "It depends. I would want to make sure our basic needs like food and shelter were met. If so, I would probably save it for a rainy day."

"Wise choice," replied Professor Williams. "Do you know what these people do with the money?"

Adam shook his head.

"They squander it. They will throw a party and buy beer and cigarettes. Sometimes they purchase frivolous gadgets or expensive clothes. Rarely do they consider spending it on basic needs, and it is even more rare that they would save it for a rainy day. Trivial items are almost always bought before food. Even if they did spend the money on food, they refuse to buy nutritious staples such as beans, rice, and canned vegetables. God forbid they cook their own meals. No, they spend the money on processed junk."

"I don't understand the logic..."

"Precisely because there is no logic to those decisions. They are, by definition, bad decisions. And poor decisions constitute the majority of the choices these people make. Taxpayers provide them with free education, free postsecondary education, free food, free healthcare, subsidized childcare, subsidized wages, and despite all of this, they rarely ascend to the next income bracket. Despite the myriad of opportunities we synthesize for them, they continue to make poor decisions. Then, they raise their children to be even worse." Adam looked at the professor and noticed his neck veins pulsating. His cheeks and forehead reddened. Never had Adam seen the professor deliver such a passionate tirade.

"The middle class and upper-middle classes are only marginally better," continued the professor. "Most of them were raised in middle class families, and never had to face true adversity. But if they did, the result would not be significantly different than what you see here. A little money can hide many problems."

Adam considered asking a question, but was afraid of further riling the professor.

"About sixty years ago, a survey asked, 'if given two weeks, could you come up with $1000?' They could use savings, credit cards, family members, and friends. Now keep in mind, at the time, median household income was about $50,000 per year, and the survey included people who made hundreds of thousands per year."

"What percent couldn't come up with $1000?"

"Nearly two-thirds," replied the professor. "A similar survey was given a couple years ago, and the proportion had grown to over eighty percent."

"So most people are living paycheck to paycheck? Why is it that hard to save a little money each month?"

"Some would argue that our economic system does not provide ample opportunity for everyone."

Adam nodded.

"There is truth to that statement, but high-income earners also live paycheck to paycheck. Politicians will not mention this, but the real reason is because people are reckless and impulsive. Rather than save money to repair a vehicle that allows them to get to work, they buy a bigger house. Even more disheartening is the fact that these people vote. And who do you suppose they vote for?"

Adam's eyes shifted upwards. He pondered for a moment before replying, "They vote for the people who make the most ridiculous promises."

"Precisely," stated Dr. Williams. "Their dimwitted decisions can affect the entire country."

The car continued touring Chicago; each neighborhood was as dismal as the last. Occasionally, Professor Williams would point at a couple thugs dealing contraband, or opine about the incompetent masses. Before long, the car arrived at the airport, and the sun had started to rise over the silhouetted skyscrapers. Adam and Professor Williams stepped out of the autonomous vehicle and walked towards the airplane.

Before boarding the airplane, Adam turned to the professor and queried, "Dr. Williams, surely there are more efficient ways to make your point. Was it really necessary for us to fly to Chicago so you could show me that people are stupid?"

"Chicago's woes are emblematic of the country's woes."

"But surely you could have shown me a video or pictures of Chicago's despondency."

"Adam, it is important to observe the situation firsthand. You are missing the larger message."

"Then what is the larger message?"

Adam and the professor boarded the airplane. They sat and buckled their seatbelts. The professor continued: "Once upon a time, our economy relied on these people. They were smart enough to complete their jobs, but dumb enough to not realize they were being taken advantage of. They were granted the illusion of freedom, but in reality, they were fettered by their own impulses and economic circumstances. As technology progresses, these people become increasingly obsolete. For too long, these troglodytes have been allowed to make their own decisions, within the confines of their environment. Their poor decision making skills have nearly driven our country to the ground many times over. Erebus has been recruiting the best and brightest for decades, and soon, our time will come. No more will we be stuck cleaning up the messes of those who refuse to cleanup after themselves. They need people like us to make decisions on their behalf. We will take care of them and we will not let them breed incompetence. The message, Mr. Carter, is that the environment is ripe for change. Erebus will make the world a better place."

The professor's audacity could not be understated. Adam found himself agreeing with the premise, but not the conclusion. Who would not wish to make the world a better place? But a few words lingered in the back of Adam's mind: *a better place for whom?*

17

Friday, August 10, 2068

Even though Adam promised to remain discreet about any Erebus activity, he felt obligated to divulge every detail to Will and Sahar. He also felt safer knowing that Will and Sahar had full disclosure. Like Adam, they wondered what test he would face.

It was a busy week for Adam. Two weeks earlier, the ASB approved his appointment to study boundaries, and earlier that week, he unilaterally redrew the borders in an attempt to garnish more representatives that sided with Will and Sahar. This, on top of the so-called 'dead-week,' when professors seemed to assign the most time consuming projects. The week culminated with the monthly Erebus meeting. Every month the location of the meeting changed. It was a tactic meant to avoid suspicion. The day of the meeting, the location would be passed personally between members. Since Adam had not yet learned the identity of many members, after social studies, Professor Williams personally delivered the message to Adam. "Top floor of the library," the professor furtively said. He handed Adam a small black box. "Turn this on before you leave your dorm. And do not get caught with it."

Adam arrived at the library at 9:50 p.m. Several people were already present, though this time most of their hoods were lowered. Adam recognized some of the faces as students he had seen on campus, but he knew few of them by name. There were several adults, including Dr. DiPrima, Dr. Rush, and even Dr. Tait. A large display powered on, and several more faces appeared on the screen.

The only digital faces Adam recognized belonged to Michael Cane and Jack Holden, though other visages looked familiar. One of the nearby members muttered, "Test, test…" He turned and extended his thumb. "Okay, our connection is secure."

Professor Williams called the meeting to order. "Let us begin by introducing the two newest members to Erebus." The professor turned towards Adam and gestured at him. "Adam Carter." Then the professor turned the opposite direction and gestured towards a hooded student. The student removed his hood. "And Jett Holden."

Adam clenched his fists. He wished he could be surprised by the organization's choice candidate, but it was obvious why Jett had been chosen. He was precisely the shady type Erebus habitually recruited: one willing to set his own morals aside to achieve ostensibly greater outcomes.

Jett looked at Adam and subtly chuckled. "I knew you'd come around," he said.

"Please," spoke Dr. Williams. "Be seated." Everyone took a seat around the large oval table. Dr. Williams continued, "Our first order of business is the initiation test for our two new recruits. The location has been established, and the test will commence the Sunday following finals week. Adam Carter and Jett Holden are to report to Arcadia gardens at 7:00 p.m., Saturday, August 16. From there, they will be given further instructions." Adam and Jett nodded in affirmation. "Mr. Carter, and Mr. Holden: wear plain clothes to your initiation. Bring no personal belongings. You are dismissed."

Adam exited the library and crept through the silent halls, back to his room. To his surprise, the desk lamp shined brightly, but Will was absent. A handwritten note lay on the desk. It read:

> I am 'studying' at the library. I hope to come back filled with knowledge.
> -Will

Adam rummaged through his desk and dresser drawers, only to find no trace of the original disruptor. *Will must have taken it*, he thought. Given the situation, going back to find Will could only cause more trouble. The best option, he thought, was to wait for Will's return, and hope that that Will would practice prudence.

Meanwhile, at the meeting, Will had concealed himself in a crevice between two bookshelves. Given that all the material was digital and most of the books were in desuetude, it was a mystery why the library retained so many antiquated artifacts. The vast volumes contained within the library walls, once emblematic of the academy's prestige, had become no more than expensive, outdated, dusty decor. And perhaps it was their lackluster qualities that allowed Will to hide so seamlessly among them, without so much as earning a second glance from any of the Erebus attendees.

Will's crouched position prevented him from discerning any faces, so he closed his eyes and listened carefully to the voices of self-absorbed men hash out their maniacal plans.

"What's the status of the vaccines?" said an aged voice.

"Still waiting to deploy," replied another man.

A third adult chimed in with great concern: "The virus has spread much faster than anticipated, and is affecting far more livestock than we predicted. It was initially designed to harm cattle, but has since evolved to infect pigs. There are reports in Iowa of chickens facing nearly identical symptoms. If—"

"So it's more effective than we thought. Is this a problem?"

"If the virus continues to mutate, our vaccine may be rendered useless. We must deploy the vaccine to halt the spread."

"Stop the virus before the election? If our candidate is going to win this election, he needs a public crisis."

"But sir—"

"Have you forgotten how fickle and ignorant the average voter is? If the virus is exterminated while the current president is in office, all credit will be ascribed to him. If he receives credit, he will not be voted out of office."

"But there are other crises that present excellent platforms—"

"Yes, for the state senators and representatives."

"With all do respect, I don't think you understand the gravity of the situation."

"No, good sir, it is your feeble mind that fails to comprehend the gravity of the situation. Every proverbial planet is nearing perfect alignment. Never have we had so many crises at once. If all goes according to plan, our people will hold majorities in the House and Senate. We control four of the nine Supreme Court justices, and soon we will control the executive office. Our companies have man-ufactured updatable neural implants sufficient for nearly eighty percent of the population. All is well."

"I thought we were only offering neural implants to school-aged children?"

"And once parents see how well their children perform in school, they will want one for themselves. Imagine, capitalizing on someone's desire to obtain new job training via a simple download. Once an ample number of citizens obtain the new neural implants, we can supplant their voting preferences, or any other preferences, for that matter. In other words, if we can take this election, we will never have to worry about winning another election. We can make people act decent and civil. The world will be molded into our vision of a better place."

"How many people must starve for us to achieve this vision?"

"We all knew there would be costs. But imagine how many lives we will save when the propensity for violence is displaced by an inclination for civic duty. All of this is possible with the new neural implant technology."

"And if this virus mutates and begins infecting humans?"

"Then they will be sacrificed for a noble cause. Don't tell me you're growing squeamish."

"No. Not at all. I only want to be thorough; to make sure we have carefully considered every option at our disposal."

"We have, and we determined this is the best outcome with the minimal collateral damage."

Will's muscles ached from sitting in such a cramped fashion. His legs trembled. The conversation had distracted him from the pain, but the momentary silence removed that distraction. He lifted his left leg to attempt to turn himself around, but he clumsily banged his knee against a bookshelf.

"Did you hear that?" sounded a voice. Will muttered a curse word under his breath. "It came from the bookshelves over there." Will's heart raced. His position obstructed his view of the meeting. He turned in an attempt find a better view, but inadvertently knocked a book from the shelf. Time seemed to slow. The book fell towards the floor. With one hand, Will grabbed a bookshelf for balance while he extended his other arm to catch the falling book. He swept the book from the air, thus avoiding any unwarranted noises.

"Must be my imagination," said the same voice. Will closed his eyes and sighed in relief. He relaxed his muscles. He was unsure of what happened next, but the consequences soon became apparent: at least one or two-dozen books tumbled from the shelf to the floor. Before Will could comprehend and react to the situation, several adults surrounded him.

"What do we have here?" one of the adults asked rhetorically.

Eric Holden stepped in and spoke, "I know this little twerp. He's one of Carter's playmates. The name's Will."

"What should we do with him?" asked another adult.

"I can take care of him!" said Eric Holden. He grinned and cracked his knuckles. "And I'll make sure no one finds him!"

Will remained silent. His eyes furtively searched for an escape. Then Dr. Williams stepped in and spoke, "Gentlemen, surely we are more civilized than that. We must not arouse suspicion."

"You have a better idea, Professor?" spoke one of the adults.

"As a matter of fact, I do." The professor reached into his pocket and produced a small bottle of pills. He looked at Eric Holden and said, "Fetch me some water."

Holden left the book crevice and returned a moment later with a water bottle.

"Good," said the professor. "Now hold him steady." The adults seized Will by the arms and legs, making his attempts to wriggle away futile. One adult gripped his chin, while another forced the pill into Will's mouth. The same adult held his mouth open while the other poured a small amount of water down Will's throat. Water spilled over his face and shirt. Finally, the adults held his mouth shut and plugged his nose until he swallowed the pill. After he swallowed the pill, the adults released him. Will coughed and fell to his knees.

"You will fall asleep soon," said the professor. "And when you awake, you will not remember anything that happened over the last few hours."

Will attempted to stick his finger into the back of his throat to trigger the gag reflex, but the adults thwarted him.

The professor kneeled to Will's level. "Listen young Will: I do like you as a student. Consider this treatment a symbol of my appreciation; you are still alive. I also enjoy your friend, Adam as a student." The professor stood again. "Though some wonder if he can be trusted. No matter: if he fails his test he will meet the same fate as the boys who made an attempt at his sister: his existence will be erased."

Will wiped the water from his mouth. "What do you mean?"

"If you look at our nation's most prominent leaders, there is nothing they would not do for their country. Similarly, our best CEOs will sacrifice everything for their company. Unfortunately, this trait is difficult to observe. Like any problem, we developed a solution: several decades ago, we devised a test. Well, in truth, we borrowed it from the ancient Greeks. Every inductee to Erebus must pass a blood test: kill a random citizen without getting caught. However, unlike the Greeks, we do not have helots in the strictest sense of the word, though the general public seems to occupy a status somewhere between free men and slaves. We cannot have any evidence linking our organization to the murders. Those who fail are never seen or heard from again. All records of their existence are expunged."

"So you're building a network of elite, maniacal extremists?" Will spit in disgust. "For what purpose?"

"Do not be foolish. Our network is already built. Now, we simply maintain it and wait to press play. Our purpose is to create the most effective governing force in the history of mankind."

Will scoffed at the professor. "And what makes you think you're fit to rule three hundred fifty million people?"

"You must understand: every society needs people to rule, and people to obey. Arcadia finds the smartest people in the country, and Erebus winnows that pool even further. We have the best of the best. Tell me Will, would not you wish the people running your country to be smarter than you?"

"Not if they're zealots like you! You're missing one of the most important traits of intelligent people." Will slowly blinked. His head wavered. A sudden drowsiness plagued his consciousness. He blinked and jerked his head.

"And what measure would that be?"

"The ability to recognize faults in your own logic. To accept that humans are prone to errors and subject to limitations!"

"Every decision we make is calculated. Unlike the general public, we refine our cognitive processes before we miscalculate. Our logic is sound."

Will swayed left and right. Balancing was becoming exponentially more difficult. "You overestimate your ability to predict outcomes. Mark my words: your arrogance will undermine you!" Will swayed and struggled to sit up straight.

"You must understand: we are not as bad as you believe." The professor paced in the narrow crevice while speaking. "We are building a better society. We can eliminate crime, poverty, obesity, drug addiction, the boom and bust business cycles, you name it. We will maximize the welfare of the entire country."

"And what about freedom? The freedom to pursue our own interests?"

"Freedom? And which freedoms are you referring to? The freedom to kill each other? The freedom to breed troglodytic children? The freedom to pay oneself five hundred times what the average worker makes? The freedom to pay for illicit drugs before paying to feed one's own children? The freedom to exploit workers and the environment? Tell me how this 'free' society is better?" Before Will could answer, the professor continued his polemic. "The people will still believe they are free. Every decision they make will feel like it is their own. With neural implants, we can alter preferences. There will not be high-school dropouts. Advertising will become useless. No more will young girls watch MTV only to be indoctrinated into believing that their bodies are their greatest assets. We can preprogram them to watch something more intellectually engaging—or for that matter, to read a book! No more will blue-collar workers prefer to eat greasy fast food for lunch each day. Imagine the money saved from a healthier population. People will desire exercise. People will not litter. Manhattan can be the cleanest city in the world. Do you understand how much greater our country will be? Imagine an entire population making good decisions on their own accord, considerate of how their actions affect fellow citizens."

"And I suppose, when a man becomes too old, you can program him to take his own life."

"When a man passes his prime, he will gladly take his life for this country. He will no longer consume public resources, burdening future generations. But more, he will be exalted for his sacrifice."

"Who will work the dirty jobs? Surely a country of snobs will be too proud to clean toilets." Will's vision blurred.

"In a few more years those dirty jobs will all be automated. But even if that were not the case, not everyone is created equal. A neural implant cannot cure stupidity. Our fools and half-wits can clean toilets. But the new neural implants will make them *want* to clean toilets. And they will believe they are acting on their own accord."

Will swayed and spoke with a slight slur. "But how many people must die for your great society? How many have starved to death because of your artificial food shortages?"

"All great societies are born from the blood of patriots. Those who perish do so for the greater good."

"But—"

"Speak no more. You will soon lose consciousness, and when you awaken, you will remember nothing." Dr. Williams pointed at the adults, then at Will. Two adults lifted Will and sat him at an empty table. They opened a book and placed it next to Will. Will gave every effort to keep his eyes open, but his eyelids grew heavier by the second. "Ironic, is it not? You are the only person outside of Erebus to hear of our plans, but tomorrow morning, you will have no recollection of it. Perhaps, with due time, you will come to agree with us. Erebus could use someone like you, but you are not yet ready."

With that final statement, Will drifted into unconsciousness.

~

The next morning, Adam awoke to find a nearly empty room; Will had not returned. Concerned over Will's absence, Adam journeyed to the library. Once there, he walked to the top floor where the Erebus meeting was held. He peered around the corners but found no trace of Will. Adam continued searching the library for several minutes before venturing to a lower floor. Two floors down, seated in a chair with his face buried in an open book, sat Will. Adam approached Will and lightly shook his shoulder. Will did not react.

"Will!" whispered Adam. He shook Will harder. Adam continued his attempts to wake Will, but to no avail. After several tries, he propped Will upright and lightly tapped his face. "C'mon Will, wake up." Again, the efforts were futile. Adam "Sorry Will," he said, expressing discontent with a hint of guilt when. Holding Will upright with one arm, Adam cocked his other arm back and forcefully slapped Will across the face. Will awoke in a panic and fell out of his chair. He scrambled on the floor, then blinked his eyes a few times and felt his face.

"Where..."

"You're in the library, Will."

"What am I doing in the library?"

"I was hoping you could tell me. It's Saturday morning. You didn't come back to the dorm last night."

Will stood and looked at the table. An open book and a few closed books sat on the tabletop. "Was I?" Will blinked. "Was I studying all night?" he asked.

"I assumed you were trying to spy on the Erebus meeting last night," replied Adam. "You left our room after curfew, you took the disruptor, and you left a note."

"I don't remember any of that," said Will, scratching his head. "What did the note say?"

"It read, 'I am 'studying' at the library. I hope to come back filled with knowledge.'"

"It sounds like I was studying."

"Then why did you write 'studying' in quotation marks?"

Will shrugged his shoulders. "Maybe because I didn't expect to get much done? I don't know."

"You must remember something from last night?" Adam said, growing slightly agitated.

Will shook his head. "I just feel tired. I think I'll grab some breakfast, then go back to bed."

"Doesn't this situation seem strange to you? Erebus also met in the library last night."

Will shrugged his shoulders again. "It's not the first time I fell asleep in the library. During the first midterm week I fell asleep while studying. I awoke in the middle of the night, but was afraid I might trigger an alarm if I attempted to leave the library. So I just slept under the table. It wasn't the most comfortable place to sleep, but it sufficed."

"And you don't think it's strange that you can't remember anything?"

"I'm naturally forgetful," replied Will. He stretched his arms. "Can we get breakfast?"

Adam rolled his eyes. He realized that the puzzle pieces did not fit, but acknowledged that no more progress could be made by interrogating his forgetful friend. "I suppose we should," he replied.

18

Friday, August 17, 2068

"That's game!" said Jett, triumphantly raising his hands into the air. He turned away from the green wooden table. The boy on the opposite side of the table slammed his paddle against the table and swore. Jett circled the table and approached the boy, then said, "You owe me twenty dollars." Jett extended his hand waiting for the boy to pay.

The boy gave a blank expression, then demanded, "Double or nothing."

Jett considered the proposition, and then replied, "You're on!"

They took their positions and volleyed the Ping-Pong ball back and forth across the table. Several minutes and several points later, a series of low thuds echoed from the stairway. The footsteps ceased and Eric Holden entered the dimly lit basement. He surveyed the room. Several boys sat on a couch playing video games. Other students slouched along the sofas.

"Everyone out," he commanded, pointing to the door. "I need to speak to my brother."

"You serious?" one of the gamers derisively asked.

Eric approached the boy and stood directly in front of him, blocking the gamer's view of the television. "Don't make me tell you twice."

The gamers looked at each other, and then back at the domineering figure standing in front of them. Then one of them spoke, with a slight quiver, "Only ten minutes until curfew."

"Right," said the other gamer. "We should get back to the suite."

The room cleared, leaving Jett and Eric alone.

"What gives?" said Jett, tossing his arms up. "I was about to win forty dollars off that kid!"

Eric stepped closer. "Williams has too much faith in Adam Carter. I don't trust him, and I'm not the only one."

"He's a loser, so what?" replied Jett.

Eric's eyes grew concerned. "You don't know what the test entails, do you?"

Jett shook his head.

"You're going to find some poor sod and put him out of his misery; for his own good, and for the rest of society."

Jett's eyes widened. "You mean I have to..." Jett drew his finger across his throat. Eric nodded. "Jesus Christ!" said Jett. "Nobody told me this!"

"And when you find out, you're going to act surprised. I'm not supposed to be telling you this."

"Then why are you telling me?" asked Jett.

"You hear how Carter's sister died?"

Jett shook his head.

"She was someone else's test," said Eric. "Williams is confident that Adam will never put the pieces together, but there's a small cabal of people within Erebus that disagree. We think it's too risky letting Adam into Erebus." Jett said nothing. After a few seconds of silence, Eric continued speaking. "I've been told to tell you to neutralize Mr. Carter."

Jett's heart raced. "Why me? How am I supposed to do that?"

Eric scoffed. "His death needs to be subtle. You're smart, you can figure it out." Eric turned and marched toward the basement.

"Wait," said Jett. Eric paused and turned towards his brother. "Everyone in Erebus has to do this?"

Eric nodded.

"Who was your target?"

"He was a nobody. Some provincial, sleazy, Jew." Eric took a deep breath. "Is that all?"

Jett hesitated, and then asked, "What was is like? You know, killing someone."

Eric laughed. "Don't worry about it."

~

Saturday, August 18, 2068

It was the day after finals week ended. The second semester was not nearly as bad as the first. Once the proper habits were established it became another rote sequence. The material had become more demanding, but most students, including Adam, were inured to the grueling workload.

Adam arrived at Arcadia gardens at precisely 6:55 p.m.—five minutes early. A minute later, Jett arrived.

"I suppose we're paired again," Jett mocked.

"Always a pleasure," replied Adam with a cheeky grin.

A few minutes later, a bald man wearing a black suit, black tie, and sunglasses entered the garden. He stopped in his tracks, robotically turned to Jett and Adam, and monotonously commanded, "Follow me." Jett and Adam trailed the bald man.

"Where are we going?" asked Jett with a hint of enthusiasm. The bald man did not reply.

Jett and Adam followed him off campus. They stopped along the sidewalk. The bald man looked left, right, and across the street. He then peered at his watch, but otherwise stood motionless. A moment later a black sedan with tinted windows stopped in front of the party. The bald man stepped forward and opened the door. He held it open for Jett and Adam and said, "Get in." Adam entered the vehicle and noticed a pistol holstered in the bald man's belt. Once Jett and Adam were in the car, the bald man boarded the front passenger seat. Another man wearing a black suit and sunglasses drove the vehicle.

"So, where are we going?" Jett asked, less enthusiastically than before. The men in suits ignored the query. Jett shrugged his shoulders. "Wake me when we get there." Jett adjusted his position, then tilted his head back and rested his eyes.

Adam stayed alert. For thirty minutes he watched. The surrounding area became less populated and urban. The new landscape contained fewer cars and buildings and more trees and rolling green fields. The sedan slowed and took a right turn. A few minutes later, it stopped in a parking lot surrounded by tall, wide trees. Pine needles covered the dirt and sidewalk. A light breeze blew, causing some tree branches to dance. In front of the car stood a small stone facility with a door on each side. A few crows perched atop the building.

Jett opened his eyes and stretched his arms. He yawned and asked, "We there already?

The bald man turned to Adam and Jett. "Follow me." He exited the vehicle and walked to the trunk of the car. Jett and Adam followed. From the trunk, the bald man took two small cloth bags. "Take these." He handed a bag to Adam and another to Jett. "Put these on and place your old clothes in the bag." He then pointed towards the facility.

Jett and Adam entered the facility and went into separate stalls. From the other stall, Adam could hear Jett quietly ask, "Can I be frank?"

Adam candidly responded, "Based on prior experience, I would say not likely."

"What I mean to ask, is can I make an honest statement without eliciting judgment?"

"You can try."

Jett took a deep breath. "I have a bad feeling about this. I asked my brother about the test, but even he wouldn't share anything."

"I know what you mean. Something isn't right."

A moment of silence passed while Jett and Adam changed. In a shaky voice, Jett said, "If something comes up, I mean... umm... we might have to... you know... put our differences aside... and... uh... work together. I mean, if worse comes to worse. We can go back to hating each other later."

"If we have to," muttered Adam.

Adam finished changing into the new clothes: an off-white shirt, a plain pair of tennis shoes, and denim jeans. He left the facility and waited by the sedan for Jett.

Jett came out of the facility expressing disgust and staring at his new attire. "I like my old clothes better," he stated.

"They probably cost five times as much," replied Adam.

Jett smirked. He held his arms out and looked at himself. "Look at me! I look like I'm part of the Wal-Mart crowd!"

The bald man took the bags of clothes and locked them in the trunk of the car. Again, he opened the passenger door, looked at the boys, and then hinted at the sedan. Jett and Adam entered the car. The sedan drove away. Adam attempted to keep track of their bearings and potential destination, but his eyes grew continually more tired. Eventually he ceased trying and fell asleep.

When he awoke it was dark. Without a watch he was nearly clueless about the time of day, though it was definitely after 9:00 p.m. They rolled along a two-lane road traveling sixty miles per hour. The car slowed and turned right on a street intersecting the highway. Then the car stopped and both men exited the vehicle. From the trunk, the bald man removed a few items. Jett and Adam exited the vehicle too. The bald man turned to the boys, extended his arm, and handed each boy a small black rectangular object. "These are disruptors," he said. "Keep them with you at all times, and make sure they are on. This will prevent you from being seen on any SSD footage. Our sedan has a built-in disruptor. You've been off-grid since we left D.C. Any questions?" Jett and Adam shook their heads. "Good. We need these back when your task is complete." The man turned back to the car trunk, took an additional item, then turned back towards the boys. He extended his arm, revealing a sheathed knife. The bald man then unsheathed the knife and displayed it to the boys. A solid black hilt and a stainless steel six-inch blade, serrated near the hilt, reflected not a shimmer of light. The perfect weapon for a clandestine murder.

"Awesome!" said Jett. The bald man sheathed the knife, and then gave it to Jett. He took another one from the trunk and gave it to Adam. Adam hesitated, and then took the knife.

"Gentlemen," stated the bald man. "Your mission is simple: find a target from the general populace and eliminate your target. Leave no witnesses. Do not be seen. If someone sees you, eliminate him or her. You are to be back at this location, precisely at sunrise, Monday. Questions?"

Adam and Jett looked at each other, then back at the bald man. Both boys shook their heads.

"A word of advice," said the bald man. "On the small of the back, just left of the spine and next to the kidney: stab someone there, and they will be instantly paralyzed. They won't be able to make a sound, and they will die in a few seconds." Adam shivered. "And boys: if you know what's best for you, you will not fail. Erebus will avoid implications at all costs." With that, the bald man climbed back into the car and drove away.

It took a few minutes for Adam and Jett to fully comprehend the situation. "They want us to kill someone?" questioned Jett. "Am I understanding this correctly?"

Adam nodded. "I believe so."

"No wonder my brother never wanted to talk about his test." Jett scratched his head. "I don't understand. Why do they want us to kill someone?"

"My best guess," said Adam, "is they need to see who is worthy of joining Erebus. They want people who will follow orders without question. People who will do whatever it takes to advance their cause."

"It's the perfect crime," replied Jett. "There's no evidence linking the murders back to Erebus, only hearsay."

"What do we do?" asked Adam.

"I don't even know where we are. The first thing we should do is uncover our location."

"Then we should walk back towards the main highway. We'll stay off to the side of the road so we can hide if we hear any cars approaching."

~

Adam and Jett walked next to the straight stretch of pavement for roughly forty minutes, though it was difficult to know for certain. Neither Adam nor Jett had a device for telling time. If the sun were shining, Adam could roughly discern the time of day by observing the position of shadows. Unfortunately, it was still dark. At least he was able identify the star, Polaris, and determine true North.

The long walk afforded Jett and Adam ample time to reflect. Adam considered his circumstances and recalled previous events: Hannah's murder, the face of the unknown boy in the yearbook, the encoded message given to Sahar, and the covert meeting with Jeff Locke. It did not take long for Adam to connect the dots: his sister, Hannah, was killed as part of an initiation right. It seemed likely that Sahar's father was killed for the same reason. Assuming every Erebus member had completed the same initiation ritual, that meant there were likely hundreds of powerful people who were also cold-blooded killers, and two of them had their sights set on the presidency and vice presidency. The only problem was lack of evidence. Without any evidence, these people would continue to roam free. As Jett and Adam walked, Adam's hands trembled. Jett noticed, but did not comment.

They continued their trek for a while longer before one of the boys finally spoke. "I once killed a quail," said Jett. "I was hunting with my brother and father. At first I felt bad about it, but after a couple days, it stopped bothering me." Jett paused. "How long do you suppose it takes to stop feeling guilty if you kill a person?"

"It probably depends on the person," Adam solemnly replied.

"The person doing the killing, or the person being killed?"

"I imagine both, but I was referring to the person doing the killing. I imagine it also depends on how the person kills."

"I remember our combat instructor discussing this," said Jett. "The greater distance between the killer and the victim, the easier it is to kill. Soldiers during the Civil War rarely killed by stabbing with the bayonets, they almost always slashed. And during World War One, most casualties occurred when the enemy fled and had their backs turned. Snipers and bombers found it much easier to kill than soldiers on the front lines."

"I suppose technology has made it easier for men to kill each other. It creates a vast emotional distance between people. Unfortunately, it's not going to help us. We have one of the oldest tools known to man. They might as well have given us rocks to carry out the task." A medium sized fallen tree lay near the side of the road. Jett and Adam carefully climbed over it, and then Adam continued talking. "But it seems to me the point of this exercise is to carry out a difficult task. Senators send troops to war."

"But the senators don't see the faces of the dead soldiers," interrupted Jett. "If we kill someone... Well, I don't know how you shake that image from your mind."

Adam breathed deeply. "If it were that easy to shed a traumatic experience there wouldn't be so many soldiers returning with PTSD."

"Maybe the new neural implants can be programmed to suppress those images."

"Maybe," Adam pondered for a moment. "But wouldn't that also suppress their emotions? I don't know enough about how the brain works, or how neural implants work, but I can't imagine much good coming from emotionless soldiers."

Jett stopped, and then Adam stopped and turned towards Jett. "Do you hear that?" asked Jett.

Adam listened. "It sounds like a car is coming," he said.

"The bald man said we are to stay out of sight," said Jett.

Adam scoped the area, looking for a place to hide. Jett pointed away from the road, towards a group of trees. "Behind those trees!"

The boys quickly trudged through the terrain and ducked behind some trees. The vehicle drove past without hesitation.

"I don't think they saw us," said Adam. His heart raced.

"We're safe," said Jett. "It's dark; there's no way they saw us."

~

Before long, they arrived at what appeared to be a small town. It did not look entirely dissimilar from Cammalot: cheaply constructed houses, unkempt lawns, and businesses with weathered signage. By the time they had reached the city, the temperature had dropped considerably. Neither boy was shivering, but every time the breeze touched them it produced goose bumps on their arms.

"I've been meaning to ask," said Jett. "That boy you killed in the bathroom, what was it like?"

"How do you know about that?" said Adam, surprised by Jett's knowledge. He suspected Jett may have learned about it from Eric.

"I only heard rumors, I still don't know the full story."

Adam frowned, and Jett looked away. Adam paused a few seconds before responding. "I was attacked in the bathroom. I had fallen to the floor, but they kept kicking me. They stopped for a second, and it gave me a brief moment to push one of the boys. I was only trying to get him out of the way so I could escape, but he fell and hit the back of his head on the urinal."

"I see. What was it like?"

Adam cocked his eyebrow and looked at Jett.

"I mean, what's it like killing someone?"

"I suppose killing him was the easy part." Adam took a deep breath. "Living with yourself, after you've committed such an atrocious act is the hard part—even if it was an accident, and even if he brought it onto himself."

"Do you still think about it?"

"I try not to, but I still do."

"How often?"

"Honestly? Every night."

The farther into the city they walked, the more difficult it became to find concealment. Eventually, they stumbled upon a vast open field, circumscribed by a short chain-link fence. A large pavilion drew the eye to the center of the park. Ten yards from the pavilion stood a play structure. Beyond the pavilion was another covered area with a set of wooden ramps.

"Let's camp out by the skate park," said Jett, pointing towards the covered area beyond the pavilion. Adam agreed, and they jogged across the field, past the pavilion, and hid under one of the ramps.

Once they were seated and comfortable (as comfortable as they could be, given the situation), Adam spoke: "I've also had a lingering question, and I don't know how to ask in a nice way... but you've been acting different. Why are you suddenly not acting..."

"Like an ass?"

"Well, yes, that's a good way of stating it."

"I wanted to get an invitation to Erebus. My brother said that you can't show any weakness, and you have to be willing to bend some rules. Plus, my father said if I don't get into Erebus, he wouldn't pay for college. He really wants Eric and me to follow in his footsteps. He's always talking about the family name."

"So you act like a jerk so you can get college paid for, and to 'protect' the family name? Moral turpitude aside, don't your actions hurt your family name? I mean, everything you do, good or bad, reflects on your family name."

Jett scowled at Adam and retorted, "I'm just stating it like it is! I don't need you to go all evangelical on me!"

Adam accepted the signal and discontinued what Jett perceived as a verbal attack. But in truth, Adam was simply trying understand Jett's actions. They sat in silence for a minute before Adam hesitantly asked, "What are we going to do about this situation?"

Jett reflected for several seconds, and then solemnly responded, "I don't think we have much choice in the matter. We have to follow through with our task."

"We always have a choice," said Adam, "but the consequences might be equally unpleasant."

"I don't like our situation," said Jett, "or even condone it. I'm saying that it's either kill or be killed." Jett unsheathed his knife and rubbed his finger along the side of the blade.

"Are you certain they would kill us? Maybe your father could convince them to make an exception."

"I wish. He would rather see me dead than ruin the family name by becoming an average Joe. Callous bastard."

Adam looked down in disappointment. Finding an easy way out of the predicament was wishful, unrealistic thinking. Adam searched his mind for a nonviolent approach to the issue, but contemplated no feasible strategies. Then Jett suggested, "If we have to kill somebody, maybe we should find someone who deserves it."

"What do you mean?" asked Adam.

"What if we could find a sex offender or some sleaze ball convict that's no longer in prison?"

"Even if we could locate such a person, does that make the act any more humane?"

Jett shrugged his shoulders. "No one takes pleasure in putting down a rabid dog, but they do it out of necessity. In the same light, no soldier enjoys killing enemy soldiers, but he does it because he has to. We don't denounce those actions. Even police officers shoot criminals—"

"After they've exhausted all other options!" interrupted Adam.

"I'm still waiting for your recommendation," said Jett. Adam said nothing. "Suppose we don't kill someone. Then what? We run and hide for the rest of our lives? The bald man said Erebus would avoid implications at all costs. That means they will search for us until we're dead!" Adam looked down, and again, refrained from speaking. "Like I said, I don't like the situation any more than you do. But if we have to kill someone, let's kill someone evil. At least we can say we made the world a safer place."

"Marginally safer," muttered Adam.

"But safer, nonetheless," argued Jett.

"Don't you see a problem with this moral reasoning? Trying to maximize general welfare is oppressive and relies on arbitrary standards! We can't kill someone for the sole reason that their absence satisfies the general population. By that logic, it was acceptable for the ancient Romans to feed Christians to lions because it entertained the populace. It follows that slavery is acceptable, as long as the cumulative happiness of non-slaves is greater than the happiness of the slaves. You don't need to be a history major to understand how infective and oppressive that utilitarian logic is. It's led to the death of literally millions of—"

"I get it, but you're overextending the logic!" asserted Jett. "According to your argument, we shouldn't imprison people because they are being used as an end to a means, namely, a convict is oppressed and imprisoned to make the general population safe."

"Then I suppose the difference is that a prisoner willfully transgressed."

"Exactly!" said Jett.

"But haven't they served their time?"

"Maybe, but do you know what fraction of prisoners regress?"

"Too many," replied Adam. "But I'm growing tired of this debate. I need to rest."

"Before you rest," said Jett, "let me beg one more question: does a convict have the same right to life and liberty as a general citizen?"

Adam momentarily relapsed in silence before responding, "No."

"And that is why, if we're going to kill to survive, we commit an abhorrent act upon someone abhorrent."

"Good night," muttered Adam. He reclined against a post and closed his eyes. Jett did the same.

~

Adam awoke just as the sun shimmered above the distant hills. A light mist hovered above the grass field. The moisture had just begun to evaporate. The hairs on Adam's arms stood in response to the light chills. He stretched his neck side to side, attempting to rid his muscles of the unpleasant kink that resulted from the cement bed. A few feet away lay Jett, awkwardly contorted on the pavement. Adam scooted towards Jett and lightly nudged his shoe. Jett let out a low moan, and then rubbed his eyes. He sat upright and yawned. "I'm hungry," he complained. "How about you?"

"I'm famished, but I don't know how we're going to find food."

"Why don't we steal some?" suggested Jett.

Adam shook his head. "We can't risk getting caught," he said. "You heard the bald man."

"Then we won't get caught."

"If only it were that simple."

"It is that simple," said Jett. "No one uses video cameras anymore, it's all SSD footage." He reached into his pocket and pulled out the disruptor. "And the disruptors will keep us off-grid."

"We don't know for certain if video cameras are used or not. Facilities in my hometown still used video recorders."

"Really?" Jett laughed. "I suppose people still drove their own vehicles as well."

Adam nodded and Jett chuckled again.

"You really did live in the stone age."

"The point is," said Adam growing impatient of Jett, "we don't know anything about this place."

Jett looked around, then back at Adam. "Well by the looks of it, we shouldn't have any trouble finding dirt-bags to kill."

"Just because their parents aren't governors doesn't mean they're dirt-bags."

"Did I say that?" said Jett, mockingly.

"You certainly implied it."

"Just look around: they're too lazy to take care of their yards and houses. I can only imagine the havoc they wreak with their attempts—or lack thereof—at raising a family." Adam clenched his teeth. He wanted to stand and fight for the underdogs of that town, but judging from his experience at Cammalot, there was a certain element of truth in Jett's statement. Many of the parents were completely inept or lazy (sometimes both).

"We still don't have a plan for anything," said Adam. "But I thought about your suggestion, and I think you're right: if we must kill someone, let's kill someone who deserves it."

"Good! Now how should we find someone who deserves it? Do we look for the messiest yard?"

Adam frowned in disapproval. "I have a better idea: every library has public computers with Internet access. And sheriff's websites usually compile a list of the worst sex offenders in the city, and which neighborhoods they reside in. All we have to do is search online."

An expression just short of a smile captured Jett's face. "I like it," he said. "Why don't you work on that, and I'll work on finding food."

"Okay," said Adam. "But we need to be as prudent as possible. I don't think the world will end if someone sees us, but we need to blend in such that we're not noticed."

"And we shouldn't meet here. It may be crowded later."

"Then let's meet just outside of town on the road we came in on. We'll secure ourselves in the trees."

"Let's regroup around noon," said Jett. Adam agreed.

~

Everything went according to plan: Adam found a library and searched the county website for a list of local sex offenders. No one gave him a second glance. His attempt to look average kept him concealed. The sun ascended progressively higher and Adam trekked towards the edge of the city. Adam arrived at the proposed location just as the sun reached its zenith. Jett had already arrived.

"Here," said Jett, handing Adam a donut and a pint of milk. "I got some donuts, milk, candy bars, and bananas. It should satisfy our appetites for the time being." Adam took the donut and milk and bit into the donut. "You find what we needed?" Adam reached into his pocket and produced a small folded pack of papers, which he then handed to Jett.

Once Adam finished chewing his food he spoke, "I printed a list of candidates, their addresses, and a map showing their locations. Now we need to choose the victim." Jett unfolded the papers. Adam pointed at one of the mug shots. "This guy's the worst on the list. He's the only level-three sex offender in the city. He's a child molester and a repeat offender."

"I don't know," said Jett. "It says he's six foot five and two-sixty. He's a big guy."

"He's a giant, but as long as we get him by surprise, it shouldn't be an issue." Adam took another bite from his donut.

"If you think we can take him, then let's do it! By the looks of it, he's a despicable person." Adam hesitated for a moment. Jett noticed Adam's awkward expression. "What is it now?"

"You said he's a despicable person," Adam breathed deeply. "If we're going to go through with this, we have to stop thinking of him as a person."

Jett nodded. "You're right," he said, "no person is capable of crimes he committed. He's a person in name only. From now on, we'll call him what he is: a monster." Adam nodded in agreement.

Jett smiled. "If it were up to me, all child molesters would be required to carry a piece of dog crap in their back pockets at all times."

Adam cocked an eyebrow. "I don't follow," he said.

Jett attempted to conceal his laugh, but could not help but laughing out loud in the middle of his sentence: "In case someone asks them for ID!" Adam laughed and shook his head.

Once Jett stopped laughing, Adam asserted, "If we're going to succeed, we need a plan of action."

"I agree. We should attack this evening."

For the remainder of the afternoon, Jett and Adam proposed different strategies until they finally hashed out an agreement. Then, they practiced techniques so that every move would be muscle memory. Before leaving their pseudo-encampment, they ate the remainder of their food. They skies had been gray all day, but in the last hour winds speeds had increased and brought a slew of dark clouds.

At approximately 8:30 p.m. (by Adam's best estimate), they stealthily trekked into the town and prowled through the sleeping neighborhood until they found the correct dwelling. To call it a house would degrade the value of other houses: it was a singlewide manufactured home, perched on a gravel lot. Rust and mold tarnished the siding. A shoddily constructed plywood cover wrapped around the lower edge of the dwelling. The roofing material curled on the slightly oblique top, indicating years of neglect. Off-white blinds in every window obscured the inside view. The nearest dwelling was several blocks away. Adam and Jett lay prone on the opposite side of a small gravel mound.

"Looks like there's only one door," whispered Jett.

"That might make a stealthy entrance difficult. We could try one of the windows."

"But we can't see inside."

The boys kneeled and stared at the house for a moment before Adam suggested, "What if one of us lures him outside while the other person sneaks inside?"

"That might work," said Jett. He looked at Adam, whose hand was trembling, but ignored it. "Which one of us sneaks inside?" They stared at each other for a moment.

"Rock, paper, scissors?" suggested Adam.

Jett nodded. "One round only."

They readied their hands. Adam's heart pounded. The game seemed to proceed in slow motion. Adam considered what Jett was most likely to play. *One.* His first thought was rock. *Two.* But what if Jett is expecting that, and Jett chooses rock? *Three.* Adam randomly selected a strategy and displayed a fist. Jett's extended his index and middle fingers in scissor formation.

Jett cursed under his breath. Adam's muscles relaxed. A sudden relief swept through his body. "It looks like I'm sneaking inside," said Jett. They quickly finalized their plan. Jett crept over the trailer and hid behind one of the corners, close to the entrance. Adam gathered the largest rocks he could find.

From behind the mound, Adam threw one of the rocks at the trailer. It hit the sidewall, barely missing the window, and produced a clash. Adam waited, but nothing happened. He took another rock and hurled it at the same window. The second rock shattered the window and penetrated the dwelling, but still, nothing happened. Adam picked up a third rock to hurl, but before he could throw it, the front door burst open. A tall heavy and greasy looking man wearing a tight, stained, white ribbed tank top and torn denim jeans stood in the doorway. His hands clenched a shotgun. His red eyes scowled and scanned the premise until his eyes met Adam's. Adam held his arm cocked back, ready to hurl the rock. His heart pounded. He stood still, as if his legs were frozen. Guns had been confiscated, and he never considered the possibility that this felon may be in possession of a shotgun. The man stepped off his two-stair porch and shouldered the shotgun. The barrel pointed directly at Adam. Adam recognized the threat and ducked behind the gravel mound. A loud bang resounded. Pieces of gravel flew past Adam and dust filled the air. Adam listened carefully and recognized the sound of the shotgun pump. He hastily peered around, searching for a covered exit, but nowhere did he see anything that could be used for cover. Another shot fired and more gravel flew over Adam. He heard footsteps approaching, and another round entered the chamber of the shotgun.

Adam scrambled to his hands and knees and prepared to dart towards the house. It seemed to be the best of the worst options. Another shot resounded, but it created no dust. The gravel sat still. A low-pitch, blood-curdling howl echoed from the greasy man. Adam slowly stood to see the man drop to his knee. Jett stood behind him, but before Jett could back away, the man swung the butt of his shotgun around and hammered Jett in the face. Jett stumbled and fell backward. With one arm, the man grasped his lower back. He used the gun for balance and tirelessly climbed to his feet. Blood stained the back of the man's shirt. Jett lay on the ground, stunned from the harsh hit to his face. The man stumbled, and shouldered the shotgun. Adam realized that Jett was about to become shotgun fodder, so he darted towards the convict and feebly attempted to tackle the man. Adam shoved his shoulder into the man's lower back, the shotgun fired, and Adam practically bounced off of the massive man. Fortunately for Adam, the man's injury caused him to drop the gun and keel. The stain on the man's shirt grew darker and wider. He cringed and nursed his side, breathing rapidly and shallowly. Adam and Jett watched, frozen as if they had been turned to stone by Medusa's snake-hair. The man fell to his side. Gurgling sounds rumbled from the man's mouth. Blood saturated his lips and teeth. He quivered and trembled for what seemed like eternity, until finally, his muscles relaxed. No more twitches. No more unpleasant sounds. Only a burly, blood soaked corpse.

Harsh tremors permeated Adam's body. No words came to mind. He fell to all fours and spewed vomit into the gravel. He closed his eyes, hoping to waken from the nightmare. But when his eyes opened, the bloody corpse was still laying in the gravel.

Jett broke the silence: "Someone probably heard those shots. We need to get out here!" Adam stood and extended an arm to Jett. Jett rose to his feet. He bent over and picked up the bloody knife, then wiped the blade on the greasy man's shirt. After sheathing the knife, he nodded at Adam.

Adam and Jett ran as fast as they could. The sun had nearly set, gracing them with many shadows to use for cover. They continued running until they were safely out of town, stopping at the original makeshift encampment to rest.

Both boys breathed heavily. "That's not how I envisioned our strategy penning out," said Adam, his voice wavering as he spoke. His hands continued their chronic trembling.

"Me neither," said Jett, "but it could have gone much worse... Look at the bright side: the world is now rid of one more monster, thanks to us."

"Let's rest a few more minutes, then head to the area where we're supposed to rendezvous with the bald man."

Adam slouched against a tree and closed his eyes. He wanted to believe that every one of his transgressions was necessary to make the country a better place, that infiltrating Erebus and preventing Holden and Cane from assuming the executive office would help millions. Even some of history's greatest heroes killed their fellow human beings. But in the core of his conscience, he knew that if his mother and father were still alive, they would be deeply disappointed by his actions. He kept telling himself that someone else killed the burly man. But even if the fatal stab had come from Jett, Adam still twisted the dagger.

A brief sound of shoes scuffling through the dirt became apparent. Adam ignored it until the scuffling grew louder. He opened his eyes. Jett stood a few feet in front of him, wielding a knife. Adam's heart raced. "What are you doing?"

"Sorry, Adam. I don't have a choice. I wish I didn't have to do this, I truly do. Don't take it personally." Jett lunged towards Adam. Adam sidestepped and stumbled, but recovered and hid behind the small tree.

"You don't have to do this," said Adam. Jett said nothing and lunged again at Adam, slicing Adam's arm with the steel blade. Adam ran several steps, drew his knife, and assumed a combat stance. "Don't make me hurt you," threatened Adam, though the quiver in his voice obviated the threat.

Jett approached Adam and assumed a combat stance. The two boys circled each other. Jett swung his knife wide and Adam dodged it by leaning back. Jett rushed in. Adam attempted to side-step Jett, but tripped over a root. He stumbled, dropped his knife, and fell to his back. Jett seized the opportunity and relentlessly kicked Adam. Adam blocked a few of the kicks, but soon lost his strength. When Jett stopped, Adam was barely moving. He lay on the ground and groaned. Jett straddled Adam and raised his knife.

As the knife drew close, Adam mustered every remaining ounce of strength and grabbed Jett's wrist in an attempt to block the knife. The knife continued its downward trajectory, but at a slower pace. Adam could feel the tip of the blade poking the upper left side of his chest. The tip of the blade slowly pierced his shirt and tore the skin. In a last ditch effort to save himself, he screamed and rolled to the side. The knife cut through Adam's shirt and sliced his chest. Jett's arms buckled and his face planted into the ground. The knife fell to the dirt. While Jett was stunned, Adam took the knife, punched Jett, and then slid the knife into Jett's ribs. Jett let out a blood-curdling scream and twitched in the dirt several minutes before releasing all signs of life.

Adam looked at his trembling bloodstained hands. He screamed and pounded his fists into the ground. For months, he felt the proverbial blood on his hands, but now he could see it. His breaths became rapid and shallow. He felt a sharp twist in his gut, and then keeled over. Bile rushed through his throat and spewed from his mouth. The rancid taste stained his tongue. He sobbed and cursed. He knew that the next time he closed his eyes to rest, one more face would haunt his dreams.

19

Monday, August 20, 2068

Upon arriving at Arcadia, Adam was escorted directly to Dr. William's office. Adam paid little attention to his surroundings. His main focus was concocting a believable story that would explain Jett's absence. The men in suits closed the door and stood by it. Adam stepped forward. Dr. Williams stood, and then slowly approached Adam. His nose twitched as he walked near Adam. It had been three days since Adam had bathed or changed clothes. "Report," demanded Dr. Williams.

"We killed a sex offender," said Adam. He tried to maintain eye contact with the professor, but his eyes drifted towards the floor.

"And?" questioned the professor.

"There's no evidence to implicate us, sir. We covered our tracks well." Adam breathed deeply.

Then the bald man spoke, "His story is accurate. We intercepted the official police report."

Williams nodded at the bald man, then fixed his eyes on Adam. "Where is your partner?"

Adam's heart raced. He cleared his throat, and then looked Professor Williams in the eye. "Jett tried to kill me."

"He tried to kill you?"

Adam nodded. "Yes, sir."

"Did he say anything?"

"He said he was sorry. He said he didn't want to, but someone ordered him to." The professor stared at Adam, waiting for more.

Adam grew tense. He had thought about the situation the entire ride back. The truth might be enough to avoid implication, but a simple lie could destroy another heinous enemy. He considered the ninth amendment: *thou shalt not bear false witness against thy neighbor.* But Adam had murdered another boy. Lying to eliminate someone evil seemed to be a minor offense compared to murder—and more humane. "Jett said he was ordered to kill me by his older brother, Eric." Adam paused. "That was all, Professor Williams. He didn't say anything else. And I didn't have a choice. I tried to talk him out of it, but he wouldn't listen. I—"

"That is enough." Dr. Williams looked at the men in suits. "We have a dead child on our hands. This cannot lead back to us. Take care of it." The men nodded and egressed, closing the door behind them. The professor turned back to Adam. "Do you have any idea what you have done?" the professor rhetorically asked. Adam bowed his head in shame. "You may have given Jack Holden the greatest gift yet."

Adam's eyes widened. He looked at the professor in shock. "What? How?"

"According to Gallup polls, the majority of people find it difficult to empathize with Jack Holden. You may have just solved that issue." The professor smiled. The evil in his eyes glimmered. "We will make Jett's death look like an accident—a car accident. Jack Holden will hold a press conference and shed a tear for the camera. It will be the biggest spectacle since the Lindbergh baby. Sympathetic voters may win us the election."

The tremors in Adam's hands returned. He clenched his fists. It took every ounce of self-control not to scream in frustration. "What will he do when he finds out I killed his son?"

Dr. Williams cocked an eyebrow at Adam. "You do not know about Jett, do you?" Adam shook his head. "Jack Holden's marriage is purely political. He and his wife despise each other. And every time Jack looked at Jett, all he could see was a cheating wife." Adam stared at the professor. The professor nodded. "Exactly. Jett is not Jack Holden's biological son. The boy is a bastard."

"If Jack Holden hates his 'son,' why did he storm into the school and defend Jett when Jett was about to be expelled?"

"Politics, Mr. Carter," said Williams. "A scandal like that could destroy his shot at the presidency."

Adam nodded. "I suppose I don't need to worry about Jack Holden, but what about Eric? Eric will want my head on a pike."

"If what you say about Eric Holden is true, then there may be a cabal within Erebus. I will personally investigate this issue. Let me worry about Eric," said the professor. "But Adam, if I find out you are lying—"

"I know," said Adam. "If I were lying, this is the last place I would want to be."

The professor smiled. "I'm glad we are understood." He walked to his desk, opened the drawer, and grabbed a small object. He approached Adam and handed him the object. A round silver pendant dangled from the leather chord. A set of laurels surrounding a flame were inscribed on the pendant.

"What's this?" asked Adam.

"A necklace," said the professor. "In Ancient Greece, laurels were awarded to victors. To the Romans they signified martial victory and triumph. Every member of Erebus wears one of these necklaces. The laurels represent former and future achievements."

Adam fingered the pendant. To him, it was a reminder of his most recent atrocity and moral turpitude. He reluctantly fastened the necklace. It dangled from his neck. "What does the flame represent?" asked Adam.

"Against the will of Zeus, Prometheus stole fire from Olympus and bestowed it for all of humanity to benefit. Erebus will give humanity the greatest gift of all: a perfect society." Dr. Williams smiled. "Adam, now that you are officially a member, it is time you became privy to our plans. Keep in mind, our plans are difficult to sell to the average voter. Drastic ideas require radical measures, hence our test. When you completed your task, you demonstrated that you will do all that is necessary for the greater good."

Williams slowly paced. "Years ago, our scientists created two strains of a virus: one strain to destroy crops, and one to kill livestock. We waited patiently for our members to ascend the corporate ladders and major political offices. We waited until our technology progressed to match our ideals. Finally, we waited for Americans to dig themselves into another hole: the financial crisis. The planets aligned, we released the virus, and after this election, we will hold majorities in both chambers of congress. Cane and Holden will secure the executive office."

The professor walked to his desk and sat at his chair. He beckoned Adam to sit across from him. Adam obliged. "You have to understand," said the professor, "it takes a crisis for people to change their hearts. Fortunately, this will be the last financial crisis. We have enough neural implants to distribute to eighty-five percent of the population. With the latest version, we can give people the will to learn any skill they need. We can supplant their personal preferences, and they will never know! Best of all, they will still believe they are free. No more will greed swallow the entire country. We can eliminate crime and poverty. No more drugs, alcohol, or obesity. Sexually transmitted infections will become a thing of the past. Abortion will not be an issue—every pregnancy will be planned. Homosexuality can finally be cured. Only the worthy will breed. The unworthy will willingly take their own lives. With an obedient population, religion will become obsolete. The economy currently does not provide enough jobs for every person, but that will change. We will not have to fight to redistribute wealth. If we need more taxes, we can increase taxes. If there is a shortage of plumbers, we can almost instantaneously fill the gap. A doctor shortage? Not a problem. And best of all: once the neural implants are received, we will never have to fret over winning another election."

"It sounds like I'm too late to help," said Adam.

"Not at all," replied Dr. Williams. "Our plan will only work if we have the smartest people running the country. We take the best of the best and train them from a young age. You, Adam, will be one of the few elite technocrats running our country. Erebus will be at the helm."

Adam scratched his head. "That's a lot of power for a few people. Aren't you worried about people abusing their power?"

Dr. Williams shook his head. "People are inherently venal," he said, "but every one of our members will have a neural implant that suppresses greed and stimulates altruism. We will finally have genuine benevolent dictators. Until recently, this ingredient existed only in theory."

Adam pondered the situation. He tried not to think of the many flaws in the professor's logic—he would have plenty of time to do that later. But his inner dialogue could not help but ponder a simple query: *Erebus wishes to make life better... better for whom? And at what cost? Even if they succeed in creating a world without suffering, what would it mean without freedom?* He pushed these thoughts aside. People were dying because of a virus created by Erebus. Some of society's highest-ranking officials were psychopaths and murderers. Adam's blood boiled, but he gave no indication of it.

"Professor," said Adam. "What happens next? I mean, what happens to me?"

The professor looked at Adam. "I will update your file with the most recent information and send the results to senior members." Adam nodded. "Other members may contact you from time to time to complete certain clandestine tasks. Meanwhile, I will investigate the possible cabal within Erebus and have Eric Holden detained until the investigation concludes. Any more questions?"

Adam shook his head. He expected to feel guilty that Eric Holden would be detained, but something about it felt right. Adam smiled and said, "I look forward to serving."

~

Saturday, August 25, 2068

For many days, Adam kept attentive to the news. The story of the man's murder did not progress beyond the town's local report. Only the most miserable stories garnish enough viewership to be reported, and it seemed that the death of a known child molester did not fit the criteria. Nonetheless, the success of the ordeal pleased senior members of Erebus (according to Dr. Williams, who was pleased that Adam had uncovered a cabal within Erebus) thereby completing Adam's induction to Erebus. Just as the professor claimed, Erebus fabricated a story of Jett's demise. "Arcadia student dies in car accident," read the headline of the article published in the school paper. No one asked questions, and no one seemed to miss Jett's presence.

Saturday, Will and Sahar returned from their first week of summer vacation. Upon their return, Adam divulged the details of the task.

"Let me understand this correctly," asked Sahar, "you did not directly kill the convict?"

Adam gave a solemn expression. "I might as well have," he said. "The plan was my idea, I suggested him as a target, and I had the chance to stop Jett from killing him, but I did nothing."

"It was technically self-defense," added Will. "He was shooting at you."

"I doubt God will spare me judgment based on a technicality. Plus, the man wouldn't have shot at me if I didn't throw a rock through his window. And even if I didn't kill the convict, I still sunk the knife into Jett."

"But still," said Will, "having a rock thrown through your window isn't grounds to shoot someone. And you did the world a favor by taking Jett out of the picture."

"I hope so. But Professor Williams thinks Jett's death will be a boon to Cane and Holden's campaign. I may have made matters worse." Adam spoke slowly, with his head down. His hands trembled. "I'm not happy with the decisions I've made."

Sahar rested a hand on his shoulder. "We all knew that this task would not be easy. We knew in advance that we would have to make difficult decisions. Still, you have born the brunt of the burden, but we must continue, lest our actions be in vain."

Adam took a deep breath. "It was easier to continue when we had a clear goal in mind. For the last several months, our goal has been to infiltrate Erebus. But how am I to find proof of their wrongdoings? If I openly oppose them, I expose myself as an accomplice to murder. I'm already on thin ice. It's only a matter of time before they discover that I lied to implicate Eric Holden. Plus, there's no direct evidence linking the crimes back to them."

"They must keep evidence somewhere!" said Will. "Even drug dealers are known to keep books. We just need to find out where they keep their information, and how to get access to it."

"How do we do that?" Adam frustratingly said. "The presidential election isn't until November, but Erebus only meets once per month—the second Friday of each month. That means I have two meetings, September and October, to find evidence of their secrets and expose them."

"And most people vote electronically now. Many are voting a month before the official election," added Sahar. "Realistically, that means we need to expose Cane and Holden by the beginning of October. That leaves one meeting, two if we are lucky."

"There must be a location where they keep files," stated Will. "We need to find out where."

Sahar leaned in. Her eyes shifted up to the left. Adam and Will watched in anticipation, hoping for an epiphany. "We need to think about this logically. Who are the highest ranking members?"

"Cane and Holden must rank high," said Adam. "They likely know more than lower ranking members, and they are undoubtedly part of the network, but their roles are different. It's safe to assume that the organization is run efficiently, and it wouldn't be efficient for Cane or Holden to keep track of the information."

"Well," started Will, "we know Dr. Williams is a high ranking official, though we don't know who he reports to."

"The highest ranking officials always have scapegoats," said Adam. "They try to avoid direct links to their subordinates in case their subordinates make a mistake. It's the best way to avoid accountability."

A curious look captured Sahar's face. "But they do not give the tasks to anyone," she said, "It has to be someone who is trusted, and has earned his place. It is almost a universal organizational principal: the secretary knows every important detail, and reports to the manager, but if the manager wants to throw someone under the bus, the secretary is the perfect culprit."

"Then it would seem," said Will, "that Dr. Williams either knows this 'secretary,' or he plays the role."

Adam adjusted his posture. He raised a finger. "Come to think of it, when I last spoke with Dr. Williams, he mentioned 'updating my file.' That means he might have a hard copy." Adam's eyes grew wide. "If Will's hypothesis is correct, where do you think Professor Williams would keep this information to ensure its safekeeping?"

Will leaned in and replied, "Somewhere close, but secretive. His office would be too obvious."

"But there may be clues in his office." Sahar, who had started to slouch, sat upright. She continued speaking, "Perhaps we ought to search for these clues."

"Do you mean to suggest we break into his office?" said Adam.

Sahar nodded. "This is a task the three of us can complete."

"And you have two disruptors now, right?" asked Will. Adam nodded. "Good, Sahar can take one, the two of us can take the other, and we can meet at Dr. Williams' office."

"Tonight?" questioned Adam—astounded by Will's suggestion.

Will shrugged his shoulders. "Why not? We're running out of time, and tonight is just as good a night as any. Plus, we need to act quickly."

"I agree," said Sahar. "We need to move quickly."

Adam shrugged his shoulders. "I suppose we've come this far… If we stop now, our whole mission was in vain."

~

At eleven p.m. Will switched-on the desk lamp. Adam rubbed his eyes and squinted while they adjusted to the abruptly illuminated room. Will had already dressed and was eager to leave. "Let's go," he whispered excitedly, but quiet enough that it would not wake his other two roommates. Adam clumsily climbed out of his bed and dressed. Will took the disruptor from the desk drawer. "We're meeting Sahar in less than ten minutes!" Adam grabbed his baseball cap and secured it on his head, then turned off the lamp.

It was not the first time either boy had snuck out in the middle of night, and the experience was nearly identical to the previous times. A cool placid air filled the halls. Every footstep, no matter how delicate, threatened to shatter the absolute silence. A faint light shone through the windows at the end of the halls. They trekked close together, to the end of the hall and down the stairs, for only one boy carried the disruptor.

Once they reached the bottom of the stairs and passed the wing of the Water Hall, they entered the hub of campus. The central staircase spiraled upwards. Dimly lit floodlights sustained visibility within the hub, while the moonlight shining through the glass ceiling dome illuminated the staircase. Will and Adam treaded lightly up the stairs and diverged from the staircase upon reaching the fourth floor. They continued down the hall until they reached the door with a nameplate that read, "Professor Williams."

"Here it is," whispered Adam. "Should we wait for Sahar?" At that moment, Adam and Will both felt a light tap on their shoulders, causing them to jump. Adam turned to see Sahar.

"Sorry," whispered Sahar, "I didn't mean to spook you. I wanted to stay out of sight until you arrived."

"What did you expect!" retorted Will, who had begun panting. "My heart feels like a battery-operated drum set!"

Sahar smiled and whispered, "We can talk about our feelings later, but now, we have a mission to complete." Will scowled at Sahar. She smiled, and removed two hairpins from her pocket. One had been broken in half and bent into an 'L' shape. Sahar inserted both of the pins into the keyhole on the doorknob. She fiddled with the pins for nearly a minute while Adam and Will watched.

When it appeared that Sahar had not progressed, Adam suggested, "I think we need another plan." At that moment, a small 'click' sound emanated from the doorknob, and the door slowly opened.

Sahar turned her head to Adam and smiled proudly.

"Where did you learn to do that?" asked Adam.

"Once, I misplaced the key to my bicycle lock, so I found a 'how-to' video on the Internet that described how to pick a simple lock."

The three students entered the office and closed the door behind them. Light from the outside street lamps shone through the window, providing limited visibility. A desk littered with papers sat in the middle of the room. Tall shelves extended against each of the sidewalls. Books, papers, and journals, filled the shelves in a seemingly haphazard fashion. The prospect of finding something relevant among the continuous rummage looked bleak. Each student utilized their small flashlights and sifted through the material in the office. Adam and Will searched through the bookshelves, but nothing stood out. Sahar picked the lock to Dr. William's desk. Inside, she found a set of small, unlabeled keys. "Look," she said, extending her arm and holding the keys.

Adam glanced around the room, then spoke, "There aren't any file cabinets. What do you suppose the keys are for?"

"Unlocking something," mocked Will.

"Thank you captain obvious!" said Adam with a sneer. He rolled his eyes.

"An obvious question yields an obvious answer!"

Then Sahar butted in, "Will you two clowns stop?" Adam and Will bowed their heads in shame. "We need to find out what these keys are for. They are not labeled, and there are no filing cabinets in this office."

"Let's keep searching," said Adam, "We're bound to find something of interest."

They continued searching for several minutes. Adam scoured the shelves again, peering behind and around the myriad of objects. Will stood on the desk and lifted the ceiling tiles, hoping to find something hidden above the ceiling. He stood on the tips of his toes and shone his flashlight over the tiles, but only found an abundance of dust. He replaced the ceiling tile, but then momentarily lost his balance. Will's foot swung wide and brushed a paperweight that sat on the desk. The paperweight fell from the table and struck the floor, producing a loud thud. While attempting to regain his balance, Will inadvertently dropped his flashlight. The flashlight hit the floor, causing a low-pitched echo. Will regained his composure. The loud noises drew stares from Adam and Sahar. Will mouthed the word, "Sorry," and gave a guilty expression.

"Did you hear that?" Sahar softly spoke.

"The whole campus probably heard that," whispered Adam.

"No," said Sahar, "did you notice the difference between the two sounds?" Will climbed down from the desk. Adam and Will looked at each other in a completely clueless manner. "The paperweight fell and created a dull thud. But the flashlight fell, and I heard an echo." Sahar stood over the area hit by the paperweight, then bent down and knocked gently on the floor tiles, creating a flat sound. Adam kneeled over the area where the flashlight hit, and copied Sahar. A low echo resounded below the tile.

"It's hollow," said Will. "We need something to ply the floorboard." Sahar searched through the desk and found a flathead screwdriver. She delicately pried the edge of the tile. Hiding in the shallow crevice was a small metal box. Adam pulled the box from its crevice. At once, all three students' eyes were drawn to the keyhole. Sahar took one of the keys. It slid perfectly into the box's keyhole. She twisted the key, and the lid popped open. Inside was a small plastic object, much smaller than a book. "Looks like an external hard drive."

"Are we going to take it?" asked Adam.

"We have come this far," said Sahar.

"What if it's not what we're looking for?"

"And what if it is?" said Sahar. "Either way, we have already put ourselves in great danger. At this point, our best option is to continue as planned, and hope for the best."

"I agree," said Will. "Just like Cortez, we sunk our ships long ago. We have landed, and there's no going back."

"Good," said Adam, "I wanted to make sure we're all on the same page." Adam took the hard drive and slipped it into his pocket. "We need to place everything back where it was—exactly."

Carefully, they replaced each item (except the hard drive), leaving almost no trace of their trespass. Soon afterwards, they hastened back to their dorm rooms. For the first night in a long time, Adam slept well. After months of struggle, he had finally accomplished something worthy.

~

The next morning, Will, Sahar, and Adam met for breakfast. The best breakfast meals were always served Sunday mornings: bacon, eggs, sausage, and biscuits and gravy. It was a favorite for most students.

Once the three students were seated, Sahar asked, "What did you find on the hard drive?" Before Sahar finished the question, Will had dug into his food. Adam frowned.

Will munched his food, and then held his hand in front of his mouth while speaking. "Nothing," he said, while simultaneously chewing. "It was encrypted."

"Can you break it?"

"I don't know," replied Will. "I mean, I could try, but some of these hard drives have a failsafe, meaning, if I mess up, the contents could be permanently deleted." Will took another humungous bite of food.

"We need to find someone trustworthy who can hack the contents of the hard drive," suggested Sahar. "The question is, who?"

Will looked to Adam. With a mouth full of food, he asked, "What about Jeff Locke?"

Adam scratched his chin. "Maybe," he replied, "but can we trust him?"

"Why not?" said Will, shrugging his shoulders. "He has helped us so far."

"What if he has his own agenda?" said Adam. "Plus, I don't know how to contact him—other than mailing the hard drive to his company, or making the trek across the country to find him. Both options sound like an invitation for trouble."

"If not Locke, then who? I'm not comfortable handing it over to anyone on campus," said Will. "Until this is over, we shouldn't trust anyone."

The group continued eating their food while pondering. After a few moments, Sahar suggested, "What about Henry?"

Will's eyes lit up, then he spoke, "He's good with computers, right?" Adam arched an eyebrow.

"Do you think he could hack the hard drive?" asked Will.

"Possibly," replied Adam, "but, I don't want to get Henry involved in this. I've already lost my sister and parents. If something were to happen to him, because of me… I couldn't live with myself."

"With all due respect," said Will, "We all got our families involved when we started investigating Erebus. They involved Henry the moment they decided to murder your sister. Whether you like it or not, Henry is already involved."

"True," spoke Adam, "but I'm not willing to place Henry in the vanguard. Even if I offered him the choice, I don't think he would understand the implications. He may be able to solve complex problems in quantum physics, but he is still only emotionally as mature as a four year old. And again, that leaves us with the dilemma: we either trek to Cammalot amidst the riots, or mail the hard drive and hope it arrives safely. And if we decided to make the journey to Cammalot, when would we go?"

"Well," said Sahar, "we still have one more week before classes resume. We could leave this week, and be back in time for class."

"How?" said Adam. "We don't have any money for food or transportation."

"I could use my smartphone to pay," said Will.

"Why do you even have a smartphone?" asked Adam. Will look puzzled. "Never mind," said Adam, "that's beside the point."

The group continued eating without speaking.

After a few minutes, Adam took a deep breath, and spoke, "I will consider it. But I would like us to think about other options."

"On a different topic," said Will, "how was everyone's break?" He looked at Adam, and then quickly reiterated, "I mean, aside from the incident last weekend."

Adam shrugged his shoulders. "It's been quiet on campus. Most people went home for the break. Other than the incident at the beginning of break, nothing new has happened around here."

Then Sahar answered, "My trip home was pleasant, though I must admit, driving near the riots was a bit scary. I visited with my family, but did not do anything exciting."

"My experience was pretty similar," said Will. "Though it was nice to have a break from classes. When you're off campus, the economic downturn is much more noticeable." Will chewed another bite of food, and then asked, "Have you heard from Henry or your grandmother lately?"

"My grandmother sent me an email recently. They are well, for the most part. Henry is working through graduate level physics textbooks, and he still spends much of his time toying with the computer. My grandmother complained about food prices, but said everything else is well."

"Good," said Sahar. "And are you okay?"

Adam shrugged his shoulders. He had killed three people (four by some counts). Every night their apparitions tortured his mind. It was not a question of whether he was "okay," but whether the battle was worth fighting. His friends seemed to think it was, but they were not suffering like him. Sahar noticed the tremors in Adam's hand as he lifted his fork to grab a piece of food. Adam looked at her, and then solemnly replied, "I'll live."

20

Monday, August 27, 2068

A hasty decision was required. To trek from Arcadia's campus in Washington D.C., all the way to Aegis's headquarters in Greenwich, a five hour train ride, or from D.C. to Cammalot, North Carolina, a seven hour trip by car (but no direct public transit route). Given the circumstances, a trip to Cammalot would have to be at least partially completed by walking, and could require several days of walking. Even though Adam was still skeptical of Jeff Locke's intent, asking his help seemed to be the better option. Plus, Adam was still reluctant to involve Henry. Thus, Monday morning, with backpacks containing food, water, clothes, laptops, and two disruptors, Adam, Will and Sahar set out for the train station. They hastened past the sleeping protestors and deadbeats, and arrived at the train station at 8:30a.m. Will used his smartphone to debit most of the funds from his bank account, and purchased three tickets to Greenwich.

The train ride was mostly dismal. The most unpleasant parts of each city seemed to be located near the train tracks. Every major city they passed—Baltimore, Wilmington, Philadelphia, Trenton, and Newark, and even the once great New York City—was plagued by urban blight. Graffiti covered entire buildings. Wide cracks slashed through the streets. The crumbling infrastructure left vestigial traces of once great metropolises. Despite advances in technology and the capabilities of SSDs, the cities still looked like bedrooms of thieves and thugs. Adam had heard that SSDs reduced crime nationwide, but the urban cesspools indicated otherwise.

Greenwich, however, was another story. Instead of dilapidated buildings and crumbling infrastructure, every structure was immaculate and well kept. The sidewalks appeared brand new. Adam and his party departed the train near Greenwich Plaza. They scanned their surroundings. Herds of well-dressed adults nonchalantly brushed past them. Just when Adam thought he spotted someone who may have had the courtesy to give directions, his efforts to steal a moment of attention were promptly ignored. As condescending as it felt to be relegated to the status of an invisible child, he quickly realized that none of the offenses were personal. When you live near the city that never sleeps, the constant clamor of desperation and the incessant echo of preoccupied professionals becomes nothing more than background noise.

Will analyzed his phone. "I think I found it," he said. "It's only a few blocks from here." Adam and Sahar followed Will.

Outside of the train station, homeless folk perched on the sidewalk. They seemed to be the only humans who gave the children a second glance, but it was only to beg for money. After walking four blocks, Adam grumbled, "I thought you said it was only a few blocks away."

"A few blocks, give or take five. Don't worry, we're over half way there."

They traversed one block north and around the corner and arrived at the edge of the Aegis Technology Complex. It stretched over several blocks and up several stories. Decorative flora and tidily cut grass embellished the entryway. Marble stairs led the way inside the building. Aegis's unstated goal was embodied by the modern architecture: always be on the frontier of innovation.

Adam and his party walked through the main entrance. Towards the end of the foyer, security personnel gathered around scanners. Beyond that was a massive lobby with a decorative marble fountain in the center. A young receptionist sat on a stool at the large curved wooden desk to the right. The students approached the receptionist.

"How may I help you?" she politely asked.

Sahar replied, "We are here to see Mr. Jeff Locke."

"Do you have an appointment?"

Sahar looked to Adam. He shrugged his shoulders.

"No," replied Sahar, "but it is very urgent. Please, we will only take a few minutes."

"I'm sorry, but Mr. Locke is incredibly busy. The best way to meet with him is to schedule an appointment. Now let me see..." The receptionist turned her attention to her computer, fiddled with it for a few seconds, and then looked back at Sahar. "The earliest available time is next week. Will Tuesday work for you?" Sahar hesitated.

Adam stepped forward. "Excuse me, Ms. Martin," he said, reading her name badge. "We traveled all the way from D.C., and we found something that Mr. Locke has been seeking for a long time. Can you please send him an email to let him know that Adam Carter is here to see him? We only ask for a few minutes of his time, and we can wait here until he is available."

The receptionist hesitated. "I can send him the email, but I can't guarantee that he will be able to see you today. But you are welcome to have a seat and use the facilities, if needed."

"Thank you," said Adam. Then Sahar and Will promptly thanked the receptionist, too.

"And what should I say is the nature of your visit?" asked Ms. Martin.

"Can you let him know that we found evidence? He'll know what it means."

"Alright... and I'm sorry, your name again?"

"Adam Carter."

"Thank you," she said with a smile. Adam smiled back.

The three students walked to the couches near the receptionist's desk and sat.

"What now?" asked Will.

"I don't know," said Adam. "I never planned for this."

"We can't wait around Greenwich for a week. And we don't have enough money take the train back. We went for a Hail Mary and dropped the ball."

"I suppose," said Adam, "that I should have learned by now: nothing ever goes according to plan. I don't know what to do... should we call our parents to come get us?"

"If my dad discovers I squandered my entire savings for a trip to Greenwich, he'll kill me!"

"Will you two stop bemoaning?" said Sahar. Will and Adam looked at Sahar in shock. "We hit another bump in the road. So, what? We give up? Just like that? When in human history has victory ever been easy?" Will sunk into his chair and slouched his shoulders as Sahar continued her lambaste. "If you are looking for an easy job, go work at McDonalds. We have a great burden, but an even greater responsibility. Who but us can solve this problem? We are top students at the best academy in the country. We can figure this out, but I do not want to hear any more talk about quitting!"

An awkward silence passed. In the background, Adam heard the receptionist's phone ring. She looked at the group of students and quietly said, "Yes, they're still waiting here... okay. Yes, sir." She hung up the phone.

"Okay," said Will. "Let's brainstorm."

"Alright. Let's just take a minute to think." said Adam.

A moment later, a man wearing a suit approached the students. He was tall, formidable, and unintentionally domineering. "Adam Carter," he spoke. "Please come with me; your friends too."

"Are we in trouble?" said Adam, quivering.

"Not at all," said the man. "Mr. Locke wishes to see you." Adam glanced at Sahar and Will. Their eyes lit up. They sprung to their feet and followed the man through security, past the decorative fountain, and into a glass elevator. From the elevator they could see much of the facility. They disembarked on the top floor and followed the man through large double doors crafted from Brazilian rosewood. A large conference table crafted from more exotic wood sat in the center of the room. A sizable window past the far side of the table offered a spectacular view of the city. To the left was another door. The man held the door for the students and beckoned they enter.

Inside the room, Jeff Locke sat at a desk, eagerly awaiting Adam's arrival. He sprung from his seat and greeted the trio. "My name is Jeff Locke," he said, shaking each of their hands. "You must be Will, and you must be Sahar."

"It is an honor to meet you sir," said Sahar.

"The pleasure is all mine," Locke charismatically replied. "Thank you, Wes." The man nodded and left the office. Locke turned to Adam. "Tell me, is my information correct? Were you able to find something of value?"

"I think so," replied Adam. He then explained everything to Locke, starting with the secret meetings, then following to the initiation task, and finally, culminating with the retrieval of the encrypted hard drive. Adam reached into his backpack, removed the hard drive, and handed it to Locke.

"Quite impressive," spoke Locke. "My computers are constantly analyzing petabytes of data collected throughout the country. Often patterns emerge that are nothing more than coincidence. But over a decade ago, what started as an ostensibly random correlation became increasingly robust. A handful of people who spent most of their time at Arcadia would disappear from the grid for several days. During that time, seemingly random murders occurred." Locke turned to Sahar. "That is why I suspected Eric Holden killed your father." Sahar looked down, and Locke continued speaking. "At first, I thought the pattern was a fluke—there weren't enough data points to draw any valid conclusions. But each year we got more data points, and the pattern became statistically significant. Once I began looking into it, my company received high volumes of cyber attacks. Keep in mind, there have always been people trying to steal our trade secrets, but after I started investigating, the cyber attacks increased exponentially. That's when I knew for certain that something sinister was happening through Arcadia."

"Well, now we know why the murders occurred," said Adam. "Erebus wants to recruit people who will do whatever it takes to advance their cause. The initiation task sends a nearly perfect signal."

"The larger question," said Locke, "is what is their endgame?" Will and Adam looked at each other in bemusement.

"What do you mean?" asked Will.

Locke answered, "They must have a larger goal in mind. We know that several members of Erebus have infiltrated multinational companies and organizations; we know they have members in high-ranking government offices, but for what purpose? Arcadia alumni already occupy such positions. Why put yourself through such an ordeal, only to achieve the same status? I suspect they have a larger goal in mind, and it's only beginning to burgeon."

"What goal would that be?" asked Sahar.

"What does someone with infinite wealth and vast amounts of power want?"

"More wealth and power," answered Will.

"And what else?"

Adam answered: "An ideal society."

"Ideal by what standard?" asked Sahar.

"Exactly!" spoke Locke. "These people all suffer from, or more like revel in, a god complex. They're always correct, and they can do no wrong. I've spent enough time with the rich and powerful to see it. Each one has his or her vision of what society should look like, and who should be in charge. According to their views, a utopia is possible as long as the right people are in power. Of course, history has shown us what results from these purported utopias."

"Well," said Adam, "I hope the hard drive contains proof of their wrongdoings. The public needs to know how monstrous these people are. Do you think you can decode it?"

Locke smiled and winked. "With both eyes closed and one hand behind my back."

"How long will it take?" asked Will.

"If we start immediately, it should be decrypted by tomorrow. In the meantime, I'll have my staff clear one of the dorm rooms and make beds for each of you. You'll each be given a card that will allow you complete access to the facility, including the dining halls. You must be famished from your journey."

"Starving!" said Will. "I could eat a whole cow!"

Locke laughed. "My staff will escort you to your dorm, and bring some food to assuage your hunger."

Sahar smiled. "Thank you Mr. Locke," she said.

Locke walked to his desk, picked up a phone and requested some escorts. A moment later, Wes returned.

"Wes will give you a brief tour of the facility, then show you to your dorms," said Locke. "When I discover what's on the hard drive, you will be the first to know." Locke held the door open, and everyone else departed.

Wes led the party through the lobby, around the dining hall, and past several computer labs, where adults worked. The students were given an inside look at select experiments in the research and development departments. Some were quite boring, while others sparked an interest.

"What's happening in that lab?" asked Sahar.

"Ah," replied Wes, "the Turk 2.0. Our physicists have been experimenting with properties of Bose-Einstein condensates with the goal of building a personal quantum computer."

"Why do they call it the Turk 2.0?"

"The Turk was a fake chess-playing machine constructed in the late seventeen hundreds. The name is an ode to that machine."

"I see," said Sahar. "And what is a Bose-Einstein condensate?"

"When you cool matter to near absolute zero temperatures, it starts exhibiting very strange properties. We hope some of these properties may be used to construct a viable quantum computer. But that day is still far away."

They continued the tour, passing a lab that was not pointed out by the tour guide. Heavy metal doors protected the entrance. Solid walls blocked the view inside. Adam asked, "What's in that lab?"

Wes hesitated, and expressed an awkward look. "That area is classified. It involves cybernetics and organic computing, and that's all I can tell you."

The conversation effectively ended, and the tour continued. Along the way to the dorm, Wes pointed out the dining hall, and within a couple minutes, the party arrived at their dorm room.

"The three of you will have to share this room. Normally, we would give each of you your own room, but all other rooms are occupied. Here are your key cards," said Wes, handing each student a card. "If you have any questions, use the phone in the room to call the front desk. Meals will be provided for you shortly." The students thanked Wes and he departed.

"This place is much more spacious than our dorm rooms at Arcadia!" said Will. Adam looked around the room. Despite three separate double beds and large dressers, space was abundant. "Look! A walk-in closet!" Will peered around the room, then gravitated towards the large flat-screen television (and gaming console). Adam sat on the couch.

"And a bathroom," said Sahar.

Adam peered out the window. The view was less than spectacular: the tall buildings blocked the site of the city and created a small alley. A group of crows feasted on scraps they pulled from the dumpster. Adam turned back and asked the blanket question, "What do you think of this place?"

Sahar shrugged her shoulders. "It is all very luxurious..."

"And?"

"It makes me wonder what they are hiding."

"Everyone has secrets," said Will. "But I'll bet Locke is better than Cane or Holden. I wouldn't worry too much about it."

Food was soon served. After stuffing themselves, the students set up their computers, checked email, and enjoyed an evening of video games, a pleasure they were not afforded since entering

Arcadia. By 9:30 p.m. it was dark, and the three students went to bed. Will and Sahar quickly fell asleep, but Adam always had trouble sleeping when unanswered questions roamed his mind. That night, there was only one question roaming his mind: *what's behind the metal doors?*

~

A blaring siren that repeated at regular intervals abruptly awakened Adam. He opened his eyes. Darkness shrouded the room. The faint moonlight shone through the window. A red light flashed.

"Is that the fire alarm?" asked Will, half yawning. Adam peered out the window, and Sahar cracked the door open and peered into the hall.

"I don't see any smoke outside," said Adam. "Nor do I see anything unusual."

Sahar closed the door. "There is no smoke in the hall," she said. "But people are running around in pandemonium."

"We should get out of here," said Will. "Let's grab our stuff and go."

Packing was easy, as barely anything had been unpacked. Each student grabbed their backpacks, exited the dorm, and speed-walked towards the glowing exit signs. They reached the stairwell. A voice from behind cried, "Wait!" They turned to see Wes running towards them. He caught up to them and handed Adam a white plastic-covered hard drive. "Hold on to this. It's a back-up of the hard drive you gave us."

Adam hesitantly took the hard drive. "What is happening?" he demanded.

"The drive must have had a locator beacon that was triggered when we attempted to access its contents. We're being raided. Jeff Locke sent me to escort you."

"Is he okay?" asked Sahar.

"I don't know," said Wes. "But heavily armed men are swarming the facility—and they're searching for that hard drive. We need to leave."

"Are they U.S. military?" questioned Adam.

"I couldn't tell you. They might be military or they might be mercenaries. Either way, I'd rather not find out. Now come with me." Wes briskly led the way and the students followed. They reached the stairwell. Wes peered over the ledge and saw a squadron of armed men climbing the stairs. "We need to find another way out! Quickly, to the other stairwell!"

They shoved past a crowd of panicked people and reached the other stairwell. Wes peered over the ledge. "All clear, let's go!" He descended the stairs and the students followed. They veered off-path upon reaching the second floor, and then took a detour through a little-known route. They rushed through an empty hallway, down another set of stairs, through a large kitchen, and out a back door. Dumpsters sat against a wall. The alley was absent of guards, but vehicles sparsely surrounded the building. Helicopters hovered above the facility, shining their floodlights down on the campus.

The party briefly hid in the shadows of a building corner to rest and hash out a plan. "Listen to me, and listen carefully," spoke Wes. "I saw the secrets on the hard drive. Our most important goal is to find a way to release the contents. But in order to do so, you need to escape." Wes reached into his jacket pocket and produced a wad of cash. He handed the cash to Sahar. "This should be enough for you to travel wherever you need to go. I am going to distract the armed men so you can stealthily escape."

"What about you?" asked Adam. "Why can't you take it? Or better yet, come with us."

"We won't make it out of here without a distraction," said Wes, looking ahead. "The contents of that hard drive are more important than any of our lives. When you see the opportunity, run and don't look back. Understood?" All three students nodded. "Good. The fate of our country rests in your hands."

Wes slid his jacket back, revealing a holstered pistol. "Those are illegal!" said Will. Wes smiled.

"Don't worry about me," he said.

Wes walked into the open. All the guards' eyes were drawn to him. Adam and his party crept closer and waited for the opportune moment. "Freeze!" shouted a guard. Wes kept walking towards them. "I said freeze!" Guards pointed their weapons at Wes.

"Now's our chance!" said Will. "Let's go." Will, Adam, and Sahar scurried along the building's edge, away from the guards. The sound of shouting guards reverberated, but none of the students looked back. They stealthily leapfrogged away from the facility, using parked cars and trees for cover. Gunshots resounded from Wes's position. Will and Sahar stopped to look back, but parked cars obfuscated their view. Adam, realizing Will and Sahar had stopped, turned back towards them.

"We can't stop moving! It's not safe."

Sahar stared in shock. Will gently grabbed Sahar's arm, and tugged. She looked at Will, and then turned her gaze to Adam. He gestured with his hand, urging Will and Sahar to hurry. Sahar snapped out of her trance, and followed Adam. They dashed across the faintly lit street and into a nearby park. Sahar stepped on a small flat object. Her right foot slid forward, causing her left knee to drive into the pavement. She was normally the least clumsy of the group, but her mind was distracted. Adam and Will helped her to her feet, then continued running—not stopping until they were several blocks away from the facility.

Adam paused at an intersection and attempted to find his bearings. He turned right and started to run, but Will grabbed his backpack. "Adam!" Adam turned back and looked at Will. Will's eyes hinted towards Sahar. She stood upright. A blank stare encroached her face. Her breathing grew rapid and shallow. "We need to stop and gather our composure."

"We're not stopping until we're safe!" commanded Adam.

"Sahar is hyperventilating! And look at her leg." Adam's eyes shifted to Sahar's left knee. Blood saturated her jeans.

He promptly ignored Sahar's injury. "Have you forgotten that the entire country is under curfew? We could be arrested for walking down the sidewalk! Now let's go!"

"Just give her a minute—"

"We don't have a minute! Those guards were looking for us, and if we stop they will find us!" Sahar started to walk towards Adam, but nearly collapsed when she put weight on her left foot. Will caught her before she fell.

"She can barely walk!" argued Will.

"Death is on my shoulder!" cried Adam. "He has followed me and harrowed me at every corner! My mother, my sister, and my father are all dead! I failed to prevent their deaths, but I will be damned if I let death bestow the same fate upon my two best friends. If we rest now, we rest forever—our country rests forever! I will carry her if I have to, but I will not rest until we are safe."

"You're right," Will gravely spoke.

Adam nodded. "Now help me carry her."

Will and Adam stood on opposite sides of Sahar and hoisted her arms around their shoulders. Using Adam and Will as crutches, she was able to continue forward, albeit, at a slower pace. They hobbled several more blocks unnoticed, and stopped at another small park.

"I think we're far enough away now," said Adam. Adam and Will helped Sahar sit. Sahar's breathing returned to normal. "Are you okay now?"

Sahar paused and blinked slowly. "I think so," she said. "Can you get the first aid kit from my backpack?" Adam rummaged through Sahar's backpack and found a sealed plastic bag containing Band-Aids, gauze, and other supplies. He handed the bag to Sahar. "In the front pouch is a pocket knife." Adam found the pocketknife and gave it to Sahar. She gently tugged on the blood-soaked part of her jeans, just next to the knee.

"What are you doing?" asked Will.

Sahar used the pocketknife to cut a hole into the jeans. She then ripped them enough to reveal her knee. "They are already ruined," she said. "And the jeans will not roll up far enough."

Will watched Sahar clean her wound.

"Do you need any help?" asked Adam.

"No. Thank you."

As soon as Sahar wiped the blood away it reappeared almost immediately.

"Holy cow!" said Will, staring at Sahar's knee. Adam elbowed Will and subtly glowered at him. "I mean... it's not that bad."

"As long as I wrap it with gauze and keep my leg straight, it should heal. I do not believe it will require stitches."

"Your knee is okay," said Adam, "but are you okay?"

Sahar shrugged her shoulders. "It was frightening... to say the least. I will be fine, but I do not understand how you are so calm."

"Because I need to be," said Adam. "After everyone I've lost, and the atrocities I committed... I think about it every night. I want to quit. I wish it all would end, but I need to keep my composure." Adam took a deep breath. "I never mentioned this before, but when I hid in the crawlspace after my parents were murdered, and I found my father's revolver..." Adam paused. "I considered ending it. The gun was loaded. I cocked the hammer, and placed the barrel in my mouth, but I couldn't do it. I wanted to, but then I thought about the people I was leaving behind. What would happen to my brother and grandmother? What about my friends? What would they think of me? I thought about how my father gave his life to protect my mother and me. I thought about how my innocent sister was murdered. I realized how selfish my initial thoughts were. My family and friends have done so much for me. My father died for a noble cause; surely, I can live for one." Will and Sahar said nothing. They sat in silence, absorbing Adam's words. Adam took another deep breath. "Battles are won, not by emotions, but by strength and logic. Right now, my mind is a train-wreck. But if we want to win, I know that I need to push everything aside, and focus on what's important."

"Your motives are noble," stated Will. He paused. Adam knew there was more for Will to say.

"But?"

"I worry about the implications of your approach."

"Such as?"

Will hesitated. "The toll it may take from your psychological health... no offense intended."

"I understand," said Adam. "But there are more important issues. I knew, going into this, there would be sacrifices. But I can't worry about it now."

"But we worry about it," said Sahar. "We worry about you. The burden you must feel from—"

"From killing?" interrupted Adam. Sahar nodded. "Living with blood on my hands has been the most difficult part of this charade. I hope that neither of you will ever have to do what I have done, but I don't want you to worry about me. Doing so will only distract us from our goal."

"What is our goal now?" asked Will. "I mean, I know we're trying to stop Holden and Cane, and achieve justice for the murders. But what's our next move?"

"New York," stated Adam.

"What's in New York?" asked Will.

Sahar's eyes lit up. "Two of the largest media networks in the country: the New York Times and the Wall Street Journal."

Will gave an 'ah' of comprehension. "If we can get our information to them, they can disseminate it," he said. "And the whole country will learn the truth about Cane and Holden." Will paused. "But won't those guards be looking for us? I'm assuming someone knew we were at the Aegis facility."

"Maybe," said Adam. "They will certainly be searching for the hard drive, but I don't know if they realize we have the hard drive. The disruptors have been on, so we won't be seen on any SSD footage. However, someone at the facility may have seen us."

"Then we must approach this like we are wanted by the law," affirmed Sahar. "We need new clothes."

Adam sat upright and with a newfound strength stated, "Tomorrow, we embark for New York."

21

Tuesday, September 11, 2068

A dark-haired man shoved Professor Williams against a bookshelf. "Care to explain how this happened Williams?" he censured.

"Care to be more specific?" the professor calmly retorted. He brushed his hands against his shirt, smoothing the newly created wrinkles.

"Our records. You were responsible for ensuring the safety of the hard drive. How does a hard drive hidden in a small office in D.C. find itself in Jeff Locke's facility in Greenwich, Connecticut?"

"It was stolen, obviously," replied Williams.

"Wipe that smug grin off your face or you will be the next artifact to go missing." Williams stared solemnly at the dark haired man. "Now, explain to me what happened," demanded the man.

"As you wish." Williams paced. "One of our new recruits turned renegade. He did not appear on SSD footage—it seems that he was using a disruptor. However, when he entered the office he tripped the motion detector. My digital camera caught all three perpetrators."

"I thought you said it was one recruit?"

"Only one of them was a member. It seems that he brought two non-member friends."

"Do you have their names?" said the dark haired man.

"Yes. All three students were in my social studies class. And before you ask, warrants have already been issued for their arrest. Their portraits should be on every major news outlet this morning." The dark haired man nodded and smiled. He unclenched his fists and relaxed his shoulders. Williams leaned against the desk. "You were there when the raid happened. What did you decide to do with Jeff Locke?"

"It's better if you don't know. But as far as the public is concerned, Locke was arrested for corporate espionage and high treason. We tell the public that he is a political prisoner."

"Good start," said Williams, "but what about the raid? Surely word about it will reach the public."

"Have you forgotten who controls the media outlet?" said the dark haired man, rhetorically.

"He has many employees. What shall we do with the people who work for him?"

"They have been arrested as enemies of the state. As we speak, they are being transferred to a labor camp in Missouri."

"It seems that the situation is under control," noted Williams.

"We seem to have salvaged your blunder. But the situation will not be under control until we catch those students," said the dark haired man.

Professor Williams opened his office door and beckoned towards the dark haired man. "Take care Mr. Holden," he said.

Jack Holden exited the office. On his way out he said, "You're lucky I like you. But if you are ever responsible for another blunder like this—especially one that threatens my shot at the presidency... well, let's just hope that does not happen."

"I assure you, it will not."

~

By 10:30 a.m. Adam, Sahar, and Will had purchased new clothes, copied the contents of the hard drive to each of their computers, and boarded a train for Manhattan. They all wore hats and sunglasses to cover their faces, and agreed not to discuss the hard drive while people were nearby.

A split second before the train doors closed, a young woman narrowly squeaked through the doors and boarded the train. She wore jogger's clothes. A hat and sunglasses shielded her identity. She passed the students and dropped an envelope. Adam reached down to pick up the envelope, and was about to return it to the woman, but written on the envelope were the words:

`Do not look back. We are being watched.`

She sat in the seat behind the students. Once the train departed she leaned forward and softly spoke. "I know you plan to share the hard drive with major media networks. Do so with caution: Erebus has infiltrated every major network. If you get it to the right person, you may be able to spread the information."

"I'm sorry," spoke Adam. He turned towards the woman. "I think you have the wrong—"

"Keep your eyes forward!"

"You have the wrong people," said Will.

"We don't have time for this. You see that man in the black suit, at the end front of the cabin, reading an e-book? He is one of their agents. There's another one at the back of the train. They are looking for you."

"Why would they be looking for us?" Adam concernedly asked.

"Because your mug shots are plastered everywhere. Supposedly, you're wanted for murder."

"That's ridiculous," scoffed Adam.

"Don't believe me?" The woman furtively passed her smartphone to Adam. Several news websites were open in the browser, and each one ran a story about murders committed by three Arcadia students. Sure enough, photos of Adam, Will, and Sahar plastered each article. Adam slipped the phone back to the woman.

"Who are you?" he demanded.

"We met at the Aegis Technology facility."

"Ms. Martin?" asked Will incredulously.

"You may call me Melissa, but yes."

"How did you escape?" asked Sahar.

"Another time," said Melissa. "I am disembarking at the next stop. I suggest you take notice of the piece of paper in the envelope."

A moment later, the train came to a halt. Melissa nonchalantly disembarked. More people entered the train, and the journey continued. Adam looked towards the agent at the front of the train car. The agent's lips moved, but his voice was inaudible. He did not appear to be talking to someone nearby, and it was generally the homeless (not the well-dressed) who carried conversations with themselves in public. Adam grew suspicious. He opened the envelope and pulled out a piece of paper. Written on the paper was a single piece of information: a Manhattan address. No name, no phone number, no email address.

"What do you make of it?" asked Will. Adam shrugged his shoulders. Will pulled out his smartphone and searched for the address. It appeared to be a small office in a large building downtown—nothing spectacular.

Adam and Sahar stared at the address. It took a minute for Sahar to internalize the threat. Her eyes grew wide. "Has that been on the whole time?" she said, referring to Will's phone.

"Since we left Arcadia," replied Will, without taking his eyes off the phone.

"That is probably how those agents found us! They tracked the cell phone! Turn it off!"

"I already deactivated the locator."

"It does not matter, they can still track it! Now turn it off!" Will fumbled with his phone.

"I have a better idea," he said. "If you're right, they've already tracked the phone, and it doesn't matter. When we get off the train, we use it as a diversion. Have faith."

Sahar begrudgingly complied. "Okay, she said. But the larger question is, can we trust Melissa?"

"We're looking at this the wrong way," said Adam. "We keep deliberating on one option versus another, but there are three of us: we need to split up."

"Should we really risk splitting up?" said Will. "We won't be able to communicate. If we're apart, we're more vulnerable."

"But our plan will have a better chance of succeeding. We have to put the plan before ourselves."

"I agree," affirmed Sahar. "Now let us plan. Does either one of you have suggestions?"

For the remainder of the train ride, the three students hashed out a plan. Sahar would make for the New York Times headquarters, Will would make for the Wall Street Journal headquarters, and Adam would head to the mystery address. When the train arrived at Penn Station, they dashed past the agent and disembarked. Immediately after passing the agent, Sahar intentionally dropped the same envelope that Melissa had dropped. The agent reached down to retrieve the envelope. He opened it, and read the piece of paper inside, containing an address to NBC headquarters. The agent touched his earpiece and communicated this information to his comrades. He stood and followed the students.

Will and Sahar followed Adam around the corner and up the stairs. Two agents followed closely behind. Upon reaching the top of the stairs, Adam, Will, and Sahar sprinted away in different directions: Adam continued up the stairs, while Will and Sahar ran opposite each other, towards other subway routes. When the agents reached the top of the stairs, they saw all three students running in opposite directions. One sprinted after Sahar. The other sprinted after Will.

Sahar ran through the crowds, ducked under the turnstiles, and towards another subway route. With little effort, she eluded the agent chasing her, but upon entering the subway, another man in a suit apprehended her. She squirmed and screamed. The agent signaled via his earpiece. Sahar's screams drew attention. "Let go of me!" she shouted. "You are not my father and I am not going with you!" She repeated this chant multiple times. Several bystanders approached.

"Is there a problem here?" asked a bystander. Sahar continued squirming and screaming.

"No," said the agent. "My daughter didn't take her medication today. Thank you for your concern."

"Please, help!" screamed Sahar. "I do not know this man, and I do not take any medications!"

"Sir, maybe you should take your hands off that girl," the bystander sternly stated. The agent glared. Multiple bystanders slowly converged towards the man. With one arm gripping Sahar, he used his free arm to reach into his suit jacket and pull out a pistol.

"Get back! All of you!"

As he waved his gun back and forth, pointing it at bystanders, Sahar used her teeth and bit into the agent's arm. By reflex, he released her. A shot fired from the pistol. Several people screamed. Sahar stomped on the man's foot, stepped back, and with full force, side-kicked him in the crotch. He fell to his knees, allowing Sahar to narrowly escape onto the disembarking subway train.

~

Meanwhile, the second agent pursued Will. Will entered another terminal and hid behind a column. The agent entered the terminal and surveyed the area. He looked at his tracker, which indicated Will was nearby. When the moment presented itself, Will chucked his phone through the open train door. The train disembarked the terminal, taking the phone with it. The agent alarmingly looked at his tracker, and then swore. He paced a few times, muttering curse words and exhibiting frustration. The distraction worked and Will was able to sneak out unnoticed.

~

Of the three students, Adam was the most vulnerable. There were only two disruptors and they were with Will and Sahar. Once the SSD software recognized his face, it would not be long before authorities converged on his position. As quickly and cautiously as possible, he trekked through the bumbling streets of Manhattan. He soon realized that he was completely lost.

"Excuse me," he pleaded, hoping to obtain directions.

One man bumped into Adam. "Watch it kid," he muttered. Everyone else ignored Adam.

Adam looked left, then to the right. Ten yards down the street was a slew of taxicabs. Adam approached a cab. The driver rolled down the window. "I need to get to this address," said Adam. "Can you take me there?"

The cab driver replied with a thick accent. "That is by Upper East Side." He nodded. "Yes, I can take you there." Adam opened the back passenger door and entered the vehicle.

The acceleration of the cab thrust Adam's head against the headrest. He gripped the door handle to prevent himself from being thrown side to side every time the cab turned. They drove several blocks and stopped behind a herd of stalled cars. The cab driver hammered the horn with his fist. Every second stopped in traffic was time that could have been spent earning more fares. Adam looked ahead and could see the green traffic lights, but the cars did not move. The rearview mirror showed images of armed men honing in. Adam's heart pounded. His hands trembled. He looked left and then right. He opened the door and disembarked the cab.

"Hey!" yelled the cab driver. "You owe me money!" The driver continued blaring the horn and shouting.

Adam crept between the cars and slipped into an alleyway. He could see the street on the opposite side of the alley, so he briskly jogged towards it.

"There he is!" shouted a voice from behind him. He did not look back, and instead, increased his pace. As Adam sprinted like his life depended on it; he thought the months of PT were finally paying-off. But then he heard the footsteps of the men behind him grow louder. The end of the alley was close—only a few more yards. If he could make it to the other side, he could disappear into the crowd. But in a moment's notice, his last shred of hope disappeared. More armed men poured through the exit in front of him. Adam attempted to reverse directions. His shoes skidded across the pavement. His arms flailed in a feeble attempt to halt his forward momentum. Armed men approached from both directions, and blocked every exit.

"Adam Carter," spoke one of the men. "You are under arrest." Adam raised his hands and waited to hear the famous Miranda rights, but they were never spoken. He remembered hearing the lines in movies. *You have the right to remain silent. Anything you say can and will be held against you in a court of law. You have a right to an attorney...* The men handcuffed Adam and led him towards a black sedan, but never spoke the Miranda rights. The message was clear: there would be no trial.

"Do you have the hard drive?" asked one of the men. Adam could not think of a good reason to resist. The battle was lost.

Adam despondently nodded. "It's in my left jacket pocket."

The man reached into Adam's jacket pocket and removed the plastic hard drive. The man smiled. He tossed the hard drive to the ground and stomped on it until it lay fragmented beyond repair. He then placed the pieces in a plastic bag and handed it off to one of his subordinates. The front passenger door of the black sedan opened and Dr. Williams stepped out. "You disappoint me," he said to Adam.

Adam glowered at the professor. "Why?" he said, shaking his head. "Why did your team engineer a virus to destroy crops and livestock?"

"I have already told you: we are going to reform the country and we need a crisis to do so," said the professor. "Something that is directly observable and impacts the general public."

"The financial crisis was not good enough for you?"

"Frankly, no," replied Dr. Williams. "The crisis will provide an excellent running platform for our congressmen and state governors, but we need more."

"How many members does Erebus have in government and business?"

"Even if we fail to gather enough support for this election cycle, there are enough of us. Every member is willing to do what is necessary to make his country better. And fortunately for us, the current president made our jobs much easier by suspending habeas corpus. He was only attempting to restore order. I suppose you could consider the confiscation of firearms and detention of political prisoners an added bonus. Now we can easily arrest anyone who opposes us. The asset seizures helped replace tax revenue lost during this recession. We never imagined how much the current administration would inadvertently play into our goals."

Adam scoffed. "Even if you take the presidency, I fail to see how you will get the entire population to agree to implant electrodes in their brain."

"You underestimate American sloth. Most of these people want to better themselves, but are too lazy to do so. We offer them an easy way out: a free neural implant that can almost instantaneously give them the missing skills they need. Naturally, many of them will realize that such a device can be used to subjugate the incompetent, but every man believes he is smarter than the average man. He will never imagine himself being subjugated."

"Do you really think this plan will work? How can you place your faith in a small group of technocrats? No one is capable of sustaining such a complex system. Such systems have always proven ineffective and oppressive. How will this system be any different?"

"The difference is that now we have the right people and the necessary technology," said Dr. Williams. "These two ingredients have always been missing from past regimes. We can eliminate crime, poverty, war, and suffering with the simple flick of a switch. Can you honestly tell me that people would not want that?"

"What about freedom? What about choice?"

"Those are fine concepts, in theory. But what happens when people make the wrong choices? The allegory of the perils of free will is ancient. Look at the book of Genesis. The first decision mankind makes—taking fruit from the forbidden tree—is the wrong decision. Freedom is what allows evil to enter the world. Evil is not some arcane, ancient force. There is no God and there is no devil. Evil is the result of people making poor decisions."

"And freedom is what allows people to make good, moral decisions. Without freedom, morality does not exist."

Dr. Williams laughed, "I suppose that someone who acts holy because he fears the consequences of acting unholy is considered righteous? Or does he act holy because he expects a reward from God? Either way, it's completely self-serving. Tell me how that is moral."

"And your vision of the world is not self-serving?" countered Adam. "Can you honestly say that you intend to make the world a better place for people other than you? Surely, your new system will require the technocrats to rule. What will prevent these people from using their power to solely benefit themselves?"

"All of us will have neural implants that suppress greed," replied Dr. Williams. "We are making the world a better place for everyone. Everyone with a neural implant will be happy. It does not matter why they act good—the result will be the same."

"What about those who resist? What do you plan to do with them?"

"They can finish their days in labor camps. Of course, more drastic actions may be needed against those who actively resist... there may be a few bumps in the road." Dr. Williams stepped aside. "Speaking of which, it is time for you to leave. I truly wish circumstances could have been different; you would have been a great asset to our team."

The man who handcuffed Adam opened the car door, and beckoned Adam to get inside. Adam complied.

~

Adam was driven to an undisclosed location. He estimated the drive was at least one hour. The car stopped next to a train. Crowds of people were loading into one of the boxcars. One of the men driving the car stepped out and opened the door for Adam. He unlocked the handcuffs.

"Where are we?" asked Adam.

The man looked at the people boarding the train, then looked at Adam. "You're an enemy of the state."

"You didn't answer my question."

"And I don't intend to. You will be joining the rest of these people—more enemies of the state—at a labor camp in the Midwest."

"I want my phone call."

"Sorry kid, but your rights ended when your sedition began. Enemies of the state are not afforded due process like ordinary citizens."

"What will happen to my family?"

"You're dead to them. If they can accept that, they can continue living their lives with minimal interruption. If they start asking too many questions, they will be joining you."

"And my friends?"

"The other rebels? Once we apprehend them, they will be joining you." Adam bowed his head indignantly.

"No more questions," said the guard. "Time for you to board that train."

Adam was the last person in the crowd to board the train. Once the freight door closed he saw only darkness. It was warm outside, but even warmer inside the boxcar. A putrid stench comprised of sweat and iron permeated the air. Hundreds of perspiring bodies generated thick, humid ozone. Breathing became difficult. No one spoke. Adam leaned against the sidewall and slid down until he was seated. He closed his eyes and prayed to God for a miracle.

22

Wednesday, September 26, 2068

Adam had spent two weeks at the labor camp—or facility M601—and he was already noticeably skinnier. Everyone was fed the minimum two thousand calories, but through thirteen-hour days of backbreaking labor, two thousand calories did not suffice.

Upon arriving he only knew one person at the camp by name: Melissa Martin, the receptionist at Aegis Technology, though he recognized several faces from his visit at the Aegis facility. Over the past two weeks, he had begun cultivating friendships with some of these people.

The facility was relatively small. It was larger than Cammalot Middle School, but smaller than the Arcadia campus. There were enough bunks to house several thousand people, but less than one thousand people were present. Chain-link fences topped with razor wire circumscribed the facility. However, anyone would have been insane to attempt an escape: dry, dusty planes stretched as far as the eyes could see. A single-lane dirt road paralleled the train tracks. It was the only other manmade path to or from the facility.

Another boxcar of laborers arrived that day. Adam stared from behind the fence. In the midst of the crowd he spotted Sahar and Will. For a moment he was glad to see more familiar faces, but also saddened because his friends would be suffering a similar fate. Will, Sahar, and the other prisoners were taken inside. Adam did not see his friends until that evening. Fortunately, the three were reunited and housed in the same quarters.

During dinnertime, the guards typically showed the news. However, that night's feature story was remarkably different from any news story that Adam had ever seen. In explicit detail, it chronicled the atrocities committed by Erebus, including the manmade virus, the plot to control people via neural implants, a list of previously unsolved murders (and their purpose as an initiation rite) committed by members of Erebus, the raid on Jeff Locke's facility (and his subsequent murder) and finally, the names and current positions held by every member of Erebus (including congress members, judges, CEOs, and more). Apparently, an unknown source had leaked the information online. While the content of the broadcast was disturbing, it provided a shred of hope for M601, hope that the leak would incite change.

Upon hearing the news, the prisoners of M601 cheered with joy. Adam's eyes gleamed with optimism. He embraced Will and Sahar in a group hug.

When the cheering ceased, Will scratched his head and commented, "I don't get it. The hard drive was destroyed, my laptop was confiscated. It wasn't Jeff Locke, he was murdered. Everyone from Aegis who could have helped is at the prison. Who leaked the information?"

Sahar stepped forward. "I have a confession to make," she said, almost guiltily. Adam and Will looked at her, waiting for her response. She looked Adam in the eyes. "I know you wanted to keep Henry out of this conflict, but I did not know what else to do. I was afraid that I would be captured before reaching the media outlets, and that even if I did reach a news outlet, Erebus would suppress the information." Sahar took a slow deep breath. "Since we copied all the information onto our laptops, I mailed my laptop to Henry, along with directions. And as a backup plan, I sent a letter to Julie, informing her of Henry's situation." Adam stared blankly at Sahar. "I know I put everyone's lives at risk," she said, "but I did not know what else to do. I hope that you can forgive me."

"Forgive you?" said Adam. He paused and attempted to comprehend the situation. He looked down at the floor, then back at Sahar. Upon making eye contact, he stepped towards her, and embraced her with a tight, affectionate hug. "We owe you everything," he said. Sahar smiled and hugged him back.

~

Tuesday, November 13, 2068

Despite the data leak, Michael Cane and Jack Holden still managed to garnish over thirty percent of the electoral vote, but they ultimately lost the election. There was speculation about how Holden and Cane could have possibly won so many votes. Some speculated that the election votes were stolen. Others blamed the notoriously short-term memory of American voters. "They should have waited a month to release the data," some said ("they" were still unknown). Some conceded that Holden and Cane had too many apologists—that people accepted Erebus's plan and behavior because it would achieve the desired end. Adam pondered the latter explanation. He remembered learning about the twentieth century psychologist, Abraham Maslow. In Maslow's hierarchy of needs, safety was the second most important desire, just above basic physiological needs. Once the physiological needs such as food, water, shelter, etc., are taken care of, people seek security: a steady job, good health, physical protection, etc. Cane and Holden preyed on this primordial desire. The financial crisis eradicated financial security for many. Then Erebus exacerbated the situation. Finally, Cane and Holden promised to heal everyone's wounds. They offered a fresh start and promised security for all. In a moment of desperation, some people accepted.

Ironically, the people of M601 had every basic need taken care of. They were given adequate food, water, and shelter. They had no financial burdens. Crime within M601 was nonexistent. Before being released, they had developed friendships and fostered respect amongst each other. With their limited free time, they were able to play games and solve puzzles. According to Maslow, these people would have been at the top of the hierarchy. But one obvious concept was absent: freedom.

EPILOGUE

Despite Adam's victory, there was still cause for concern: large factions of the population were apologists for Erebus. They believed that the desired outcome, the illusion of freedom, a decline in violence, crime, drug-use, sexually transmitted infections, out-of-wedlock births, obesity, poverty, and income inequality, and increases in innovation, student performance, and educational achievement, justified Erebus's tactics. Undesirables would not reproduce, and the elderly would willingly take their life when they passed their prime. Social security and healthcare spending would not bankrupt the country. The rich would gladly pay higher taxes. An obedient population would obviate the need for religiosity. The apologists argued that a neural implant could create a benevolent dictator. Further, they believed that the U.S. could be an exemplar for other countries. If enough people were given neural implants, war could be all but eliminated.

Erebus attempted to create a utopia with minimal terror and collateral damage, but even their attempted utopia was not without great cost. The initial virus, engineered and distributed by Erebus, mutated several times. It was contained, but not before killing nearly fifteen percent of the U.S. population (directly, from exposure, and indirectly by destroying food sources). And despite Erebus's attempts to subjugate the population, people continued "upgrading" their brains with neural implants. The massive surveillance system, capable of predicting crime, became even more ubiquitous (though its capability of predicting and detecting crime was greatly diminished when criminals began using disruptors). Those whose firearms were confiscated never saw their firearms returned.

Erebus's plot had been foiled, but every economic crisis would provide more opportunities for men with grandiose promises of utopia. A democracy is necessary, but not sufficient to keep despotism at bay; it is not the source of power that matters. Even Adolf Hitler was democratically elected. With each administration overextending its power and using political muscle to disenfranchise opponents, the barrier between fascism and freedom attenuated until it was as thin as the good faith of elected officials. The environment was still ripe for change. For better or worse would depend on the people.

ACKNOWLEDGEMENTS

Several people provided invaluable feedback during the editing process. My wife, Kelly, my mother-in-law Kathy, my colleagues Janet, Ruth, Liana, Tracy and Katie: thank you for finding mistakes, typos, inconsistencies, and more. Several students volunteered to "beta-test" the early version of the book. Ashwin, Ryan, Haylie, Andrey, Clayton, Evie, Max, Brenden, and Rebecca: thank you for your input. Finally, thank you to the multi-age literature circle groups for your critical analyses.

ABOUT THE AUTHOR

Daniel Mershon was born in Portland, OR in May of 1988. His father was an airplane mechanic for the Air National Guard, and his mother was a photographer. A few years later, his brother Micheal was born. In 1993, the family moved from a Portland suburb to the backwoods town of Carson, WA. He spent many hours outdoors with his childhood friends, and cousin Sean. At the age of six, Daniel and his friends were running through the woods when he fell on a small branch that punctured his kidney. He spent several weeks in ICU, lost a kidney, gained a gigantic scar, and missed a couple months of school, but eventually recovered. Later that year, his parents divorced.

In 1997, Daniel's younger brother was diagnosed with terminal brain cancer. When his brother could no longer walk, Daniel spent his life savings to purchase his brother a Nintendo 64. Even though his brother was only able to enjoy video games for a couple months, Daniel still claims, "That was the best $300 I ever spent." Micheal died May 2, 1998.

Daniel continued working hard in school and outside of school. He bought Pokémon cards and sold them individually for a profit. He continued caring for neighbors' pets, recycling beer cans, scrubbing decks, mowing lawns, and washing cars. By the age of fourteen, he worked as a dishwasher in a local restaurant. At fifteen, he landed a job at the local grocery store, and worked there until graduating high school. At sixteen, he squandered his savings on a 1985 Z28 Camaro and a cheap acoustic guitar. He taught himself to play, but was disappointed that he could only afford a low quality instrument, so he set out to build his own (which was later completed as a senior project—and it's sound quality still surpasses any factory-made guitar). It was his senior year when he started dating his (future) wife, Kelly.

Daniel saved more money through his job, and earned enough scholarship money to pay for his first year of college at Concordia University (he was fortunate to live with his grandparents that year). He later transferred to Washington State University, where he majored in Mathematics. Through a combination of scholarships and work, Daniel graduated college debt-free in 2010, married Kelly in 2011, and began teaching that same year. He will be leaving the teaching profession to attend graduate school at the University of Notre Dame, starting Fall 2015.

www.ingramcontent.com/pod-product-compliance
Lightning Source LLC
Chambersburg PA
CBHW021230130626
46554CB00004B/1427